forever

forever

forever

A Friends Novel

New York Times Bestselling Author
MONICA MURPHY

Cover design © Hang Le byhangle.com

Interior Design and formatting by

E.M.
TIPPETTS
BOOK DESIGNS

www.emtippettsbookdesigns.com

everafter ROMANCE

chapter one

Tuttle

It's pure torture, having her so close, knowing I can't talk to her, touch her, kiss her. Whisper in her ear all the dirty things I want to do to her.

I can't do any of that.

None of it.

I'm the bastard who broke her heart. I'm the jerk who can't commit. I told myself to stay away from her. Though she still tortures me even in my thoughts. I close my eyes and I see her. Her scent seems to fill the air when she's not around. My mind plays tricks on me, and I can't make it stop.

So I watch her when I can. When no one's paying attention. When *she's* not paying attention, which is a rare occurrence. I'm pretty sure she's as aware of me as I'm aware of her.

Friday night football games are the worst. Like right now, I'm standing on the sidelines, watching our defensive line with a critical eye, dying of thirst. I need a drink, and the only one who's working the hydration station is Amanda. Kyla, the other girl who works the hydration station with Amanda, isn't here tonight.

Just Amanda. All by herself. Hustling her cute little ass in those tight jeans the entire game, running around making sure we're all hydrated. Except for me.

"Fuck it," I mutter as I toss my helmet onto the ground and stalk toward the hydration station. Amanda is talking to one of the JV players, being too nice as usual while the kid blatantly stares at her tits. She complains they're too small, but I think they're perfect. *She's* perfect.

The asshole staring at her chest? He's too close.

I want to smash his face in. I don't even know the kid's name, but it doesn't matter. I don't like how he's looking at Mandy. My Mandy.

You can't make that claim anymore—you rejected her. Remember?

The nagging voice inside my head irritates me so much, I actually growl. Out loud.

The JV player spots me first and his eyes go wide, no doubt because of the mean look on my face. And maybe he heard me growl too. Who knows? Who cares? I glare at him and he leaves without a word while Amanda is still talking, and she makes this cute, exasperated noise, shaking her head.

"How rude," she says, turning toward me with a faint smile. That smile fades in an instant when she sees it's me.

That hurts. More than I ever want to admit.

"I need water," I practically grunt, sounding like a primitive caveman. But what else can I say to her? *I need you? I want you?*

Yeah, that won't fly.

She raises an eyebrow and grabs a water bottle, thrusting it toward me. "You haven't said one word to me in two weeks, and the first thing you choose to say is, 'I need water'? You didn't even say please."

My knees are weak. Seriously. I'm six-foot-two of solid muscle. People tend to run when they see me coming, especially when I'm in a crap mood like now, and I'm scared shitless of this girl. "Please?" I add, my voice soft, my heart racing, my entire body on edge from her nearness.

"That's better." Amanda steps closer, so close I can smell her. My legs shake. Maybe it's because I'm dehydrated. Maybe it's because I'm in love with a girl I can't have.

I take the water bottle from her and my fingers graze hers. That brief connection sends a jolt through me that makes every fine hair on my body stand on end.

"Thanks," I say before I start to drink. I drain practically half the bottle before I stop because she's laying into me.

"You shouldn't drink so fast. You'll make your muscles cramp up," she chastises, though her voice is gentle. Her gaze is too. Everything about her is soft and beautiful and right. She's wearing a navy blue polo shirt and jeans that show off those endless legs and I'm tempted to fall to my knees and beg for mercy. Would she take me back?

Or is she already over me?

But I don't fall to my knees. And begging's not my style. Instead, I return the water bottle to her and start to walk away, eager to make my escape when she says my name. Not my last name either.

"Jordan."

Pausing, I glance over my shoulder to find she's watching me, her dark eyes extra big, her mouth curved downward. She looks sad. Hopeless. I know what that feels like. I'm right there with her. "What?"

"I—I miss you." She hesitates.

My heart starts beating extra fast. I can't believe she just said that. I want her to say more. So much more.

"Do you miss me, too?"

Those last words are a faint whisper. Like it took everything out of her to admit that.

I say nothing. I can't. I messed up. I let her in and it cost me. More than she'll ever know.

More than she'll ever understand.

I give the slightest shake of my head and leave her standing there. I can feel her eyes on my back as I walk away, and I know she's mad. How does that old saying go? If looks could kill? Well, I'd be a dead man for sure. She's probably plotting my future murder.

"Hey, jackass. Ready to play?" Ryan appears out of nowhere, shoving my helmet into my stomach extra hard, making me cough.

"Asshole," I mumble as I take my helmet from him.

"I'd be a lot nicer if you got your head out of your ass and focused on the game," Ryan tells me. "Don't let that girl mess with your mind, man. We need this win."

"She's not messing with my mind," I say, though I'm lying. She's totally messing with my mind. I can't think about anything else. Just Amanda.

Why did I walk away from her again?

"She is," Ryan says firmly. "It's been weeks since you two split. Move on, dude. She's not worth it." He shifts closer to me, his face practically in mine, though I'm taller, so I have the advantage. "Think about your future. Don't worry about some girl who wouldn't give it up to you. She's using that to control you. I bet if you'd already boned Amanda, you wouldn't be all twisted up inside over her. You'd be ready to find the next girl."

It takes everything within me not to tear his face off. He's saying this type of crap to get a rise out of me. I know it. But I refuse to take the bait. "You don't know what you're talking about."

Ryan grins. "I think I do. But whatever, man. Keep fooling yourself. Just don't let your misery affect the team. We need you, Tuttle. We've made it to the playoffs. We need to keep winning."

He's right. I want to win. We all do. I need to get over this. Over her. Focus on my future. Win the division championship, clinch a scholarship at my school of choice and get the hell out of here. Screw my dad. Screw my mom—though she doesn't care what I do, as long as I'm gone.

Amanda will just hold me down. Distract me. Ryan nailed it. She's still messing with my mind and we're not even together anymore.

Were we ever together in the first place? Was that hopeful thinking on my part? I wanted her so badly. I still do. Despite everything I've done, everything I've said, everything she's said, I still do.

And I think she wants me too.

"Let's go," I tell Ryan when the defense comes off the field. Almost the end of the second quarter and the score is three to zero in our favor. "We need to score a touchdown."

"Now you're talking!" Ryan shouts as we run out onto the field. "Let's go kick some ass!"

I become the quiet, intense quarterback in the blink of an eye. The untouchable leader. It's what they expect, what my team needs. It's amazing how easily I fall into the role, how it fits me like a second skin. How I become Tuttle the QB, the star. The legend in the making.

It's all bullshit. But that's okay. I'm just going through the motions, doing what I need to do in order to survive. I need no one. Just myself.

Maybe if I keep thinking it—saying it out loud, even—I'll eventually believe the words.

chapter two

Amanda

"I despise working the hydration station." It's the first thing I say to Livvy when I spot her after the game's over.

Livvy frowns as she watches me approach. She's waiting for me so we can go find Ryan's car together. He's our ride back to her house since I'm spending the night, which I think Ryan secretly hates. He'd rather have Livvy all to himself.

"I thought you enjoyed it?" Livvy asks. "Flirting with all the football players. Keeping tabs on that asshole Tuttle."

I ignore her calling him an asshole. I'm the only one who's usually allowed to call him that, but right now, I'm so furious, I don't care. She could put a hex on him and I'd encourage her. I'd probably build the voodoo doll and everything.

Oh my God. My thoughts are so incredibly random, I'm making no sense.

"I hate him," I tell Livvy. "I don't want to keep tabs on him." Oh, I sound like a Bitter Betty, don't I? I can't help it. His earlier rejection still stings.

Why'd I tell him I missed him? Why, why, why? I'm such a fool. I get within a few feet of him and it's like I can't even help myself.

Clearly I have major issues.

"Please." Livvy rolls her eyes. "You do not. You're madly in love with him and super pissed because of what he did."

"Don't remind me." I start walking and she falls into step beside me. "I just want to go home."

"Ryan should be out any minute." She starts texting him and I keep walking, headed for the parking lot in search of Ryan's perfect white BMW. I hope we're not stuck here too long. I don't want to sit around and wait for Ryan while he talks with his football buddies. I'm afraid I might see Tuttle again.

Ew. No.

…fine. Swoon. I'd love to see him again, as long as he didn't open his mouth and say something stupid. Though it's more like I'm the one who needs to keep my mouth shut and not say something stupid. More like everything he says is infuriating.

I can't be with you.

I don't know how to be a good boyfriend.

I don't know how to show my feelings.

I don't know how to love you.

All those words, all the pretty lies and sweet and sexy promises that dropped from his perfectly kissable lips were nothing but total bullshit.

"I'm so glad they won," Livvy says when I remain silent. She's practically running to keep up with my strides and I don't slow down.

The farther away I can get from the football field, the better. "Ryan's always in a good mood when they win."

Wait a minute. "Am I ruining your plans tonight?" I ask her, coming to a complete stop and making Livvy trip over her own feet. "If you want to take off with Ryan, I totally understand."

The look Livvy sends me is pure skepticism. "Yeah right. I won't ditch you in your time of need."

A month ago she would've ditched me for Ryan without hesitation. Livvy's changed. I knew she had a good heart buried deep down inside. It just took her a while to dig it out.

"Are you sure?" I know what it's like to have a boy you want to spend all of your time with. I sort of felt that way with Thad. I totally felt that way with Tuttle.

I still feel that way about Jordan Tuttle.

"Ryan will have to live without me. He can make a date with his hand tonight." Livvy giggles, making me smile. "I'm hanging out with you. We can eat popcorn and watch a scary movie."

"Make it ice cream and you've got a deal," I suggest.

Livvy shivers. "It's too cold for ice cream. And anyway, aren't you sick of it, working at Yo Town all the time?"

"Frozen yogurt and ice cream are two different things," I point out, going for logic, though I know I'm annoying her.

"Not really, but whatever." She rolls her eyes then loops her arm through mine, steering me toward Ryan's car. "We'll have ice cream. Hopefully Ryan will let us stop at the store on the way home so we can grab some."

"I'll buy. My treat," I offer.

"You're just saying that so you can pick out the flavor."

My new best friend already knows me so well. "Valid point. One I won't deny. But I'll make sure it's something you like too."

"Gee, thanks." Livvy glances over her shoulder, her smile growing just before her gaze meets mine. "Ryan's just behind us. And he's alone."

Disappointment and relief hit me. I almost wanted to see Jordan, but...why? So he can say something awful? So he can watch me with his beautiful, vacant blue eyes?

Ugh.

Ugh.

Ugh.

I need to get over him. Find someone new. I'm surrounded by hunky, gorgeous football players on an almost daily basis, so I have plenty to choose from. The season is almost over so I'm running out of time.

"Ladies." Ryan's deep voice comes from behind, and he wedges his lean body in between us, forcing Livvy and me to let go of each other. He slips his arms around our shoulders, squeezing us close to his sides, and I let him. Ryan annoys me sometimes, and sometimes he doesn't. Like right now. He smells good and he's in a great mood, so I can tolerate him. "I hear I'm your chauffeur for the night."

"Right. You're taking us to the store for an ice cream run, and then you're taking us home," Livvy tells him.

Ryan leans in and kisses her, never missing a step. Never releasing his hold on my shoulders either. The guy is smooth. "That sounds so boring, babe. Come on, let's go dig up a party. I hear Cannon Whittaker is having one tonight."

"Tuttle's not having a party?" The words fly out of my mouth before I can stop them.

Ryan sends me a knowing look, and I'm not sure how to interpret it. What does Tuttle tell him? They're close—as close as Jordan allows anyone to get to him, which truthfully is pretty far. But I'm sure they've talked about me. What does Jordan tell Ryan? Does he say awful things about me?

I can't imagine it.

Does Ryan say awful things to Jordan about me? I wouldn't put it past him.

Maybe.

"Cannon's mom is out of town," Ryan finally says. "So we all convinced him it's finally his turn to host the after game bash."

"Well, count us out," Livvy says, leaning forward so she can shoot me a look. "Amanda and I are having a girls' night in."

Ryan makes a disgusted noise. "Boring."

"Life isn't an endless party, you know," Livvy points out, sounding prim. Meaning she sounds very un-Livvy-like.

"Says my girlfriend who loves to party," Ryan teases, squeezing us both closer to him. "Come on, girls. Forget moping about a certain someone over ice cream."

I frown. Yep. He's got me all figured out.

"He won't be there." When I glance up, I find Ryan studying me. "Tuttle. He won't show up. He doesn't like going to parties, unless he's hosting them."

"He went to your birthday bash," Livvy reminds us.

"That's when he was chasing Amanda." Ryan's gaze never leaves mine. "I don't think he's chasing you anymore. Do you?"

I slowly shake my head, not liking his tone of voice. Or the look in his eyes. "And I'm not chasing him either."

"Right," Ryan drawls, pulling me in so close to him, my face is smashed against his very hard chest. I shift away, flustered. I'm not attracted to him, but being held so close to a guy is making me miss it.

The closeness that comes with having a boyfriend. A relationship.

Damn it, I miss stupid Jordan Tuttle so much, it hurts.

"She's definitely not chasing him," Livvy says firmly, rushing to my defense. "She's over that douchebag."

I wince. I'm the only person allowed to bag on him and Livvy's done it twice in one night. "I am," I say weakly. I don't sound very convincing and Ryan knows it. Livvy probably does too. "*So* over him."

"We can find you someone new then," Ryan says, giving my shoulders a squeeze. "Maybe even Cannon. Guy's been down and out lately. I don't know what his deal is. He needs to get laid. Maybe you could offer up your services."

Did he basically just call me a prostitute?

Livvy slaps Ryan on the chest, making him yelp. "You're so freaking crude! Amanda isn't going to help Cannon with *that* particular problem tonight. Or ever."

"Oh. Right." Ryan starts to chuckle. "Considering she's a virgin and all. Guess she wouldn't even know how to help him."

I shrug his arm away from my shoulders and start walking ahead of them, silently fuming. Livvy immediately starts chewing Ryan out and I wonder if I should stay and listen. Gloat a little bit, maybe even add a few words. But I don't want to. Insulting Ryan in return won't give me any satisfaction.

Nothing will.

Well.

Maybe Jordan Tuttle would.

But that's hopeless thinking on my part.

Ultimately, I decide to stay out of their fight. What's the point? I don't want to get in the middle of that. They've been arguing more lately too. She's always irritated with him. He's always irritated with her. It makes me wonder how much longer Ryan and Livvy are going to last.

I've been leaning against the back of Ryan's car for five minutes before Livvy finally approaches me, her cheeks flushed, her eyes still sparkling with residual anger. "I'm so, so sorry he said that to you." She takes a step closer and envelopes me in a quick hug. "He's an asshole."

"Yeah. He is," I say against her hair before I pull away. "You don't need to apologize for him. It's not your fault he said that."

"But he's my boyfriend, so I feel responsible. I told him we're definitely not going to that party tonight. He can go alone." She crosses her arms, even makes a little "humph" noise, but I can see the worry in her eyes.

She doesn't want her boyfriend to go to a party alone. He's one of the hottest guys in our class, and he's still relatively new, considering he moved here over the summer. This makes him a hot commodity. Lots of girls would love to snag him up. And Livvy knows it.

"He's going without you?"

Livvy nods. "Yeah."

"Are you okay with that?" I ask carefully.

She throws her arms up in the air in a frustrated gesture. "What am I supposed to do, huh? Control his every move? I'm supposed to trust him, right? So his going to the party alone tonight will be a moment of trust on my part."

"And his."

"Right. And his." Livvy nods, her chin wobbly.

Like she might start to cry.

"We'll go to the party." The words rush out of my mouth quickly. I needed to say it fast or I might think too much and reconsider. "We won't go with Ryan, though. We'll show up later. On our own."

Her mouth drops open. "Why? So I can spy on Ryan? Make sure he's being a good boyfriend?" She starts pacing, and I wonder where the hell Ryan is so we can get him to take us back to Livvy's house. I'm desperate to get out of here.

"You're still mad, so if we go to the party with him, you two will just end up fighting all night. This way, you can show up looking hot like fire and he'll chase after you the entire time," I explain.

The angry spark in Livvy's eyes is immediately replaced with an excited gleam. "That's a good idea. And you should show up at the party looking hot like fire too."

"Ugh. Why?" And who cares? I know I just thought about crushing on someone new, but I'm not ready yet. Or am I? God, I don't know.

See? I'm a typical confused mass of teenage hormones.

"Amanda!"

I whirl around to see Ryan headed our way, a reluctant Cannon walking beside him. Frowning, I call back to him. "What's up?"

They stop in front of me, Cannon shoving his hands in the front pockets of his jeans, looking anywhere but at me. Weird. "Cannon asked me to ask you to go to his party tonight."

"What? I did not." Cannon shoves Ryan's shoulder, nearly toppling him to the ground. His gaze reluctantly meets mine and his smile is weak. "Ryan's full of crap."

"Okay." I draw the word out, a little thrown off by their behavior. I don't get what Ryan's trying to do. Humiliate Cannon? Humiliate me?

"Stop pretending you don't like her," Ryan says with a smirk. The murderous glint in Cannon's gaze makes me take a step back, and he wasn't even looking at me. "You should drive her home so I can talk to Livvy." Ryan turns his pleading gaze on me, oblivious to Cannon's irritation. "What do you say, Amanda?"

"Um…"

"No way," Livvy pipes up, coming to stand by my side. "I don't want to be left alone with him." She points at her boyfriend.

Ugh. Their flip-flopping relationship is exhausting.

"Come on, baby." Ryan goes to Livvy, slipping his arms around her waist and hauling her in close. "I need to talk to you."

The rest is lost in intimate murmurs and—yep, I hear lips connecting—a kiss or three. I send a sympathetic glance in Cannon's direction and he shrugs.

"I can give you a ride if you want. Unless you'd rather go with your friend," he offers, all traces of his earlier anger gone, just like that.

I part my lips, ready to turn him down, but I glance over my shoulder instead. See the way Ryan and Livvy are nuzzling each other like they're madly in love. Like they just didn't have a raging argument only a few minutes ago.

What the crap ever.

"Yes." I turn to face Cannon once more, noting the shock in his gaze. "I'll take you up on that offer. I'd really appreciate it if you could drive me home."

"Yeah. Sure. Absolutely." He bobs his head up and down like an eager puppy and takes hold of my arm, steering me toward his car.

"You're going home with Cannon?" Livvy screeches after us. Clearly my choice has stunned her.

I gently pull away from Cannon's grip and turn so I'm walking backwards. "Yes. Text me when you get home, okay?"

"I will! We'll go to the party together." She winks at me just before Ryan blocks her face with his own. As in, he's kissing her again.

Seeing them kiss makes me miss kissing a certain someone. I turn so I'm walking like a normal person.

"What was that all about?" Cannon asks, his voice low.

I shrug. "What exactly are you referring to?"

"Ryan and Livvy."

"They're fighting. Now they're making up."

"Right." He pauses. "I don't know why he said that about me wanting you at my party. It's not that I don't want you at my party, it's just..."

"I get it," I say, wanting to reassure him. He doesn't like me like that. I never thought he did. I know I don't like him like that either, so we feel the same way.

My heart—damn it—still belongs to someone else.

chapter three

I climb into Cannon's huge truck and slam the passenger side door, glancing around. It's a newer vehicle and it's absolutely immaculate. Like, everything's clean, there's no leftover change in the center console cup holders, nothing hanging from the rearview mirror, not even a bit of dust or dirt on the floorboards.

Cannon hops into the car a few seconds later, scowling as he turns to look at me. "Despite what Ryan said, I don't really like you. He's full of crap."

I'm slightly taken aback by the ferocity of his tone. "Okay."

"He's an asshole for saying that." Cannon slams his door and sticks the key into the ignition like he's trying to stab something. He cranks the car on, pressing his foot against the gas so the engine roars, and all I can do is stare at him.

What the hell is going on?

"Are you mad?"

He barely looks at me. "Just frustrated. Shit's not going my way lately."

Cannon Whittaker played a terrific game tonight, so I'm not sure what he's referring to. Maybe something personal? "Like what sort of shit?"

His mouth drops open as his wide eyes meet mine. "Did you just curse?"

I shrug, a little embarrassed. "I do on occasion say bad words. I'm not as prissy as everyone seems to think I am." Where did that assumption even come from?

"I never thought you were prissy. It's just…you're so smart. It's intimidating sometimes, trying to talk to you." He looks away. "I'm the farthest thing from smart, so I don't feel like I measure up, you know?"

"Cannon." I'm shocked he would even say such a thing, but I guess we all have our own insecurities we're dealing with. "That's the craziest thing ever. Why are you intimidated by me? I'm nothing. You, on the other hand, are such an amazing football player." His gaze meets mine once more, his brows furrowed in seeming confusion. "Seriously. You could probably get a scholarship somewhere. Anywhere you want to go."

"Aw, I don't know about that. That's what my mom says, but she just wants me to get out of here and make something of myself. Problem is my grades aren't so good." A horn suddenly honks and I glance out the passenger side window to see Ryan pulling out of the parking lot in his fancy white BMW, the tires squealing and I swear I could hear him laughing through his open window.

Such a show off.

"We should go," Cannon says as he puts the truck in reverse and backs out of the parking spot. "Give me your address. I don't know where you live."

I rattle it off and remain quiet for a while, my mind running over what Cannon said. What happened earlier between Livvy and Ryan. What happened between me and Tuttle during the game. It's been an adventurous—and mostly annoying—night and there's more to come with the party at Cannon's.

Great.

"I feel bad about you taking me home, since you're the one having the party," I finally say. "Don't you have to get things ready?"

He chuckles, his mouth curving into a little smile. "Get things ready for what? I don't need to do much."

Any party I've helped plan, there's constant stuff to be done before it starts. "Are you sure? Don't you have to like, set out food or whatever?"

"I have a giant bag of tortilla chips from Sam's Club and a couple of kegs out waiting in the backyard. Oh, and some beers chilling in the fridge, but those are for my VIP guests. Otherwise, I'm ready." We come to a stop at a red light and he turns to look at me. "It's no big deal, Amanda. Besides, you don't live that far from me. After I drop you off, I'll be home in less than five minutes."

Right. Because we don't live in the rich neighborhoods like everyone else we hang out with.

Trying to change the subject, I run my hand along the smooth, dark gray dashboard in front of me. "I like your truck."

He smiles. I can tell it's a source of pride for him. "Thanks. I treat it like my baby."

"Did you buy it brand new?"

"Yeah." His smile slips. The pride I saw flashing in his eyes is gone. Now he appears uncomfortable. "My dad bought it for me at the beginning of the summer. Called it an early graduation gift."

More like a year-early graduation gift. Parents are so weird sometimes. "Oh." I don't recall ever seeing a Mr. Whittaker come to watch the games. I don't remember ever seeing a Mrs. Whittaker there either. "So. Are you close to your dad?"

"Not really," he says through clenched teeth. He looks tense. Almost...angry. "He's not a big part of my life."

"Oh." I keep repeating myself. And I have no idea what it's like to have a neglectful parent. My parents are so involved in my life I wish they'd leave me alone half the time. "Well, he bought you a really nice truck." He must have major money to afford this.

"Yeah. I think it's supposed to make up for all the times he's never around." Cannon guns it when the light turns green, making my head jerk back and bounce against the back of the seat. "Sorry. My father is a touchy subject."

Fathers seem to be a touchy subject for more people than I realized.

"It's okay. I get it." Not really, but I want to. "How many people did you invite to the party?"

"Everyone. Like the entire football team and whoever else wants to come. My mom doesn't go out of town too often, so I had to take advantage."

"Will she be mad if she knew you were having this party?"

He shrugs, keeping his eyes glued on the road. "Maybe. I don't know. She just wants me happy, so if she ever did find out about this party, she'd probably like it. At least I'm being social. That's what she'd say."

"I think you're pretty social."

"Yeah, well, most of the time I'm hating on everyone, so I must do a good job of pretending."

I always thought Cannon was a simple guy with no problems. But he's a lot more complex than he seems. I'm starting to realize pretty much everyone is a lot more complex than they seem.

"Tuttle really cares about you, you know," Cannon suddenly says.

My entire body goes stiff. I do not want to talk about Jordan, especially with Cannon. Though I don't think they're close friends, so it's not like this conversation would get back to Jordan. "He has a funny way of showing it."

"Yeah, I guess. I don't think it's easy for him to show his feelings, which I totally get. I'm not big on it either." Cannon shakes his head as he flicks on the signal and turns right onto the main street of my neighborhood. "He never brings a girl around. Never looks at them the way he looks at you either."

My skin goes warm and I push the annoying feeling away. I refuse to fall back into that trap. "What do you mean? He has to fight off all the girls who want him." Maybe a slight exaggeration, but that's what I've always heard. Witnessed a time or two.

"Well, yeah. There are a bunch of girls who want him, including Lauren Mancini, who will probably cut a bitch if she gets in her way." He sends me an apologetic look. "Sorry. Just calling it like I see it."

"You don't need to apologize. It's true."

Cannon smiles and laughs. "Right. All sorts of girls are panting for his ass, but he really doesn't want any of them. I've never seen him go crazy for a girl the way he acts around you."

"How does he act around me?" I'm almost afraid of his answer.

"Like he can't stop looking at you. Like there's no one else in the world he'd rather stare at but you." Cannon's voice is soft. Almost reverent. "I'm not his good friend or anything, but I've spent a lot of time with him over the years, and I know what he's like."

I'm jittery. Like my hands are shaking from what Cannon said. He's just an observer. He doesn't know Jordan that well, doesn't know his thoughts. But maybe. Just maybe…

"Do you really know what he's like? Or are you just saying this to make me feel better?" He pulls in front of my house and I unclick the seatbelt, turning to face him. "I don't need any sweet words to make me feel better, Cannon. I've given up on Jordan Tuttle, because he's given up on me."

Cannon's lips thin and that ferocious look is back in his eyes again. "He's a total dumbass, giving up on you."

"Tell me all about it."

His jaw hardens as he stares at my house. "Is it wrong to want something you don't think you deserve?"

Is he talking about Jordan and me now? Or maybe someone else? "Depends on how much wanting something else ends up hurting you."

"I don't mind the pain." His smile is sad. "I just hate the waiting. And there's only so much waiting you can do until you feel like an asshole. You know what I mean?"

I burst out laughing, and Cannon eventually joins in. I can't even say why I'm laughing exactly. Maybe because it's better than crying? "Surprisingly enough, I know *exactly* what you mean."

chapter four

"I'm feeling really self-conscious right now. Just thought you should know," I tell Livvy.

"No shit. If you'd stop tugging on your skirt, people wouldn't notice that you're self-conscious," Livvy says under her breath as we make our way to the front door of Cannon Whittaker's house.

Once Cannon dropped me off at my house, I texted Livvy. She came over so the both of us could get ready before we took off to his party.

And just because she was making out with Ryan while still in the school parking lot doesn't mean they're doing well. They fought again on the drive to her house and she was still mad at him.

Like, out-for-revenge mad at him.

"I can't help it." I tug on my skirt again, hating how short it is. I don't wear dresses very often, but Livvy insisted I wear one tonight. Considering she was at my house and my closet was at her mercy, I didn't have a choice.

Plus, I can admit to myself I was secretly hoping Tuttle might show up after all and see me looking extra hot. Maybe he'd change his mind and want me back after all…

Want you back. That jerk doesn't even deserve you. You're too good for him and don't you forget it.

It's weird, but my inner voice sounds suspiciously just like my mom. Maybe because she said something very similar to me when we first split up. She was trying to make me feel better, but…

Yeah. Her words didn't really help.

"Yes, you can help it." Livvy slaps my hand away from the hem of my tight-fitting black dress, making me yelp. I don't even remember buying this dress, so I have no idea where it came from. "You're skinny with legs that are a mile long. I swear you look hot. Stop acting like a weenie and own it."

Ugh. I hate it when Livvy's logical.

"I'm owning it tonight too." She tilts her chin, a wicked gleam in her eyes. "Ryan's going to regret making me so mad."

She's also hell bent on proving to Ryan that she doesn't need him. I guess they got into a yelling match in her front yard. She didn't even care if their neighbors saw, and she told me all about it when she got to my house.

"But then I looked across the street and there he was, standing in his front yard with his mouth hanging open. I'm surprised he wasn't recording it on his phone. Dustin saw *everything*," she announced just before flopping backward on my bed. I'm shocked she's so worried over what her ex-best friend—and occasional former hookup—thinks about her relationship with Ryan. "I haven't talked to him in what feels like forever, and the first time I see him, he gets to watch me argue with my boyfriend. Talk about humiliating."

She's been quiet ever since, silently stewing over what happened. I just hope they don't get into yet another argument tonight. What she needs is a little distance from Ryan.

"Do you think Dustin is here?" Livvy asks as we enter Cannon's house. The place is small, which means it's crowded inside and the music is so loud I can hardly hear myself think, let alone hear what Livvy is saying to me.

"Who knows?" And who cares? Livvy shouldn't. But she's scanning the room, trying to be subtle but failing miserably.

And I know she's not looking for her boyfriend either.

"If you spot him or Brianne, tell me." She turns to face me. "I want to talk to him."

"Why?" When she says nothing I slowly shake my head. "Talking to Dustin while you're in an argument with Ryan is like playing with fire, Liv. Someone's gonna get burned." Probably her, but I don't say that. She's a big girl. She can figure this stuff out on her own.

"But I need to explain to him what happened." She grabs my arm and gives it a squeeze. "It's embarrassing, knowing he watched us arguing. He heard Ryan say such awful things to me. I don't want him to think we're always like that."

"Who cares what he thinks about you and your relationship with Ryan?" I pull my arm out of her grip. "You should care more about Ryan and what *he's* thinking right now."

Livvy rolls her eyes and resumes her scan of the room once more. "I have nothing to say to him. Not until he apologizes to me first."

She's being ridiculous. "What exactly did he say to make you so mad?" I'm opening myself up to a minimum two-hour conversation here, but I'm too curious to stop myself.

"He called me a moody bitch." Livvy turns to look at me, her mouth formed into a thin line. "He's supposed to love me, not call me names. Right? Or am I expecting too much?"

Valid point, but I know how Livvy works. "So did you call him anything?"

"I said he was a rude prick." Livvy crosses her arms and sniffs, her lips curled downward in clear distaste.

Ah. And there it is. They sling insults at each other, and the angrier they get, the worse the insults are. I've seen it happen a few times lately. At first everything seemed perfect between them. I thought they were total couple goals.

But after Halloween, something switched. They've been getting on each other's nerves a lot quicker. She nags him and he picks on her. I'm tired of it and I'm not even the one in the relationship.

"Hey." I grab her hand and tug her close so I can whisper in her ear. "Forget Ryan. Forget Dustin. Let loose and have some fun. Just…don't let your boy problems ruin everything tonight."

Livvy pulls away, her eyes wide. "If you want me to let loose, you have to let loose too. I know you're still down in the dumps. We should both get our drink on tonight."

"We can't get too out of control," I warn her, unable to help myself. I'm like her mother and she's my wayward daughter.

She laughs. "We won't. I promise."

Uh huh.

Livvy squeezes my hand. "Forget Ryan. Forget Dustin. Forget Tuttle. Boys suck."

I nod and release her hand. "Totally. Boys do suck."

Maybe if I say it loud enough, I'll believe it. Because yes, Tuttle really does suck.

But then again, he doesn't. Not at all. He's damaged and emotionally stunted, yet he's also smart and sweet and quick to react and...

I miss him. I want him. If he walked into this house right now and demanded I talk to him, I would. I so would. I wouldn't even hesitate.

Which is stupid. I know this. I'm a logical person. My feelings for Tuttle are illogical and confusing. Does that mean those feelings are love?

I'm not sure.

Distance helps in the healing. Somewhat. The longer I go without dealing with Tuttle, the better it'll get. Maybe I'll even forget all about him someday.

Doubtful. But hey, a girl can dream.

"Oh God, is that Dustin over there?" Livvy stands on her tiptoes, trying to see over the crowd.

I slap her shoulder, making her yelp. "Stop looking for him! What did we just say?"

Her gaze meets mine. "Boys suck?" she asks weakly.

"Yes." I nod firmly. "They do. Forget him. Let's go." I hook my arm into hers and steer her through the crowd. "Let's go find the keg. Cannon told me it's in the backyard."

Livvy is smiling and waving at every guy we pass and I want to slap her hand down. It's like she turns on the flirt even harder when she's mad at Ryan. Just so she can prove to herself she's still got it.

"Please don't tell me Ryan's in the backyard." Is she pulling me into a trap or what?

"I have no idea where he's at." I've seen that innocent look on her face before.

"Really?" That one word drips with sarcasm. I can hear it. And I don't believe her. She probably knows exactly where Ryan's at.

And if they're near each other, she'll want to start another fight. Or even worse...

She'll go in search of Dustin, mess around with him yet again, and *really* start a fight. A big one. One that would most likely result in a breakup.

Yeah. Not going to happen on my watch. Livvy is a happy drunk. She has a beer or two and she's in a good mood. That's what she should stick to. I'll maybe have one beer, then I should stick with soda or water for the rest of the night.

Drowning my sorrows in booze won't help. They run too deep.

Just as we approach the kitchen I pull away from Livvy. "I need to go find the bathroom. I'll meet you in the backyard?"

She nods. "Don't ditch me."

I laugh and shake my head. "As if I would." I watch her walk away and then head down a short hall to find the bathroom. It's occupied, of course, but after only a minute a girl and guy I don't recognize walk out. The girl's face is bright red. The guy has a smirk on his face and waggles his eyebrows at me as he passes by.

Gross.

I use the bathroom quickly, wash my hands and am about to make my way to the kitchen when I hear someone from behind me say my name.

"Amanda."

I freeze at the sound of the familiar voice, and dread slithers down my spine. I knew I'd run into him. I always do. Though he'd been avoiding me as of late, I had a feeling he might talk to me if he saw me here tonight.

Slowly I turn to find Eli Bennett standing in front of me. Just turned fifteen years old, an adorable freshman and the star quarterback of the junior varsity team, he is Jordan Tuttle 2.0 in the making. "Eli." My voice is weak and I clear my throat. "Hey."

"What's goin'?" He leans in and kisses my cheek so quick I'm left startled when he shifts away from me. The boy has nerve. "Didn't think you and Liv would show up tonight."

"What makes you say that?" I'm frowning. I can't help it. Who's he talking about us with?

"Ryan."

Oh, right. Duh. His big brother.

Eli shakes his longish golden brown hair out of his eyes. "He told me he and Livvy got in a huge-ass fight."

"They argued," I agree, not wanting to say more. He'll run and tell Ryan if I gossip about him. Besides, I would never do that to Livvy.

"Those two should just end it." He makes a face. "My brother has all kinds of hot girls lined up who want him, so it's not like he's hurting."

"Eli." I'm chastising him like I'm his mama, but I can't help it. He shouldn't talk like this to me considering how close I am to Livvy.

"What? It's true." He smiles, his green eyes sparkling. He's gorgeous and he knows it, but I am so not interested. We had that stupid moment in Tuttle's bathroom, but it never amounted to much and I'm glad. I'm not necessarily proud of that moment, to be honest. Eli is way too young for me. "They're all lining up for me too, you know."

I glance around, seeing no girls nearby. "Huh. Is this line you speak of imaginary?"

He starts to laugh. "You never fall for anything I say, do you?"

"No." I smile. "I don't."

His laughter slowly dies. "I like you, Amanda. Too damn bad you don't feel the same way."

A sigh escapes me and I take a step closer. There's something sweet about Eli. One minute he's a complete horn dog saying the worst things and then the next he's like a vulnerable little boy seeking approval. "Eli, I'm too old for you. Go pick on someone your own age."

He makes a face. "The freshman girls suck. I've dated all the ones I was interested in and they went nowhere. Gone through a few sophomores too."

"Then tackle a junior," I suggest, patting him on the shoulder. "I'm sure you can find someone who might be interested in you."

"I'm not interested in anyone else." He shakes his head, sounding frustrated. "Just you."

"Didn't we already talk about this?" I don't understand his fascination with me. I thought it was a fleeting thing. I also thought he was terrified of Tuttle and that's why he left me alone, but maybe not.

Or maybe the entire football team knows—of course they know—that Tuttle and I are no longer together and Eli is making another attempt.

Seriously, I wish he'd direct his attention toward someone else.

"You haven't even given me a chance."

Now I step away from him. "Actually, I did. Remember? The night you told me I was fine as hell?" Talk about embarrassing. That entire night is a blur to me, and Eli almost ruined everything. Well, he sort of *did* ruin everything. I appreciate his enthusiasm, but...

"You *are* fine as hell," he says, his earnest voice interrupting my thoughts. He lets his gaze roam over me, lingering on my legs, which are on full display in the too-short dress. "Tuttle was a total dumbass to let you go."

Anger starts to simmer in my belly and I take another step back. What's with everyone slinging insults Jordan's way? I'm the only one allowed to do that. "Gotta go, Eli. Talk to you later."

"Aw, don't go away mad! Come on, Amanda!" he calls as I hurry away from him.

I don't turn around, don't acknowledge what he's saying. It's pointless. He'll just keep talking, trying to wear me down and I'm not interested. I'll give the kid points for determination, though.

I head to the kitchen in search of something else to drink besides beer when I spot our host Cannon looking like a giant while he sits alone at the tiny table by the window. There is so much going on around him, and his expression is so...

Sad.

He's having a huge party at his house yet he's sitting alone so I decide to go sit with him.

"Hey, Cannon."

He glances up and smiles briefly at me, but his blue eyes are still dim. "Hey, Amanda. I didn't think you'd show up."

"I told you I would." What he didn't believe me? I know he was in a bad mood during our car ride, but I hoped the party would cheer him up. Looks like that didn't work. "And here I am." I nod toward the empty chair across from his. "Can I join you?"

Cannon's expression switches from sad to pleased in an instant. "Yeah, sure. You want something to drink. A beer? If that's not your thing, I might have some vodka stashed in the cabinet above the fridge." He starts to stand, but I wave my hands at him, shaking my head.

"I don't think I want any beer." My stomach churns just thinking about it. Why am I suddenly so nervous?

"Ah, come on Amanda. Loosen up." He points at the empty chair across from him. "Sit down. Let me get you a drink."

"Fine. Okay." I flash him a smile as I sit and he offers a weak one in return. This is a boy who used to be a total player. Now he's sitting around looking like someone kicked his puppy. Maybe I do need a beer to deal with this. "I think I'll take you up on that beer."

"Awesome. Hey, Bennett!" Cannon practically roars, making me flinch.

Of course, Eli Bennett materializes out of nowhere. I'd rather avoid both Bennett brothers tonight, but I don't know if that's going to be possible.

"What's up, boss?" Eli asks, looking—and sounding—like an eager servant.

Weird.

"Get the lady a beer." Cannon nods in my direction and when Eli spots me, he smirks. "And don't say a word to her or I'll kick your ass."

I can tell Eli knows that Cannon means business. The smirk disappears and he practically runs to the fridge, pulling out a Bud Light and running back over to deliver it to Cannon. "Here you go," Eli says before he leaves, never once looking at me.

Well. That was kind of nice.

"What's up with you two?" I ask.

Cannon hands me the beer. "He's a little punk who needed to be put in his place. So I did."

I pop open the can and take a sip. It's nice and cold, better than the warm, foamy crap in the keg. I lucked out. "How?"

"I kicked his ass." He sends me a look when I start to giggle. "For real."

Clamping my lips shut, I nearly choke on the beer still in my mouth. I carefully set the can on the table and gape at Cannon. "What do you mean, you kicked his ass for real? Why?"

"He said some not so nice things about a friend of mine." Cannon shrugs those impossibly wide shoulders of his. They're even wider than

Jordan's, and that's saying a lot. "So I wanted to teach him a lesson."

"By kicking his ass."

"Eli's a little fucker. Just like his brother." Cannon sends me an apologetic look. "Sorry. I don't mean to curse in front of you."

"I can handle it," I say, taking another sip.

"And I know your friend Livvy is dating Ryan and that Eli even tried to get in your panties at that last party Tuttle had. And then Tuttle got all pissed off and wanted to fuck him up over it." The moment the words fall out of his mouth, he presses his lips together, his cheeks turning ruddy. "Sorry. That was rude of me. I should learn when to keep my mouth shut."

This is kind of funny. It's like Cannon's proving all those gentle giant stereotypes are real, though let's not forget he kicked Eli's ass. "You're only speaking the truth," I reassure him. "But yeah. The Bennett brothers are kind of awful sometimes."

"Kind of? They're awful almost all the damn time." Cannon shakes his head, looking pissed. "Eli called my—*friend* a slut. He was even spreading rumors that she'd suck anyone's dick on the football team. All they had to do was ask her. And I know that's not true." He grimaces. "Damn, I keep saying the worst things in front of you."

"Cannon." I reach out and touch the top of his hand, trying to reassure him. "It's no big deal. Say what you gotta say. It sounds like you need to get this off your chest."

"I do. I really do." He nods in agreement, downright vigorously. "She's a nice girl. She might have a reputation around school, but I know her. We've talked. A lot. Most of the time, she frustrates me, but I think that's because she doesn't know how to take—kindness." He makes a face. "That makes no sense. But maybe you know what I mean?"

Whoever he's talking about, she's reminding me of someone. "I do know what you mean. And maybe she doesn't know how to handle kindness because no one has been genuinely nice to her before?"

"That's what I'm thinking. I'm definitely nice to her. Maybe I'm too nice. I dunno." He takes a deep breath. "I want to watch out for her. Protect her. But she won't let me."

That is the sweetest thing ever. I take a huge swallow of my beer before I ask, "Who exactly are you talking about?"

Cannon parts his lips, ready to give me an answer, when a shrill voice calls out his name.

We both swivel our heads to see Em approaching the table with determined steps and fire blazing in her eyes. I swear she's mad that she's found Cannon and me sitting at the table together. Alone. With my hand still resting on top of his.

Whoops. I snatch it back, not missing the way Em's glaring at me. Almost like she's…jealous?

Okay. This is getting strange.

"I don't talk to you for a couple of hours and this is what you do? You go running to *Amanda?*" Em aims her angry fire on Cannon and he shrinks in his seat, like little Em is scaring the crap out of him. She rests her hands on her hips, the disappointment clear on her face. "So you're a liar. Just like the rest of them."

"It's not what you think—" he starts, but she cuts him off.

"That's what you all say." Em laughs, but there's no humor in the sound. No, her laughter is bitter. Angry.

Sad.

Just how Cannon's acting.

"Hey." I stand, practically thrust myself in front of Em so she can't see Cannon. I want her to focus on me, on what I'm about to say. "It really isn't what you think."

She tilts her head back because I'm taller than her, and I swear her chin wobbles. Like she's about to cry. "I thought you were my friend."

"I am." I take her hands and give them a shake. "I just got here. I saw Cannon and thought he looked sad, so I started talking to him. I've known him a long time, you know."

Em's eyes are dark, lined with thick black eyeliner, and so wide as she studies me. She looks like she wants to believe me, but she's still unsure.

"Em." I shake her hands again, harder this time, and I lower my voice. "I'm not into Cannon at all. I'm—I'm still in love with Tuttle."

It took a lot to admit that. And I think Em knows it too.

Realization seems to flicker in her eyes. "So you're just friends? That's it?"

"Yes. We're friends. I don't want Cannon like that. And I really don't think he's into me either." I squeeze her hands one more time before I let them go and say in a low voice, "But I do think he likes you."

She blinks once, twice, like she's startled. "Really?" Her voice is a breathless whisper, and I'm baffled. These two are totally into each other. It's obvious. So why are they acting like this?

Huh. I could ask Tuttle the same question I guess.

"Yes. Really," I say, my voice flat. This is what happens when I think about Tuttle and our situation and how stupid it is. Doesn't he see that? Doesn't he realize just how ridiculous he's being by denying that he has feelings for me?

Because I know he has feelings for me. He cares about me. And he'd rather push me away. Keep me out of his life.

It's so incredibly frustrating.

And stupid.

Em glances over at Cannon before she returns her gaze to mine. "You're still in love with Tuttle?" Hearing her say the words out loud makes me wince. "You should tell him. He's here. I just saw him."

My heart trips over itself. "What? He's *here*?" I didn't think he was coming, though I'd secretly hoped. "Are you serious?"

"Yeah. When I first got here, I saw him outside, leaning against his Range Rover, looking irritated and sexy, though I don't know how he manages to do both." Em laughs and shakes her head. "You should totally go find him and talk to him. I know he'll listen to you."

Yeah right. "He already knows how I feel." My heart is racing. It never seems to remain calm when Jordan is nearby. "It's a waste of my time to talk to him."

"I don't know about that," Em says slowly, her attention focused on Cannon. Her lips curl into a flirtatious smile. "Hey, you got anything for me to drink, Whittaker?"

And that's it. I'm forgotten, which I can't blame her for, because if she really likes him, I get that. Wanting to spend all her time with the boy she wants, I've been there. I've so been there.

Walking through the kitchen, I go to the door that leads to the backyard, watching everyone outside. I spot Livvy on the far side of the yard, talking with Ryan, her expression closed off, her arms crossed in front of her like she's trying to keep him away. Her body language says it all. A breakup is imminent.

I turn away and head for the fridge, where I find another cold Bud Light. I open it and chug half of it in a few gulps, wipe a hand across my mouth before I finish it off. My head is already spinning and I toss the empty can in the sink, turning away from the fridge to glance around the kitchen.

No one's paying me any attention. I'm alone. It's like I'm invisible.

It doesn't matter what I do, because no one is going to notice me doing it. Right?

Shrugging, I go into the living room, where loud music is playing and a bunch of girls are dancing. I join them, laughing when they easily accept me. They all yell and cheer and one of them grabs my hand, pulling me into the center. We're all dancing and singing the words to the popular song currently playing. Guys start to take notice of us and they hover nearby and watch us, though they never join in the dancing.

Chickens.

Speaking of chickens, Jordan Tuttle is nowhere to be seen.

Of course.

The song ends and another fast one starts, making us cheer all over again. More girls join us and it's getting so hot. My hair sticks to the back of my neck and I lift it up, trying to cool myself off.

"Want a drink, Amanda?"

I turn to see a girl I knew from band standing in front of me with a smile, a red cup of foamy beer in each hand. I take one from her with a loud thank-you, ready to bring the drink to my lips when a hand shoots out of nowhere and snatches the cup from my fingers.

"Hey!" I yell, lifting my head to find myself staring into Jordan Tuttle's eyes. He's glaring at me, clearly irritated and gorgeous and infuriatingly sexy while gripping the red cup in his hand like he wants to crush it.

My skin tingles.

My heart flips.

He doesn't move and neither do I—until someone calls out his name.

The moment he's distracted, I turn and run away.

chapter five

Tuttle

I'm only here because I knew *she* would be here. It's like I have no control. When I got home after the game, I took a shower. Jerked off. Dried off. Thought about shaving but didn't, because I'm too lazy. Got dressed. Climbed into my car. Made the drive to Cannon Whittaker's house without even thinking about it. It was like I suddenly found myself pulling into his driveway with no recollection of making the journey there.

I killed the engine and sat there, watching the house for a while. So many people. They were everywhere. At least at my house, it's big enough you can't see them all. Here, they're all I see.

Except for the one person I *wanted* to see. I knew she was inside. I could feel it—feel her presence. Maybe she's what drew me here.

Ridiculous. Illogical. Yet here I am. Trying to come up with the courage to go find her.

After a few minutes, I got out of the SUV. Leaned against it, watching people go past, a few of them calling my name in greeting, and I nodded in return. Most of them say nothing at all, they just stare at me as they walk past. I stood outside for a solid fifteen minutes, contemplating my next move. Hesitant. Full of doubt.

Totally unlike myself.

"Fuck it," I muttered, and headed toward the house, not paying attention to anyone, not bothering to say a word. I opened the front door, pausing as I scanned the room, and she was the first person I lay eyes on.

Amanda. Dancing with a bunch of girls I didn't recognize, wearing a tight dress that revealed every curve and showcased her long, sexy legs. Her hair down, dark and wavy around her face and tempting me to plunge my hands in it. Wrap those silky strands around my fist so I could drag her back into the nearest bedroom and have my way with her.

Yeah. I'm thinking like a caveman. This is what she does to me.

I was heading toward Amanda when another girl came out of the kitchen with red Solo cups in each hand. She offered one to Amanda and I intercepted it just before she takes a drink.

From the glassy look in her eyes, I'd guess she's already had plenty of alcohol to drink.

God, she's beautiful. And this is torture. Coming here. Seeking her out. Her dark eyes go wide when they meet mine and I can hardly move. Neither can she. She sinks her teeth into her lower lip, a look I've seen her give me time and again, and I want to be the one who bites her lip. Taste her skin. Kiss her mouth.

"Tuttle!"

I turn away from Amanda to find Ryan is standing in front of me, a drunken smile plastered on his stupid face.

"What's up dude?" he asks with a laugh.

I acknowledge him with a lackluster one-finger salute, keeping my mouth shut. I don't want to deal with this guy. I need to talk to Amanda.

But when I turn back around, she's gone.

Gone.

Shoving past a questioning Ryan, I go on pure instinct, pushing through the crowd in the living room, ignoring everyone, my only focus on finding her.

The house is small. She couldn't have gone too far. I need to find her. I have to talk to her.

I have to.

chapter six

Amanda

He's chasing after me. I can feel him getting closer, and I try to push past the crowds of people filling Cannon's house to gain some distance, but it's no use. His fingers eventually close around my upper arm, halting my progress, and I whirl on him, jerking against his ever-strengthening hold.

"Let me go!" I'm yelling to be heard above the music, and I don't care if people are watching. Listening. I want to cause a scene. Maybe it'll actually force him to react. He's so cold all the time. So distant.

Even when he tries to talk to me, when he's almost desperate to make himself heard, he doesn't make much sense. He talks in circles. Claims he can't do the things that should come easy to him. How hard can it be, to love someone? What barriers are in his way?

"I want to talk to you," he starts, but I shake my head, cutting him off. I've heard this all before. We won't get anywhere.

I'm over it.

Maybe someday I'll be over him too.

"I don't want to listen to you. I'm *done* listening to you." My skin is tingling where he touches me, and I'm so annoyed by my body's reaction, I tug even harder, trying to get out of his grip. "Let me go, Tuttle."

The anger on his face is obvious. He hates it when I call him Tuttle. Well, too damn bad. "You're being unreasonable."

"*You're* being unreasonable," I throw back at him like a child ready to launch into a major temper tantrum. "You want to start fighting in front of everyone? Because I'm up for it. I can yell and scream and kick and tell them you're holding me against my will."

His expression turns dark. Thunderous. "You wouldn't do that."

"Try me," I say smugly.

The music is still playing but people have stopped dancing, talking, laughing. They're watching us with wide eyes, some of them holding up their phones. Recording the argument? Maybe they're snapping a few photos to throw up on social media? For once, I really don't care.

"You're being unreasonable." His tone softens and I tell myself not to let my resolve do the same. "Just hear me out, Mandy. Please."

I hate it when he calls me Mandy. And I really hate it when he says please because he so rarely does. Hearing him say that word makes me want to give in and let him talk to me. Let myself believe in what he wants to say.

Murmurs start and the crowd slowly parts, a fuming Cannon emerging from its depths. His face is red and his eyes are narrowed as he strides toward the two of us. I sneak a quick glance at Tuttle, but his face is a mask. He almost looks...

Bored. By the entire situation.

I'm tempted to stomp on his foot just to make him react.

"Hey." Cannon's voice is sharp as he tries to wedge his broad body between Tuttle and me. His back is to me and I can't see anything around him. He's as big as a wall. "What the hell do you think you're doing, Tuttle? Let her go."

"Stay out of it, Whittaker," Jordan says between clenched teeth just before he lets me go. I take a step back, needing the distance from the sudden testosterone-fueled air. "Leave us alone."

"We were having no problems at my party until you decided to show up." Cannon takes a step toward Jordan, looming over him. They're so close their chests are practically touching, but neither one backs down. "Leave her alone."

Cannon's voice leaves no room for argument. But seeing the look on Tuttle's face, all that earlier supposed boredom is gone. He appears enraged, his hands clutched into fists, like he's ready to throw one straight at Cannon's face.

Fear trickles through me, leaving me cold, and I wrap my arms around myself.

"Stay out of our business." Jordan's voice is hard, as is his expression. His jaw is so tight it looks like it might shatter.

"If you two have business, then take it elsewhere. You don't need to start anything at *my* house." Cannon turns to look at me, his gaze imploring. My new friend Cannon, rushing to my defense. Who knew he'd do this? Definitely not me. "Do you want to talk to him, Amanda? You don't have to."

I'm torn. Part of me wants to listen to what Jordan will say. The other part wants to tell Jordan to kiss my ass and never speak to me again.

"Say yes, Amanda," Jordan commands like he's the boss of me.

Hearing him talk like that makes me want to punch him. The fear switches to anger just like that, and I stride toward him, ready to push, punch, scream, whatever gets my point across, when someone shouts and shoves Cannon from behind.

It all happens so fast. Cannon yells. Jordan starts swinging. I hear phones clicking, flashes going off as people in the crowd snap pictures. Two of our best football players are going at it, and I'm stuck in the middle.

"Fight!"

I get caught, both boys having a shoving match with me in between them. Cannon grabs hold of my arm. "Get out of the way!"

I try to, slithering out of Cannon's loose grip before stumbling into Jordan. He grips me by the shoulders, his gaze locking with mine and I suck in a sharp breath at the anger I see on his face, in his eyes.

But I know it's not anger toward me. He's mad at Cannon.

"Let her go, Tuttle! She doesn't want to talk to you!" Cannon roars.

Jordan holds up his empty hands, sending Cannon a death look. "Give me a break. I'm not even touching her."

"Leave her alone!" Cannon continues, his face going red. I appreciate his rushing to my defense, but it's not necessary. Jordan isn't hurting me. He's not even touching me. I don't get what the big deal is.

It's a big deal though. The entire party is starting to fall apart. People begin shouting. Arguing. The music shuts off and girls scatter in all directions, screaming at the top of their lungs. I hear the crash of glass, an agonizing yowl, and I realize quick everything's fallen into complete chaos.

"This is ridiculous," Jordan mutters just before he hooks his fingers around my elbow. "Let's get out of here."

"No." My defiant tone is loud and I shake my head. "I'm not leaving with you."

"Wanna make a bet?" One brow lifts and he smirks. It's adorable.

And infuriating.

"Tuttle." Cannon steps around us, grabbing hold of Jordan's arm, but Jordan pulls back, sending his elbow straight into my left eye. He nails me so hard I fall backward, landing on the floor with a hard thud that makes my teeth slam shut and my butt hurt. My skirt is wound around my thighs and I can taste blood on my tongue. Not to mention the throbbing that's started below my left eye.

A groan leaves me and I let my head drop to the floor, my hand flying up to cover the left side of my face. The metallic taste of blood fills my mouth and I close my eyes, fighting the dizziness swamping me.

"Jesus!" I hear Jordan yell and then he's kneeling next to me, his hands roaming over my body, fingers pulling my skirt down over my thighs. "Are you okay? God, tell me you're okay."

I crack my right eye open, my hand still covering the left. "You hit me."

His expression is nothing less than horrified. "I didn't hit you."

"Your elbow hit me. By accident." I close my eyes, the beer sloshing around in my stomach making me nauseous. Everything's making me nauseous. All the yelling. The scent of Jordan's cologne. The people darting around us. I'm scared someone's going to step on me and hurt me even more. "It hurts."

"Damn it," he mutters just before he scoops me up in his arms and stands, cradling me close. "We're getting you out of here."

"Put me down," I protest weakly, but he ignores me, which is best.

I don't really want him to put me down.

I hear Cannon yelling at everyone to *calm their tits* and it makes me laugh. But laughing only makes me feel worse, so I stop. Instead I gaze up at Tuttle, studying him as he walks down the short hall where the bathroom is located, carrying me like I don't weigh a thing.

He looks so handsome and worried and furious. His jaw is still tight. I can see a tic there, hear him exhale extra hard. There's the shadow of stubble on his cheeks and jaw, his hair is unruly—he seriously needs to get a haircut—and his eyes are dark, hooded. Full of fire.

Without warning he lifts his leg and kicks a door open, making a couple kissing on the center of a bed leap apart in shock. It's got to be Cannon's room. There are posters all over the wall, some of beautiful girls wearing little clothing, but most of them are of NFL football heroes. Future aspirations, I guess.

"What the hell?" the guy yells at Tuttle, but neither of us say a word.

He starts to check the next door, but I rest my hand on his chest, stopping him. "That's the bathroom."

Jordan glances down at my hand resting on his chest before lifting his gaze to mine. "Still want to hit me?"

I slowly shake my head, waiting for the embarrassment or shame to come. But surprisingly, it doesn't. "I'm over it."

"Good."

We finally find a tiny room with only a plain desk and a narrow single bed in it. Jordan turns on the overhead light after he shuts the door behind us and takes me over to the bed, carefully setting me down. His gaze is searching, roaming all over my face, lingering on my left eye.

"Can I touch you?"

"Why?"

"I want to make sure your eye isn't worse than I think it is." He reaches out, hesitant, his hand hovering in the air between us. "Can I?"

I remain quiet, getting lost in his eyes for a moment before I finally give a tiny nod of permission.

His fingers are gentle when they land on my cheek, just below my eye. He presses down on my skin, shifting up until he's feeling along my cheekbone, getting closer and closer to my eye until I finally wince when he touches one particular spot. "That hurts?"

His voice is a low, sexy murmur that I feel right to the very depths of my soul. Even though I'm in pain with a swimming stomach, a cut tongue and a blooming black eye, he still manages to give me butterflies.

"Yeah," I whisper. "It hurts a lot. Your elbow is like a lethal weapon."

Jordan makes a face and shakes his head. "I can't believe that happened. Are you sure it wasn't Whittaker who nailed you in the eye?"

"It was you." I suck in a sharp breath when he brushes wayward strands of hair away from my forehead. I wish he wouldn't touch me like that. Look at me like that. Like I might still matter. Like he might still care. "You hit me hard."

"I didn't know you were standing that close."

"I was right in the middle of you two." I sound incredulous because I am.

"You were also beating me up." He smiles, the arrogant jerk. "Rather ineffectively, but it was cute."

I glare at him. "Don't call me cute. I was trying to hurt you."

His smile disappears, though I can tell it's a struggle for him to remain neutral. "You were trying to hurt me?"

"Yes." He touches my forehead again, like he can't help it, and I want to tell him to stop, but it feels too good. My eyes fall closed and I savor the feeling of his fingers skimming my skin, lightly searching around my eye. I wince again, and he pauses.

"I see bruises."

"I'm sure I'm going to look hideous tomorrow."

"You could never look hideous."

I can't stop the smile from curling my lips. "You haven't seen me with a black eye yet, so never say never."

He chuckles. "Where's your phone?"

"I don't have it with me." I frown. "I left it in the car."

"Whose car?"

"Livvy's. We came to the party together." My eyes pop open. "I need to find her. I need to tell her I'm okay. I need to see if she's okay." I start to sit up, but Jordan stops me, his hands going to my shoulders and pushing me back down so I'm lying on the bed.

"I'll text her," he says, his voice gentle. Soothing. "Don't worry about it. You need to rest." He pulls his iPhone out of the back pocket of his jeans and his fingers fly over the screen.

"I'm perfectly fine." *I'm also a liar.* "I don't need rest. I need to get out of here." I sit up this time, so fast my head spins and I rest a hand over my churning stomach, closing my eyes again in hopes it'll ward off the nausea. But that doesn't help either, since my head is swimming. I carefully lie back down and throw my arm over my eyes. "I think I drank too much."

"How much did you have to drink?"

"Um, two beers? Maybe three? But I drank them really fast."

"Too fast?"

"Yeah, and plus I was dancing and it was so hot and crowded in the living room. I think that's my problem. I just need to cool down."

Jordan inhales sharply and shifts on the side of the bed, coming closer to me. I can feel his body heat, smell his scent, which isn't as overpowering as it was just a few minutes ago. "You looked really good out there," he admits, his voice low and sexy and vaguely irritating.

Only because I think it's sexy. "Dancing with the girls. The dress. Your hair. You look pretty tonight, Amanda."

My heart soars at the compliment and I want to tell it to calm the hell down. He's given me plenty of compliments before, but does he actually mean them? "Thanks." My stomach makes an embarrassing noise and I rest my other hand on my belly. "I shouldn't have drunk those beers."

"Are you going to be sick?" Now he sounds a little freaked out.

I shake my head and stop immediately because ow, that hurts. "No, I think I'll be okay." I keep my hand there, as if it'll somehow calm me down. "I told myself I wasn't going to drown my sorrows tonight in booze."

"Drown your sorrows? What sorrows?"

Ugh, that he would even say that sort of pisses me off.

"My Jordan Tuttle sorrows." Thank God my eyes are covered so I don't have to see him. I'm shocked and pissed at myself for saying those words out loud. "You never heard me say that."

He's silent for a moment, most likely considering what his reply should be. "But I did." His voice is even softer than before. I think I shocked him.

"Well, act like you didn't. Pretend the words don't matter, okay?" I can't look at him, can't face the humility of saying what I just did in front of him. He's the cause of my sorrows. I just told him that. What must he think? Does he pity me? Feel sorry for me? Though I know he's said some pretty messed up things too. Yet I refused to listen.

Maybe we're even.

"Amanda—"

I interrupt him. "I don't want to talk about it. Please. There's nothing left to say between us, don't you think?"

He's quiet again, and the silence is so unnerving I'm almost desperate to fill it with meaningless words. "Why would you say that?"

I'm scrambling to come up with a reason. A good one. A strong, valid reason to make him stay away once and for all. I drop my arm from my eyes, though I still keep them closed, and part my lips, ready to say something when the door crashes open and I hear Livvy's voice.

"There you are! I've been looking everywhere!"

chapter seven

Livvy rushes into the tiny room, filling it up with over-the-top, stressed-out vibes. I crack open my eyes and watch as she approaches the bed, dropping to her knees so she can be face level with me. Her eyes are wide and staring into mine as she reaches out and rests her hand on my forearm, her nails digging into my skin. She zeroes right in on my black eye, her face crinkling in horror just before she lifts her angry gaze to Jordan.

"You did this to her?" Oh, she sounds mad as hell.

Jordan stands and takes a step away, almost like he's afraid of her. "It was an accident."

"Oh, so your *fist* connecting with her *eye* was an *accident*? How gullible do you think I am, Tuttle?" Livvy turns to examine me once more, and her voice drops to the barest whisper. "Do you want me to take you to the emergency room? Call the cops? We can make a report. I'll help you. Whatever you want to do, I'm here for you, but know this. He needs to pay for hurting you, Amanda. He can't get away with hitting you. Your eye looks *terrible*. I can't believe he did this! Has he been abusing you all along?"

"Oh my God, Olivia. Seriously. You need to chill out." I grab hold of her hand and give it a tight squeeze. She looks borderline hysterical. "He hit me *accidentally* with his *elbow*. He didn't mean to do it. I promise."

The skeptical look she sends me says it all. "His elbow?"

"Check with everyone who just watched it go down. Half of them were recording it on their phones." I try not to think about that part because talk about humiliating. I'm sure my getting nailed with an elbow is already making its appearance on everyone's Snapchat stories.

I sink my head into the flat pillow and close my eyes. I'm exhausted. My head still hurts. My eye hurts. My tongue hurts, though it stopped bleeding a while ago so that's good. "I was the one beating up Jordan first," I explain to Livvy. "I got in between him and Cannon to try and stop their argument, and the next thing I know, I'm taking an elbow to the eye."

"Wait a minute. Are you saying Cannon and Tuttle were fighting over *you?*" I crack my eyes open to see her brows are so high they're practically in her hairline. She turns to look at Tuttle. "What's going on there?"

"Ask Amanda. I don't know what's up with them."

I roll my eyes, but that's painful too, so I stop. "He's into Em," I tell Livvy. "Cannon is, I mean. He doesn't like me like that. They weren't fighting over me, I swear."

"Cannon Whittaker likes Em? Really?" Livvy shakes her head with wonder. "Who knew?"

"He acts like he's into you. He was trying to stop us from talking,"

Jordan says, his voice tight as he stares right at me. "Like I'm a threat to you or whatever."

Livvy sighs. "This is sounding way too familiar." She studies me. "Are you really okay? Do you want me to drive you home? I can. I don't mind. I'm completely sober."

"I'll take her home," Jordan says, making both of us turn and glare at him.

"Is that what you want?" Livvy asks me.

Yes. Yes, it's exactly what I want. But is it a smart move? Am I just setting myself up for heartbreak yet again? How many times can we do this to each other? How many times can I endure the back and forth with my emotions before I finally can't take it anymore?

"Hey." We all turn toward the door where Ryan is standing, looking contrite. "You okay, Amanda? I brought ice for your eye." He holds up a Ziploc bag full of ice cubes.

"I'm fine," I say as I sit up, wincing at the pain lancing through my head. "Is everything okay out there?"

Jordan goes to Ryan and takes the bag of ice from him before bringing it over to me. I take it from him and gently set it over my eye, sucking in a sharp breath from the coldness.

"Someone broke a glass vase in the living room, but otherwise, everything's fine. Cannon made everybody go out to the backyard." Ryan smiles at Livvy. "Ready to go, baby?"

I think I just threw up a little in my mouth. I hate the way he just called her baby. Not even an hour ago she was spitting fire and ready to hook up with Dustin just to prove some weird point. Now she's looking at him with hearts in her eyes like he's her personal savior.

"Amanda? You'll be okay with him?" She sends Jordan one of her famous death looks.

I shift the bag of ice over my eye, hoping this helps, because the icy cold against my skin sucks. "I'll be fine. Promise. Text me when you get home." Realization dawns. "Wait, my phone is in your car. I should go—"

"You're not going anywhere," Jordan interrupts before he turns to Ryan. "Can you grab Amanda's phone from Livvy's car for me?"

"Uh, sure." Annoyance flashes on Ryan's face, and then he's gone.

Livvy starts to giggle. "He doesn't like it when someone tells him what to do."

"I know," Jordan says smugly, making us all laugh.

Ryan returns minutes later with my phone in his hand and Cannon in tow. He's the one who delivers my phone to me, his cheeks ruddy with embarrassment.

"You okay, Amanda? I didn't mean to cause all that trouble." He sends a look toward Jordan. "We cool, man? I don't want to fight with you."

"I don't want to fight with you either, so we're cool. And I didn't mean to cause a scene. Your house didn't get trashed, did it?" Jordan asks.

"Nah, it's all good. I made everyone go outside. The temperature will drop and then they'll all bail." Cannon shakes his head with a faint smile. "This'll be the talk of school come Monday, won't it?"

"Most likely." Jordan pauses. "You mind if we stay here for a few more minutes? I want to make sure Amanda's okay before she starts moving around."

Geez, what is he? My dad? Though it's kind of sweet, how worried he is about me.

"Yeah, sure. No problem. However long it takes," Cannon says easily. "Sorry again, Amanda. I was just trying to help."

I send Cannon a smile. "I know. And I appreciate it."

"We'll get out of your hair," Livvy says, steering both boys out of the room. She glances at me over her shoulder, mouthing, "text me later" right before Jordan closes the door behind them.

And now once again, we're all alone.

He walks over to the bed and sits on the edge of the mattress, closest to the end. "How you feeling?"

"I'm okay." I run my tongue over my teeth and grimace. "My tongue hurts."

"What? Why?"

"I bit it when I got hit and I think I cut it."

He scoots closer. "Let me see."

I clamp my lips shut. "No."

"Come on. Let me see. What if it's serious?"

"Serious as my black eye? I doubt it."

"Your eye isn't black." He tilts his head to the side. "Yet."

"Whatever. You can't even see it." I drop the bag of ice beside me on the bed. "I need a break from the ice."

"You should keep the ice on your eye. It'll keep down the swelling and bruising."

"It's cold."

"That's the point."

He makes a growling sound that's part scary, part sexy. "Show me your tongue, Amanda," he demands.

I stick my tongue out at him and he leans in, examining it closely, which is just…weird. It makes me think of his tongue. How it's been in my mouth, curling around mine. How he's licked my neck, my chest, many parts of my body. How he went down on me and proved that his tongue was downright magical…

And now my head is spinning for an entirely different reason. I close my mouth and our eyes meet. "See anything awful?"

"No." He slowly shakes his head. "A tiny cut, but nothing major."

I don't know what to say. How to act. So I hold the ice against my eye once more instead. "I feel better now."

Jordan frowns. "Are you sure? You want fresh ice? Ibuprofen?"

"No, I'm fine. Really." I smile and make to get off the bed so I can stand on my own two feet like a normal person, but he grabs hold of my ankle, stopping me.

"Rest for a few minutes longer. You don't want to move too fast and make it worse," he says, his voice low, his gaze roaming over me hungrily, like he wants to eat me up.

My skin goes tight and I'm tingling. I should not be—*turned on* by the way he's looking at me. My eye is throbbing. I feel like I've been beat up. I *have* been beat up.

So why am I wishing he would just lean over and kiss me?

I must be crazy. Something was knocked loose when he hit me with his elbow.

"Why did you come to the party?" I ask him.

He appears startled for a moment, but then that smooth, Jordan Tuttle mask appears, and I can't get a good read on him. "Cannon invited me."

"Right. And you always come to parties when someone else throws them." I raise a brow. "Were you looking for someone?"

"Yeah," he says slowly. "I was, actually."

Not the answer I expected. And if he says Lauren Mancini, I will lose my mind.

"Well, maybe you should get back out there and keep looking," I suggest. Then I remember his offer to take me home and how I agreed to it. "I'll be fine by myself for a few minutes. I just want to rest."

"But I don't need to look anymore. I already found her." He's watching me like I've completely lost my mind, which yeah, is probably true. I'm torturing myself by trying to figure out who he's trying to hook up with tonight.

Did he come here tonight to find someone to hook up with? Did I get in his way? I know he said he wanted to talk to me, but that's nothing. Maybe he was just going to tell me to stay out of his way. Stay out of his business.

Not that I care. Not really.

Okay fine, I care a lot. But I can fake it with the best of them when I need to.

"Well, what are you waiting for? Go back out there and talk to her. Or whatever it is that you do to work your sexual magic on her." I wave at him like I'm shooing away a fly.

Jordan frowns, his dark brows furrowing. "Are you really feeling okay? You're not acting right."

I heave out a big sigh and pull my leg out of his grip, which makes my skirt ride up way too far on my thighs. I tug on it, not wanting to flash him my panties, and of course his gaze drops right there. Like he's trying to figure out what color my panties are.

In case anyone's curious, they're black. Like Jordan Tuttle's soul.

"I'm fine. Stop asking," I tell him before I drop my head and fixate on the tops of my thighs. It's easier than looking at Jordan. I don't know what's going on between us, and I hate how natural this feels when he is so clearly still fighting what's happening between us.

"When I said I found her, I was talking about you, Amanda." I lift my head, our gazes clashing. His face is so serious, so handsome and earnest. I try to glare, to pretend he has no effect on me, but I can feel my resolve melting when I see the tenderness in his gaze.

Why does he have to look at me like that?

"Are you saying this to make me feel better? Because you're afraid I have a concussion or whatever? Or you feel guilty because you gave me a black eye?" I reach out and rest my hand on his knee, unable to stop myself from touching him. "Be real with me. Be honest."

His gaze drops to where my hand rests on his knee and stays there for long, quiet seconds, allowing me to get lost in the moment. Pretending that we're together and he's totally into me and I'm totally into him. When he lifts his head, he's staring at me in the same way, like he can't believe we're here together and it's—nice. His gaze does a lazy perusal of me, starting from the top of my head and ending at the tips of my toes, lingering on what he'd probably consider the good bits.

Like my (nonexistent) boobs. My waist, my hips.

He's such a typical boy.

"Jordan." My voice is wobbly and I clear my throat. "Are you going to say something?"

His gorgeous blue eyes flicker with unmistakable pleasure. "You said my name."

Is that all he can focus on? Figures. "Is that it?"

He frowns. "No. I don't know. It's like I get near you, and I don't know what to say next. I can't help it, Mandy."

"Don't call me that," I snap, and he rears his head back, clearly startled at my show of anger.

Well, good. I never act angry toward him. It's about time Jordan feels my wrath.

"I'm sorry." His deep voice is quiet, reverberating within me. I love his voice. His face. His thick, dark hair and his square, masculine jaw, which is currently covered in stubble. I bet he'd give me beard burn if he kissed me for even a few minutes, and I'd also bet I'd love every moment of it.

His words suddenly sink in and I blink up at him. "What did you just say?" Did he really apologize?

"I said I'm sorry. I won't call you Mandy anymore." His gaze is imploring as he studies me. "Why did you say that earlier?"

The swift change of subject is jarring. "What are you talking about?"

"Earlier, at the game. You told me you missed me. It was so— unexpected." He shakes his head. "I didn't know how to answer you."

"So you thought the smart move was to say nothing? Thanks for that, by the way, because you made me feel incredibly stupid." Like how I feel right now, being trapped in this tiny room with him, where he seems to suck up all the air with just his mere presence.

"I didn't mean to make you feel stupid. I was the stupid one to walk away like that."

I snort in response and his lips curl into the faintest smile. His perfect face is too perfect, and *ugh*. It's positively unfair how gorgeous he is. It's also unfair how I can be so ready to forgive him when he offers me up the smallest smile as his apology.

He's stingy with those smiles. And he's even stingier with his laughter.

"You were stupid," I agree, removing my hand from his knee. I need to stop touching him. We're too close, this moment feels too intimate and I need to make it stop. Create some distance.

"I'm always afraid whatever I say to you will fuck it all up," he admits in a low whisper. "So most of the time, I think it's best to say nothing at all."

"Yes, and you somehow still manage to fuck it up, even when you're quiet." His eyes go wide at me dropping the f-bomb and I smile, rather pleased with myself. It's not easy to shock the unshockable Jordan Tuttle.

"I'm starting to realize that," he says.

"Please. There are a lot of things you don't realize." I pause. "A ton."

He arches a dark brow. "Like what?"

Men. They always want facts.

"You don't seem to ever realize my feelings."

He says nothing.

"You don't realize that it's not a bad thing, having a girlfriend." I glance down, running my fingers over the bag of melting ice, before my gaze returns to his.

His eyes are lighting up at the mention of the word girlfriend, but he's not getting an easy pass.

Not even close.

"You don't realize that you had someone who would've always been in your corner, fighting for you no matter what. Nope, you let that slip right through your fingers like the idiot you are." He flinches at my harsh words and I only feel a little guilty. I'm getting to him. My words are bothering him and that's a good sign.

"So what you're saying is that I can't get you—it back."

"No." I shake my head. "You've lost the privilege."

Jordan frowns. "I can't even earn it back?"

"How? You've stomped all over it." All over me. All over my freaking heart. "There's really no way to get it back."

"I want to try." He says this so quietly, I have to lean forward just to semi-hear him.

"Are you serious?" Unable to stop myself, I start laughing. Oh, he's hilarious, this guy. "Do you even know how to do that?"

"Do what?" His frown deepens.

"Try."

Everything comes so easy for him. Or at least, it seems to come easy. Maybe some things are hard for Jordan. This has been hard on him. What we're doing. Or at least, I *think* it's been hard on him.

I hope it's been hard on him. If not, then he's inhuman.

"Not very well," he says truthfully, along with a halfhearted shrug. "Things are just…given to me. It's been that way my entire life. I've rarely had to fight for anything. The football scholarship I want to earn to the school of *my* choice, and you. Those are the two hardest things I've ever had to fight for." He takes a deep breath and slowly lets it out. "And I feel like I'm losing both battles."

"You're losing this particular battle." I point my thumb at my chest, indicating myself. "But I think you already know that."

He says nothing. Just watches me with that pitiful little boy look he's perfected.

"I think I need to be alone for a little while. Just so I can close my eyes and rest for a few minutes before you take me home." More like I need some time by myself so I can go over what he just said to me.

He doesn't so much as budge. In fact, he shifts closer, his body nudging against mine, and I'm tempted to shove him off the bed.

But I don't.

"A few minutes? Please?"

Jordan gives the slowest shake of his head I think I've ever seen.

"Seriously?" I lift my hands palms up in pure frustration. "Are you holding me captive now? Is this how low you'll go to keep me in the same room as you?"

"I'll go even lower if I have to. Hold you down, tie you up, whatever it takes to convince you that I mean it. That I want to fight for you. That

I want—you." He sort of chokes out that last word, and I suppose him saying the word out loud should set my heart aflutter but forget it.

That stumble over the word *you* has thoroughly pissed me off.

"You talk a good game. But you never come through. Ever." I shake my head but stop because it hurts. I'm going to have a killer headache tomorrow. "How is it you can throw all of those amazing touchdowns, yet you can't seem to ever score a girlfriend?"

His nostrils flare, and I wonder if I made him angry. "I haven't met anyone I wanted to make my girlfriend before."

"Seriously?" I still have a hard time believing these sorts of statements when they come from him.

"Seriously." He hesitates, his expression softening. "Until I met you."

"Please." I snort, not caring if I sound unladylike. He's the one who sent me sprawling to the ground with his elbow. So now he gets to see me through all my good *and* bad moments. "Stop lying to me."

"I'm not lying."

"Whatever." I grab the bag of ice, but it's wet and most of the ice has melted. I drop it to the ground, feeling vaguely guilty I'm getting the carpet wet.

"Haven't we had this argument before?" he drawls.

This, of course, reminds me of our stupid argument in the guest bathroom at his house. The night he thought Eli Bennett kissed me.

"Please." The anger slips from my voice, replaced by sadness. "Just leave me alone for a few minutes."

"I'll take you home right now." He touches my arm, making my skin tingle. "You need to rest."

"I need to get away from you," I mutter, sucking in a shocked breath when he shifts position so he's sitting next to me on the narrow bed and I'm practically in his lap, my back to his front, my head resting on his broad shoulder.

How did this even happen?

What's worse is that I'm enjoying it, being in Jordan's arms again. I sort of melt into him like I can't help myself.

Which I think is my biggest problem.

"You don't want to talk?" he asks softly. I can feel his breath stir the hair at my temple, and oh God, it feels so good, sitting like this.

"There's nothing more we can talk about," I say weakly.

"You're right." He leans forward, nuzzling the side of my face with his. "Then let's not waste our breath talking."

His hand cups my cheek and turns my head toward his, and then we're kissing. His lips are soft and seeking, never pushing too hard, and I forget about everything. The fight. The elbow to my eye. Falling onto my butt in front of everyone.

All I can focus on is the texture of Jordan's lips, how damp and warm they are as they press against mine. How natural it feels to be sitting with him like this, his hand on my face, my hand on his chest.

This is dangerous for my well-being. So dangerous. Yet I can't stop. I don't want to stop.

"Jordan," I whisper when his lips drift across my face. My nose. One cheek, then the other. My knees are wobbly and I'm glad I'm on the bed. My skin feels tight. Hot. I'm trembling and I don't know what to say to make him quit.

Not that I want him to…

His mouth hovers above mine once more and I part my lips, ready—*eager*—for him to kiss me.

"Tell me you don't want me and I'll walk away from you forever," he whispers against my lips.

Like I can say that. The jerk knows I can't, too.

I remain quiet, anticipation making my breath come too fast and my heart race.

"Amanda?" I crack open my eyes to find him watching me again, an almost amused look on his face. The smug bastard. "Can you say it?"

I say nothing. Instead, I reach up, curl my hand around his nape and slowly pull him in close so his mouth brushes against mine. I ignore the pain and focus on him.

This time around, I'd rather show him how I'm feeling versus tell him.

chapter eight

Tuttle

She feels good in my arms, soft and warm—she fits perfectly. I could drown in her kiss, the taste of her, the sounds she makes, the way she inches closer, like she wants to climb on top of me. Words are bogus. Useless. I'd rather kiss her for hours and convince her that I want her.

Words just get in the way.

Her fingers slide through my hair and I groan. Her lips part and then her tongue circles mine, and I'd give anything to press her against the mattress and let her feel what she's really doing to me.

But I don't do anything like that. She's hurt. I don't want to make it worse. And I definitely don't want to push.

"Jordan," she whispers against my lips, and the breathy sound goes straight to my dick. I want her so damn bad.

I just keep kissing her, silencing her. I don't want to talk.

But she says my name again. She's struggling against me. So I loosen my hold and she pulls away. I open my eyes to find her watching me silently. Her eyes are wide and dark. Her lips are parted and swollen. The sensitive skin close to her mouth is pink, most likely from the stubble on my face.

I scrub a hand along my jaw, making the stubble rasp, fighting the possessive feeling rising within me. I marked her. For everyone to see that she belongs to…someone.

Hell. She belongs to me.

Amanda shakes her head slowly, licking her swollen lips. "We shouldn't have done that."

Her words are like knives carving at my walled-up heart. Those words bring me back to reality, remind me I have a huge task ahead of me. One I need to prepare for because I'm done losing. I'm done listening to what others want from me.

For once in my damn life, I'm going after what I want. Screw everyone else.

Screw my parents. They're the ones who try to control me. I'm over it. Over them.

"You ready to go?" My voice comes out low and gravelly, and I clear my throat, then run a hand through my hair. She watches me do it, her gaze lingering on my head, and I wonder if she wants to touch me there. I love it when she rakes her fingers through my hair.

Does she remember? Does she know that's a weakness? Does she realize she's my weakness? I don't even think she knows the all-consuming power she holds over me.

"Yeah," she says shakily as she reaches up and brushes her lips with her fingertips. Her hand is trembling. The bruise beneath her left eye is starting to darken and I know it's going to look like hell tomorrow.

The guilt that washes over me, knowing I did that to her, can't be stopped. It was an accident, but tell my conscience that.

I climb off the bed and offer my hand to help her stand. She's a little wobbly, but otherwise she's fine. I catch the wince, catch her gently touching her cheek, and I know she's in pain.

I need to make it up to her. I need to make this right.

Starting now, she'll have no doubt whatsoever how I feel about her. But will she actually believe me?

chapter nine

Amanda

"Amanda!" My bedroom door is thrown open with a resounding bang and I roll over with a moan, tugging my comforter over my head so Mom can't see me. "Your dad needs your help outside."

Mom is never subtle about waking me up early on Saturday morning. As in, she never lets me sleep in. She used to love that I was in band and would have to be out the door early on Saturdays to go to practice or marching band competitions.

Now, without band, she constantly complains that I'm getting lazy. It doesn't matter that I work the hydration station and that I'm on the yearbook staff. In her eyes, I'm not doing much at all.

Whatever.

"He needs my help with what outside?" I crack open my eyes and stare at the wall. My left eye aches. I'm sure it looks terrible.

I'm also sure I don't want Mom to see it.

"The backyard." Mom's tone tells me I should already know this. "He's digging everything out of the plant beds, and then he's going to add river rock. Remember the plan? We discussed it over dinner a few nights ago."

I vaguely remember the conversation. I haven't been around much lately, not like I used to be. I'm always busy and staying for football practice, especially since we're going into the playoffs, means I miss dinner most of the time.

"Where's Trent? Why can't he help Dad?" I close my eyes, praying for her to leave soon. I'm going to have to show my face—and my nasty black eye—sometime, and I'm hoping before I see my family that I can use foundation and concealer to hide it. Or at the very least make it look less awful.

First, I need to see just how awful it is.

"He spent the night at Zion's house. Once he comes home, Daddy's putting him straight to work too. With all three of you out there, he's hoping he'll be done by midafternoon." Mom raps on my door extra hard, and I wonder if she hurt her knuckles. "I'll make you breakfast," she croons to tempt me. "Your favorite, bacon and waffles."

For once, her promise of bacon isn't going to work. "I'm not really hungry," I tell the wall. "And before I help him, I need to take a shower first."

An exasperated sigh leaves her. "What's the point? You're just going to get dirty anyway."

"I want to, okay? I feel gross." I sound whiny, and she hates it when any of us whine, but at the moment, I don't really care. I'm still half asleep and my eye hurts and I can't get over what happened last night.

Yeah, that's my biggest problem right now. I don't know how to deal with last night. Jordan and I kissed. He told me he still wants me. He drove me home and we were quiet for most of the ride, right until he pulled up in front of my house, cut the engine, leaned over and planted a sweet, lingering kiss on my lips that almost made me swoon. He'd cradled my cheeks with both hands and whispered, "I'm sorry" while staring into my eyes.

So where do we stand? What's going on? I have no idea.

"Hurry up then." Mom's shrill voice pulls me from my thoughts. "Your daddy's waiting." She slams the door extra hard, making everything in my room rattle. I reach an arm out from beneath my peach and pale green printed comforter and snatch my phone off my wobbly bedside table, checking my notifications. I have Snapchats from what feels like everyone, including Jordan Tuttle.

I decide to keep the anticipation going and open the other ones first. Most of them are general acquaintances who were at the party, asking if I'm all right. Livvy sent a kissy face selfie with a giant blue circle around her eye and *you okay* scrawled in red across the photo.

I send her a photo of my ceiling fan with the message *I'll live.*

Finally, I open Jordan's Snapchat. It's a photo of his room, and I see his reflection in the mirror that hangs above his dresser. He's a distant figure lying on his bed, and I swear he's not wearing a shirt.

There's no message. Just the photo. So I do what every normal teenage girl on Snapchat does and screenshot that sucker before it disappears. Then I open it up in my photos and zoom in on him lying on the bed.

Yep, he's shirtless. Wearing what appears to be black pajama bottoms? Maybe black sweats? One hand is resting on his flat stomach and the other is clutching his phone and taking the photo. I can't see his face, but his dark hair is a mess. The muscles in his arms bulge. And he looks really good without a shirt on, though I already knew this.

Rolling over on my back, I sit up a little, pulling my hair over my left eye so he can't see it. I have no makeup on and I probably look like trash, but screw it. I take a selfie and quickly send it to him before I chicken out.

He immediately texts me in chat.

How's your eye?

I don't know. I haven't looked at it yet.

You're still in bed?

Yeah.

Nice.

I smile. Then scowl. Pervert.

He sends me another message.

You work today?

Oh. That's right. I do.

At three.

I'll take you.

I'm scowling again. There he goes assuming things he has no business...assuming. He can't drive me to work. We're not a confirmed thing. Nothing's changed between us just because of last night. We talked, I got mad, he hit me by accident, he kissed me, I liked it. End of story.

I don't need a ride.

I know you don't. Because I'm taking you.

Jordan, seriously. My dad can drive me to work.

Yep. I'll ask him if he could take me, though he'll probably be annoyed that I'm interrupting his yard project.

I want to do this. Stop arguing with me Amanda. I'll pick you up at 2:45. Be ready.

I don't bother answering him. What's the point? He won't take no for an answer. And deep down inside?

I sort of love it.

After scrolling through my phone for a while, I drag my lazy butt out of bed and sneak into the bathroom across the hall, thankful no one's around. The moment I spot my reflection in the mirror, I suck in a sharp breath and stare. It's like a horrific accident on the freeway—I can't look away.

The bruise around my eye is black and purple with the faintest tint of red. I look...awful.

Terrible.

Lifting my hair away from my face, I lean across the counter and get as close to the mirror as I can. Oh, it's bad. I turn this way and that, hoping I look better in certain angles, but it's no use. I need a professional makeup artist to hide this disaster on my face.

How am I supposed to go into work today and help the public? I'll freak them out. I look like I got beat up. I *did* get beat up. And my parents are going to freak the hell out when they see me. Mom will probably want to call the cops. Dad will most likely want to kick Jordan's and Cannon's asses.

Yeah. This is bad.

I hop in the shower and take a quick one, not bothering to wash my hair. Before I go to work I'll be back in here anyway, so Mom did have a valid point, but really I'm just stalling for time. Once I dry off, moisturize and brush my teeth, I throw on an old T-shirt and a pair of sweats. Then I pull out all the makeup I own, which isn't much, and start applying layers of foundation and concealer around my eye.

After laboring for five minutes, I lean back and turn my face to one side, then the other, studying my reflection. The makeup helps, but it doesn't really hide the bruise. I don't think anything can hide this bruise. I'm just going to have to face my parents and explain what happened.

Deciding the best way to deal with it is head on, I go to the kitchen, trying my best to ignore the nerves bubbling in my stomach.

"I made you waffles and bacon even though you said you weren't hungry," Mom says when I enter the kitchen, her back to me as she rinses off a dish in the sink before setting it in the open dishwasher. "There's a plate waiting for you at the table."

"Thanks," I say gratefully as I go to the kitchen table and sit down, hoping the food will help ease the nerves.

Mom turns off the faucet and shuts the dishwasher door, then grabs a dishtowel out of the drain, drying her hands as she turns to look at me. I duck my head, my hair falling over my face, but the gasp that escapes her tells me I didn't duck fast enough.

"*Amanda.*" My name whooshes out of her mouth, full of dread and shock. Her shoes click loudly across the tile floor and then she's right there, standing in front of me, her fingers slipping beneath my chin so she can tilt my head back and examine my face fully. "My God. What happened to you?"

I try to smile, but the stern look on her face prevents me from doing it. "It was an accident."

Her fingers drift over my face, and I wince. "Did someone hit you?" Her voice is quiet but with a lethal edge. Like she's ready to tear someone apart for hurting her baby girl. "Tell me, Amanda. What happened?"

Deciding not to hold back, I launch into the entire story, giving her pretty much every detail minus the reason the boys were fighting—supposedly over me—and the fact that Jordan kissed me. The more I explain, though, the more she scowls, until when I finally finish my story, I'm afraid her face is going to permanently stay that way.

"I thought you split up with Jordan Tuttle."

I thought so too, I want to say, but I don't. "I'm…confused over what's happening between us."

"He sounds like he's trouble."

"He's not that bad. Really." He's a big heap of trouble, but I'm drawn to him anyway. Can't tell her that either.

Her mouth is a tight line. "I've never liked you going to all those parties, and here's the perfect reason why. You're grounded."

My jaw drops open. "Are you serious? Why? I'm almost eighteen, Mom. You can't ground me."

"As long as you live under my roof, I can do whatever I want. And I can definitely ground you from going to those parties. They're nothing but trouble. People drinking and doing drugs and having—" Her voice drops to a harsh whisper. "—*sex*. They're not a good place for you to be."

How can I argue with her when everything she says is true? "So you're only grounding me from parties?"

"Yes." She nods. "For a month."

"A month?" That's a long time. Four weeks. Thirty days.

"Keep questioning me and I'll make it two," she warns.

I snap my lips shut and keep quiet.

"I know you have to work, and you still have a social life minus the house parties. Plus there's football, though that's ending soon, right?"

I shrug, then pick up a piece of bacon and start munching on it. "Depends on how far they go into the playoffs." I don't want to argue with her or trigger her into grounding me from everything. I need to remain neutral in order to save my senior year.

And I really don't want to miss the parties, especially if Jordan continues to host them at his house. What will he say when I tell him I can't go? He'll think I'm lame. Totally immature since I'm *grounded*.

"Well, the football season feels never-ending. It's already November."

"We could play until right around Thanksgiving if they keep winning."

"Great." Mom shakes her head. "Will you hate me if I wish they would lose?"

"Mom! You can't wish that. Some of those guys have potential full-ride scholarships hanging on this. If they win regional and even state championships in their division? They'll look like superstars."

"Hmm. Well, all this hydration station stuff takes my daughter away from me. It's not the same like when you played with the band. Then I could at least go watch you and enjoy the performance. Now when I watch the band, I get sad. And there's not much to see when you're handing out water bottles to the players."

She makes my job sound so small. And she can't get over the band thing. Even though I feel like she's baiting me, I'm not going to argue. I just keep munching on bacon and hope she drops the subject.

"I miss you," Mom says when I remain quiet. She smiles and I see the sadness there lingering in her eyes. "You're going to leave us soon. We only have a few months left before you're gone forever."

"Oh, Mom." Now she's making me feel bad. "I'll still be around. I thought you wanted me to go to community college."

"It's all we can afford if you can't get a scholarship, but you're going to get one. I can feel it. You're too smart and too well rounded a student not to get one." She reaches out and pats my hand, then gives it a squeeze. "Now hurry up and finish your breakfast so you can go outside and help your daddy. I'm afraid he's going to overdo it all by himself."

"Mom, can you tell Dad what happened to my eye?" I wince when she sends me a sharp look. "He'll probably react better when he hears it from you. If he sees me before I get a chance to explain, he'll probably want to go beat Cannon and Jordan up."

She shakes her head as she pushes the chair away and stands. "Fine. I'll go warn him for you. But be prepared. He'll probably want to talk about it. And give you a speech. Possibly even ground you."

"You already grounded me!" My appetite is leaving me with every word she says.

"Don't worry, I'll tell him that. You'll be fine." She stops and gently pats my cheek, smiling down at me. "That's one hell of a shiner, sweetie. You need to take photos every day and document it."

"Why?" I ask incredulously.

"So you can show all the photos to Jordan Tuttle and make him feel guiltier and guiltier for what he did to you." She walks away, leaving me with my mouth hanging open.

I can hear her evil laughter all the way down the hall.

chapter ten

Jordan

I send Amanda a quick text to let her know I'm here just before I pull up in front of her house. I thought about her all night. All morning. I can't get her out of my mind, though that's turned into a normal thing for me. I used to fight it, but really. What's the point?

I'm both dying and dreading to see her. I want to check out her eye. Yet I don't want to see it either. Her injury is just an actual, *physical* reminder of how I hurt her.

And I've hurt her far more emotionally than physically.

The moment I put my Range Rover in park, the front door opens and out comes her mother.

Shit.

She's striding toward my car and I roll down the passenger window, hoping she'll stay over there instead of coming to the driver's side. "Hey, Mrs. Winters," I say weakly.

"Jordan Tuttle. I want to have a word with you." She leans against the car, her head practically poking through the window as she peers at me with eyes that are the same shade as Amanda's. "You hurt my daughter."

Guess she's going to come right out and say it. "Yes, ma'am." *Yes, ma'am*? I never say that kind of crap. "It was an accident. I feel awful about it."

"You should feel awful. She looks terrible. You hit my daughter. You caused her pain. You physically marked her and now everyone will know what happened," she stresses.

If she's trying to make me feel guilty, she's succeeding. "I know," I say quietly. "I wish I could take it back, but I can't. So I'm going to do everything I can to make it up to her."

"See that you do that." She points at me. "You're lucky I'm letting you drive her to work. I should never let her see you again. You don't deserve her."

My chest goes tight. Everything she's saying is true. She's only confirming all the doubtful feelings I have about me and Amanda. "I really hope you don't do that, Mrs. Winters. Your daughter means a lot to me."

"Really?" The skeptical look she sends me says a million things. All of them starting with, *I don't believe you.*

"Really." I nod.

"Then prove it." She slaps the side of my car, turns and walks back toward the front door just as it opens, and Amanda walks out. She's wearing jeans that make her legs look ten miles long and a pale pink T-shirt that says *Yo Town* in white lettering across it. Her long, dark hair is in a ponytail, though there are a few pieces pulled out and hanging over her left eye. They don't disguise the black eye, though. It's obvious she has one.

And I feel like shit for being the one who gave it to her.

The tightness in my chest eases when our gazes connect. A tiny smile curves her perfect lips and she gives her mom a quick hug, nodding at whatever she said before she makes her way toward my car. I hop out of the driver's seat and run around to the passenger side door so I can open it for her.

"Such manners," Amanda murmurs as she starts to climb into the car, but I stop her so I can examine her eye. "It doesn't look so bad, right?"

Her hopeful tone makes me want to lie and agree with her, but I promised myself I wouldn't lie to this girl ever again. "It looks…" I touch the bruise as gently as possible, not wanting to hurt her, but she grimaces anyway.

"Bad, huh?" Her voice is quiet. She reaches up and places her fingers over mine, and her touch soothes away all the earlier worry her mom filled me with. "People are going to talk at school."

"I don't care if you don't."

"They'll assume you hit me like Livvy did."

"Have you seen all the Snapchat stories that feature it? Most everyone caught it all, right down to you landing on your butt." I even saw the moment she bit her tongue, caught the wince and the way she touched her tongue to the corner of her mouth.

"Oh, that's not embarrassing." She rolls her eyes and tries to laugh, but I silence her by resting my fingers over her lips.

"I'll protect you at school," I murmur, tracing the curve of her lower lip. "I won't let them say shit."

"You can't be my guardian angel all the time," she says against my fingers, her big eyes imploring as she watches me.

I'm filled with the urge to kiss her. To take her back to my house and back to my bed. Keep her locked in there forever so no one can touch her. Tease her. Hurt her.

But I do a pretty good job of that myself. Am I really her protector?

I don't know.

"Watch me," I say just before I lightly slap her perfect ass. She yelps, sends me a disapproving look and then I'm shoving her into the car and shutting her door behind her. "We need to hurry and get you to work. Don't want you to be late," I tell her through the open window.

I don't want to give her any more reason not to have faith in me. I need her trust.

I just flat out need her.

chapter eleven

Amanda

"...So then we talked for a really long time, and he apologized. *Finally*. I mean, that took like three hours to get a sorry out of him, but whatever. I'm over it. I think we're good now." Livvy shakes her head as we enter the senior hall Monday morning and head toward our lockers. "He's so stubborn sometimes, I swear. Why exactly do I put up with his crap again?"

"Um, because you love him?" I remind her.

"Oh yeah, that's right." She laughs. "I mean, I know I'm stubborn too, and that means we butt heads a lot, but I'm trying to be more easygoing, you know?"

Yeah right. When it comes to Ryan, Livvy is the farthest thing from easygoing.

"You guys fought the entire weekend?" I ask, not really expecting an answer, because it's obvious they did.

I wish I hadn't come to school. I don't remember the last time I felt this way. I usually like going to school. I'm weird like that.

But after everything that happened at Cannon's party, the very public fight over me, my resulting injury—yeah, somehow my eye looks even worse—I don't want to face anyone. They're all talking about it. Boys smirk at me as I walk past them. Girls curl their lips and watch me with disdain.

Honestly, I don't know why. The proof is all over Snapchat and it's also on Instagram. There are even images of Jordan's elbow making direct contact with my eye. It's obvious it was an accident.

"What are people saying about Friday night, Livvy?" I ask when we stop at her locker. "And tell me the truth."

She glances around before her gaze reluctantly meets mine. "The rumors are bad, Amanda. Really bad."

"And, what? You weren't going to tell me? I had to ask you first?" Sometimes I wonder just how loyal Livvy is to me.

"I'm trying to protect you! And I was hoping all the chatter would die down, but it looks like it hasn't." At that precise moment, a group of boys walk by, all of them coughing "slut" into their fists as they stare at me. Nice. If this keeps up, I'm going to cry. "The worst rumor I heard was that Cannon and Tuttle have—shared you in the locker room. And that one of them got jealous so they started fighting over you at Cannon's party."

"*What?* That's the most disgusting thing I've ever heard!" I look around the hallway, noticing how everyone turns away rather than making eye contact with me.

Oh, yeah. Livvy's right. The rumors are bad.

"I know. It's totally disgusting. I'm sure the rumors will die down eventually, so don't worry, okay?" Livvy smiles brightly, going for the positive, but I can already feel the tears threaten, and she sees that too. She dumps her books into her locker and turns toward me, grabbing both of my hands. "No, don't cry, Amanda. I'll shut them all down, okay? I promise."

She's only one person. How can she stop the vicious high school rumor mill? The tears finally make their appearance, springing into my eyes, and I dash a hand across them, wincing when I press too hard on my bruises.

God, I can't win today.

I wish I could go back to a year ago. When I was a nobody in the band and so happy with my group of friends. I got good grades and the teachers loved me. I was trying out a relationship with Thad and giddy with those butterfly *does he really like me* feelings. It was fun. Simple.

So simple.

"Thanks, Liv," I tell her with a watery smile. "I don't know if that'll help, but I'll take what I can get."

"Well, well, well. Looks like you actually showed up today. The infamous Amanda Winters," a familiar voice says from behind us.

I close my eyes, fighting the dread that's washing over me. Without having to see her, I know it's Lauren Mancini. I'd recognize that snotty voice of hers anywhere. I dab at the tears before I turn around to face her. She physically recoils when she spots my black eye. "What do you want, Lauren?"

"Your eye. It look hideous," she says, making all of her cheerleader friends laugh nervously. She's brought a posse with her, but why? For backup? So they can all make fun of me?

Great.

"Gee, thanks. I didn't know." Sarcasm drips from my words.

"So is it true?"

I decide to play dumb. "Is what true?"

"The rumors about you and Cannon and Jordan." I seriously hate it when she calls him Jordan. Like she has the right. "You guys are now a threesome or what? I mean, that's very...modern of you, and them." She laughs and so does the rest of her friends.

I clench my hands into fists and part my lips, but no words come. It's like I've drawn a complete blank, which is the absolute last thing you want to do when forced to confront Lauren Mancini.

"No, of course it's not true. How dare you even ask," Livvy says, rushing to my defense. "Who the hell are you to judge anyway, Mancini? We've all heard the rumors about *you*."

Lauren's eyes flicker for the briefest moment. Thank God Livvy remembers all the rumors and crap that fly around this school. "You don't know what you're talking about."

"Neither do you, so keep your thoughts to yourself, bitch." Livvy grabs my arm and starts steering me down the hall. "Let's go, Amanda."

"Wait a minute. I need to get my book out of my locker," I start to say, but Livvy cuts me off.

"Come back and get it later," she says under her breath. "We don't want to stick around here. Lauren will only make everything worse."

I know she's right, so I follow her lead, wishing we'd run into Jordan. Or even Cannon. Anyone to help set the rumors straight. But we don't. We're less than a minute away from the final bell ringing, so I run into class, settling into my seat and pretending to dig in my backpack, searching for my book.

But I know it's not in there.

The final bell rings and I go to my teacher's desk, asking if I can go get my book since I forgot it in my locker. He hands over the hall pass and I run back out into the empty hallway, thankful Lauren's not lurking around anymore with her little group.

I go to my locker and open the door quickly, noticing the folded piece of white paper caught in the door vents. My heart picks up speed as I pluck it from its spot and carefully unfold the paper behind the still-open door.

There's only one sentence scrawled across the middle of the otherwise blank paper, in slashing black script.

You look pretty today.

Lifting my head, I glance around the hall, wondering who left it, and when. Was it some creeper preparing to give me grief over the threesome rumors? I don't recognize the handwriting. And I don't know why anyone would leave me a note. Jordan and I have talked. He picked me up from work when my Yo Town shift was over and we chatted on the drive home, but we kept it easy. I felt like I was hanging out with a friend, not my boyfriend.

Not that he's my boyfriend. I can't make that claim yet.

I grab my book and slam the locker door, the metal clang reverberating throughout the otherwise empty hallway. The overhead speakers click on and the student body president starts the morning announcements, and I cringe, praying he doesn't say anything about the weekend rumors.

Not that he would. I'm just totally overreacting.

I look at the note once more as I head back to class, rereading the words. I guess it could be Jordan who wrote the note, but I'm not sure. Maybe it was some jerk hoping to rattle me. It could've been anyone really. Maybe even Lauren, though I don't know why she'd do this sort of thing. Without thought, I crumple the paper into the palm of my hand and I drop the balled up note in the trashcan as I pass by.

THE MORNING PASSES with little fanfare, which works for me. Livvy tries to convince me to hang out in the quad at lunch with her and Ryan, but there was no way I could show my face there. Lauren would gloat and say something awful. Some of the cruder boys from the football team might make comments I don't want to hear. And I have no idea where Jordan is. I haven't heard from him all morning. No passing by him in the halls, no texts, no Snapchats.

Nothing.

So I hide out during lunch in the library like old times. It's cloudy outside and the wind has picked up, so I'm glad I'm not out in the quad.

I'd rather be by myself.

"I figured I'd find you hiding out in here," Em says when she approaches my table, pulling out the chair on the opposite of my table and settling in.

"Why don't you join me?" I say sarcastically as I tear open a bag of kettle chips. My baby carrots and ranch are long gone.

"Can I have one?" Em asks, nodding at the chips.

I point the opened bag toward her. "Be my guest."

She takes a few and shoves them all in her mouth, chomping loudly. She's so loud, I'm afraid the librarian can hear her and we're clear in the back of the room.

When she remains silent, I can't take it anymore. "Are you going to ask me if the rumors are true?"

"No." She smiles. "Because I know they're not."

I frown. "How do you know?"

"I was with Cannon on Friday night. In his room." Her smile

grows. "He's definitely not interested in you."

Ha. Since he's interested in her. At least she finally realizes it. "So you two are together?"

"Oh, no. I don't tie myself down with anyone." She waves a hand, dismissing my statement. "I've learned attachments are for stupid people who don't know any better."

I think she just insulted me, but I'm going to choose to ignore it. "Well, let me just say it before you do. The rumors are bad."

"They'll blow over soon enough. There's more juicy gossip to be had. For instance, I'm sure people would love to know that a certain freshman is going around campus soliciting blowjobs before, during and after school."

My mouth drops open. "Who are you talking about?"

"Eli Bennett, of course. That boy is desperate to get laid." Em starts laughing. "He even asked *me* to blow him, but I turned him down."

"Em!" I say her name way too loud. I actually hear the shush of the librarian, so I lower my voice. "Are you serious right now?"

She shrugs. "Totally. He asked me last week. Led up to it by sending me dick pics on Snapchat. I screen shot one. Wanna see?"

Em's pulling out her phone and I lunge across the table, batting at her hands. "I absolutely do not want to see that picture. No way."

"You're no fun." She mock pouts as she shoves her phone back into her backpack. "Not that any dick pic is good to check out. They're all sort of funny looking, don't you think?"

"Definitely." This of course, makes me think of Jordan's. I didn't think it was so hideous. But there's nothing about him that's hideous, so...

"Not that you know much about dicks, am I right? You're still a virgin." When I feel my ears burn with embarrassment she starts to laugh. "I knew it. That's what's so great about this rumor. You're a tramp/slut/whore who lets two jock boyfriends tag team you all night long. It's so ridiculous, it's almost amusing."

"Yeah. Real amusing." I cross my arms and slump in my chair.

Em's laughter dies. "Oh, come on. You'll be fine. Have you heard the rumors they spread about me? At least they don't call you a hooker who does it for actual money. They've even said Livvy's mom's boyfriend is my pimp."

I frown. "How did he get drawn into your rumors?" Fine, I've heard the many rumors they spread about Em, but I blew them all off. How much of that can be true? Now that I'm dealing with my own outrageous story, I know the answer is pretty much none of it.

"There was that really short period of time when my parents took my car away from me? Do you remember that?" When I give her a blank look, she continues. "Well, anyway, I was walking home from school because no one would give me a ride, and he saw me and pulled over. Offered to take me home and so I went with him. I wasn't going to say no. My feet were killing me."

Just thinking about getting into a car alone with Fitch, Livvy's mom's boyfriend, gives me the creeps. He's strange. He gives off this weird vibe that Livvy says she can't trust. She wouldn't take a ride from him, even if it was the last ride in the world. Yet Em climbs into his car alone with him like it's no big deal.

"I can't believe you did that," I tell her.

"Yeah, well, I regret ever taking that ride because it blew up into this stupid rumor around school and I never did figure out who started it," Em complains.

"That's awful."

She shrugs. "I know it's hard dealing with the bullshit, but welcome to high school! It's not perfect. Not like it was when you were hanging out with your nerdy band friends and contemplating letting that guy feel you up or not in the back of the bus on the way home from an away game. Nah, this is way more hardcore. A lot more like real life, you know?" Em's eyes light up as she's talking. I think she's loving this. The fact that all the new, nasty rumors around school have nothing to do with her. It's like she's offering up advice to me, the newbie, while she's the old, wise one.

My appetite leaves me at her depressing words, and when I offer the bag of chips to Em she snatches it up. "How do you get past it? All the rumors that swirl around you? Don't they all just make you want to crawl into a hole somewhere far away and die?"

"Nah. You can't deal with it like that. You're just setting yourself up to fail. When you hide, you look so damn guilty everyone thinks the rumors must be true," Em explains.

"So what should I do if I were you?"

"You hold your head up high while you stroll down the hall and own that shit. Seriously, it's no big deal. You act like yeah, I did it. So what? And when you're like that, they don't know what to say, or how to deal. They feel all awkward and stuff around you, and it's great because you've totally ruined it for them." Em shoves another handful of chips into her mouth and chomps on them gleefully. "So own it. Work it, girl. You've got nothing to lose and everything to gain."

"What do you mean I have everything to gain?"

She leans across the table and talks low, like we're co-conspirators in this crazy game. "Everyone knows who you are now. No more nerdy smart girl Amanda Winters who gets good grades and is tucked into bed every night by Mommy and Daddy. Now you're the girl who took on Jordan Tuttle and broke his heart. You're the girl who gets gang banged by the entire football team—"

"Hey, take that back! I haven't heard that rumor." And if I ever do, I know who started it.

"Semantics. Whatever." She waves a hand. "Anyway, you're the girl who has threesomes with Cannon Whittaker and Jordan Tuttle in the locker room while the coaches watch. I mean, the rumors I'm hearing are just outrageous. So outrageous, I don't know who the hell would even believe them."

"The way you talk, they sound pretty convincing." My stomach is turning just thinking about all of this.

"Yeah, well, we know they're not true. Your truth is what I just said." Again she leans over the table, a giant smile on her face. "You really *are* the virginal ex-band nerd who broke Tuttle's heart and somehow has him still panting over you. You *are* the sweet girl who gets straight As and all the teachers love you and you probably *are* tucked into bed every night by Mommy and Daddy."

"That's not true," I start, but she cuts me off.

"It doesn't matter. What matters is how scandalous you *seem*. And right now, you are leading the board for most scandalous, with me just behind you and Lauren Mancini a distant third."

"Lauren? She's on the most scandalous board?" Why am I even talking about this supposed board? It doesn't even exist.

"Sure. She's one of the girls who agreed to give Eli a blowjob." When my mouth drops open, Em's pointing at me, laughing her ass off. "See? You're shocked. She *wishes* she was as bad as us."

"But I'm not bad. And she's way worse than me."

"Nope, not right now, not in their eyes. You want my advice?" When I nod, she continues. "Own the moment. Run with it. Act like you *own* those two boys. We know the truth. And trust me, the rumors will eventually fade. They always do. Especially now that we have Eli out there creating all sorts of drama. He's a rumor wet dream come true." Em shakes her head and starts laughing all over again. "Got any more chips?"

"Nope, you ate them all."

She crumples the chip bag in her hands and shoves it into the front pocket of her backpack. "Where's Tuttle anyway? I haven't seen him all day. I figured once he heard all the shit talk, he'd be knocking heads together by second period."

The thought of him "knocking heads together" on my behalf warms my heart, which means I'm a sick, twisted person. "I haven't seen him either. I hope he's all right."

Her eyes go wide. "You haven't talked to him? At all?"

"Not today," I say with a little shrug.

"Weird," Em mutters, shaking her head. "He's mysterious. I can't figure him out."

"What do you mean?"

"People may try and hide their true selves at this school, but it always comes out eventually. Always. But with Tuttle? I don't know. The mystery is real with him. Where is he today? It's a Monday. He should be in school. But he's not. Why? Where does he go? What does he do?"

I've tried not to delve too deep into the mystery that is Jordan Tuttle for fear it would make him withdraw even further. He's never been particularly open with me, and when he acts like he wants to say something, he always manages to mess it up.

"I don't know. He does a lot of things I can't explain."

"Exactly. So we need to figure out what's up with this dude." Em taps her pursed lips with her index finger, staring off into space.

"We?" I raise my brows. "Are we going in on this together?"

"Don't you need my help figuring out the mystery that is Jordan Tuttle? I mean, I could leave you on your own, but then you won't have him figured out as quick if we put our heads together."

I'm intrigued by her offer. But then again, I shouldn't sneak around with Em and try to find out Jordan's secrets—if he even has any. I should be open and honest and go straight to him when I have questions.

Though he doesn't like to answer the tough questions. He either flat out changes the subject most of the time, or even acts like I never asked the question at all. That's frustrating.

Maybe I should dig around into his background without him knowing so I can figure out exactly what he's doing when he disappears. And he disappears a lot.

Too much.

"So you in?" Em asks after I'm quiet for a few minutes. "I know this is a touchy subject, especially if you two are dating again, or whatever you want to call it. But you know he's never going to spill all his secrets to you."

"Why do you say that? Why wouldn't he?" I'm offended. I want him to tell me everything.

But wasn't that the problem before? He'd get so tight-lipped when I tried to ask questions, when I tried to...act like a caring girlfriend. He wouldn't let anything slip. He has a façade, that Jordan Tuttle mask, and he knows how to put it on so much, I'm not sure if I'm dealing with the real Jordan or the fake one half the time.

It's frustrating.

"Because he's probably afraid you'll hate him when you find out who he really is." Em grins, but there's so much sadness in her eyes. "Isn't that what we all worry about?"

chapter twelve

I don't see Jordan all day. Not in English, not anywhere in the halls or in my other classes or even in the parking lot when school lets out. Only when I go to football practice after school and help Kyla set up the hydration station do I finally catch a glimpse of him out on the field running drills.

The relief that floods me at seeing him is almost overwhelming. I was worried. And now I'm kind of pissed that he ignored me all day, one of the worst days at school in my *life*. But how's being angry at Jordan going to help matters? It's not.

Just like he needs to learn how to trust me, I need to do the same.

"So the rumors are true," Kyla finally says to me once we have everything set up. It feels like she's been holding that question in for the last fifteen minutes, just dying to let it out.

"About what?" I ask warily. If she brings up the threesome rumor or worse, a gang bang story, I'm going to lose it.

"The black eye you're sporting. Tuttle gave it to you, right? Or was it Cannon?" She glances out at the field to watch the boys run for a while before she turns to look at me. "They're such jerks. Every single one of them. I hope you realize this by now."

"Tuttle nailed me with his elbow, that's all. It was an accident," I tell her, rushing to Jordan's defense. Feeling defensive at her bitter words. "And none of the rumors are true. Not a one."

"Really?" She sounds doubtful.

I nod. "Do you really believe I'd involve myself in a threesome with Jordan and Cannon?"

Kyla bursts out laughing, her cheeks turning pink. "I've heard worse, so I don't know."

"You know me better than that. I wouldn't get involved with something so…dirty." I shiver just thinking about it. So gross. I can only handle one boy at a time, thank you very much. And the one I'm currently dealing with is a major handful.

"Sometimes things just happen, you know? You end up doing something you don't want to, but you're trying to be nice. You're trying to get along with everyone. And please that one boy you like so much. But he doesn't like you. Not like that." Kyla's voice drops and I step closer so I can hear her. She's talking in a monotone and there's no emotion on her face. None. "Yet you'll do anything to make him happy. Including getting drunk and servicing his friends, because that's what the cool girls do, right?"

Kyla bursts into tears when our gazes meet and then she's running back to the girls' locker room. Without hesitation I chase after her, the blood roaring in my ears, her words on repeat in my head.

Sometimes things just happen, you know?

God, what does she mean? I almost don't want to know.

I find her in the locker room, collapsed on one of the benches that runs between the rows of lockers. I tentatively sit down next to her, noticing the way her shoulders shake. She's crying. Great big heaving sobs that make me want to draw her into my arms and hold her close. Offer her lame words of comfort because they're all I've got.

"Do you want to talk about it?" I finally ask her minutes later. I reach out and touch her shoulder gently, but I still manage to make her flinch. "Are you okay?"

Kyla sits up and tilts her head back, staring at the ceiling. "I'm fine." She takes a deep breath and wipes at her eyes, but there's still streaks of mascara running down her face. "It happened a long time ago."

"How long?"

"Freshman year." She draws in a shaky breath and I see the tears continue to slip down her cheeks.

"We don't have to talk about it if you don't want to."

"No." Kyla turns to face me fully. "I should talk about it. None of the boys who did it to me are here anymore. They were all much older."

I'm scared to ask. But I want to know. "Did they—rape you?"

"One of them d-did. The one I liked the most." She lets her head hang, her hair falling in front of her face. "I was so young and he was so…I don't know. Mature? Definitely more experienced. He knew just how to play me. And after it all happened, I heard I wasn't the only one he did this to."

Oh my God. I can't even imagine. "Did you press charges?"

"No." She shakes her head and wipes at her face once more. "My mom doesn't even know it happened. I kept it all a secret. So that means you have to keep it a secret too, okay?"

I don't want to agree. How can she keep this to herself? Doesn't it gnaw at her mind day after day? "But isn't this eating you up inside?

Not being able to talk about what happened to you?"

"I've worked through it. I'm good now." Another shrug. Another blank smile with blank eyes and blank...everything. "We should go back outside, don't you think? They're probably looking for us."

She didn't give me much detail, and maybe I should've pushed for more, but what would I do with it once I had it? My automatic response is to tell. But she didn't. She told no one. So now she's stuck with this horrible burden that has a tendency to break out whenever she...what? Is triggered?

"Are you sure you're okay?" I ask carefully as I watch her rise to her feet. "We can talk about it some more if you want. I'm a really good listener."

Kyla doesn't even take me up on my offer. She flat out ignores it. "Duty calls. We need to get back outside and get to work." She claps her hands together and smiles, reminding me of the Kyla I first met. "Let's get to work, Winters!"

And then she's gone.

Slowly I shuffle out of the girl's locker room, walking past the lower field where the band is practicing—nostalgic pang—striding faster by the left upper field where the cheerleaders practice, until I'm finally at the edge of the football field. Kyla's already backing at the hydration station, keeping everyone hydrated, and I just...

I'm not ready to go back there just yet. My mind is whirling with too many tumultuous thoughts, all of them having to do with my new friend and her painful burden. I thought my problems were bad. Mine are just rumors and bullshit. Kyla is dealing with real life stuff...that she hasn't properly dealt with.

"Hey."

I turn to find Jordan jogging toward me, his helmet dangling from his fingers, his longish hair already damp with sweat. He's got the pads on and the white pants they wear to away games—which are streaked with grass and dirt, telling me someone has already sacked him once or twice—and his navy blue and white jersey with the number eight emblazoned across his chest.

He looks freaking amazing.

"Hey yourself," I tell him, trying to keep it easy. Nonchalant. I don't want to seem like the stalker ex-girlfriend who immediately asks where he's been.

Though I'd like to.

"How are you?" I ask instead.

"Busy," he says, sounding the slightest bit short, though I ignore it. Then his voice softens and his eyes go warm as he studies me. "But I've been missing you. Are you okay?"

And just like that, my heart blooms in my chest like a lovingly watered flower. "I've missed you too," I confess, hating how it feels like it took everything inside of me to admit that. Sometimes I'm just as walled off as Jordan is, I swear. Or is he the one who makes me that way? "And yeah, I'm okay." Sort of. Not really.

But I'm a lot better now that he's standing in front of me.

"Yeah?" He smiles and grabs hold of my hand, lacing our fingers together and pulling me closer. "I'd hug you, but I've got all this gear on."

"You look hot." The words slip from my lips before I have a chance to stop them and I slap my free hand over my mouth, feeling like an idiot.

"You think so?" He's full on grinning now and the sight of it is dazzling. He's like the sun and I'm planet Earth, forever caught in his orbit. "I wish you'd say that more often."

"Why? You never call me hot." Yikes, did I just confess I want him to call me hot? Because I so do. I want to know that he wants me. I want to hear the words. I need the confirmation.

Does that make me insecure? Maybe…

"I call you hot all the time. Though maybe more in my head, now that I think about it." He frowns and releases my hand, stroking his chin with his fingers, and I give him a shove, though he doesn't move an inch. His gaze goes to my face, lingering on my left eye. "Hey, your eye looks better."

"Thank you for your pretty lies," I say, batting my eyelashes.

"No, seriously. I wouldn't lie to you about that. I wouldn't lie to you about anything. I promise." He tucks a strand of hair behind my ear and I lock my knees so they won't wobble. His fingers touch my cheek, the spot directly below my bruise. "Your eye really does look better. The swelling has gone down a lot."

Whatever. He could say I'm a hideous troll right now and I'd probably fall under his spell.

"Tuttle!" A whistle blows and I recognize Coach Halsey's voice. He sounds pissed. "Stop mooning over your girlfriend and get your ass back out on this field right now!"

All the guys start up a collective "oooh", which only irritates Coach Halsey even more. He starts snapping at them, making them all take extra laps, and Jordan leans in while the coach is distracted, kissing me with the softest, sweetest lips.

"Looks like I need to go. Want me to drive you home after practice?" he asks against my mouth.

I nod. At least, I think I nod. I feel like I'm in a drunken stupor. "Sure."

"See you later then." Another kiss stolen and then he's jogging back out onto the field. I keep my gaze fixed on him for a long, drunken moment. He runs with ease, his body an athletic machine and he shoves his helmet on his head, covering that glorious hair of his. A sigh leaves me and I slowly shake my head.

Despite everything he's done to me, I still have it bad for him.

Glancing around, I catch someone watching me from afar. A cheerleader who looks amazing in her too-short navy blue shorts and a white tank top that hugs her perfect breasts, well, perfectly.

It's Lauren Mancini. And if looks could kill, I'd be a dead woman.

Turning my back to her, I start for the hydration station. But I can hear her running after me, calling my name, asking me to stop. God, what could she want to say now? I hurry my steps, trying to get Kyla's attention, but she's too occupied with the JV players, who all just came over to the station for some water.

Which means she needs my help.

"Seriously, you're just going to ignore me?" Lauren calls indignantly, so close now I can hear her huffing and puffing.

Screw it.

I whirl on her, coming to a complete stop so quick, she practically runs into me. "What do you want now, huh? Want to call me a slut again? Ask if I've been gang banged by the entire team yet?" I think of what Kyla told me and I become angrier. "Rape isn't a joking matter, you know. Though I'm guessing you probably don't get it, considering you're such an insensitive bitch who doesn't care about other people's feelings."

Lauren's pink glossed lips pop open as she stares at me and she slowly shakes her head. Her ponytail swishes back and forth, almost smacking her cheeks, and I hate that stupid huge bow sitting on top of her head. She looks like a doll.

"Pretty harsh, Winters," she spits out. "Talk about a low blow."

"And you're the queen of low blows, so give me a break." I turn and start toward the hydration station once more, and unfortunately she runs up so that she's walking right beside me.

"Listen, I wasn't going to accuse you of getting—gang banged or whatever." Lauren makes a face. "I just wanted to apologize for what I said earlier."

I stop walking yet again. And she almost collides with me yet again too. "Are you serious? You're *apologizing* to me? What's wrong, are you sick?"

She shakes her head, setting that ponytail to swishing again. "I'm not sick. It just ate at me all day, what I said to you."

"You don't give a crap about me." I can't believe what she's saying.

"You're right. I don't. But I don't like talking about things that didn't actually happen either. Rumors are the worst."

I'm sure she speaks from experience.

"You're right. It didn't happen," I say firmly.

"I know. Cannon told me." Her eyes go wide. "He actually threatened me over it. He must really like you."

"Only as a friend."

"And Jordan?" She raises a brow. "What's going on with you two?"

I lift my chin. "That's none of your business."

My MYOB statement doesn't stop her from talking. "You two looked pretty cozy just a few minutes ago."

"Look, I really need to go. Are we done here?" I never talk like this to anyone. I'm always polite. But all this bullshit lately has brought out the worst in me.

Or maybe it's brought out the best in me. I'm not sure.

With a sigh, she stares out at the field, her gaze locked on Jordan, no doubt. "Congratulations, Amanda. Looks like you finally caught the uncatchable one."

I haven't caught him yet. The words almost fall past my lips, but I don't let them. And I'm glad. It's okay to hold some things back. Why give your enemies ammunition? I don't need to admit anything to Lauren. She can think I've caught Jordan all she wants. The illusion is far better than the truth. Isn't that what Em meant?

But I'm starting to realize as I discover everyone's truths, it's not that easy. Sometimes the raw truth can be the best thing ever.

And sometimes the illusion can end up being a total trap.

chapter thirteen

"What time do you need to be home by?" Jordan asks after I climb into his Range Rover. Just as he promised, he's driving me home after practice.

I pull the seat belt over my lap and click it into place before I meet his gaze. "I don't know. What do you have in mind?"

"Do your parents expect you home by a certain time?" When I frown at him he continues. "I don't want to piss them off, Amanda. I know your mom doesn't like me."

"What exactly did she say to you the other day when you picked me up?" I never did ask. I was too immersed in the moment. Having Jordan back in my life like he never left it was heady stuff.

It still is heady stuff.

He stares straight ahead as he starts the car. "Do you really want to know?"

My stomach bottoms out. "Was it bad?"

"It wasn't nice." He turns to look at me. "But I don't want to be dishonest with you. I promised myself I wouldn't be."

I think of what Em and I discussed. How she sent me a text not even an hour ago that she was going on a Jordan Tuttle Google blitz, whatever that means. "Just tell me."

Jordan takes a deep breath and then lets it all out before he says, "She threatened to never let me see you again. She thinks I'm bad for you, and that I'll only end up hurting you."

Hanging my head, I twist my hands together in my lap. I wish my mother hadn't said those things to him, but then again, maybe he needed to hear it. Especially because I don't necessarily disagree with her. Jordan might be bad for me. He might hurt me again too.

But for some reason I can't explain, I'm willing to take that chance.

"Do you wanna go somewhere? With me?" He sounds worried. Almost desperate. Like he's afraid I'm going to tell him no. And maybe I should.

I lift my head and meet his gaze, remembering Mom telling me I'm grounded from parties. But hey, this isn't a party so it doesn't count, right? "As long as you don't take me to a party, we're good. But I need to be home by nine." It's already past five, closer to six. I don't know what we could do for three hours.

Well, maybe I *do* know what we could do. Not that I want to do *that.* Though my body goes hot just thinking about it.

A faint smile appears. "Want to come back to my house? No one's home."

"I don't know if that's a good idea," I say hesitantly.

The smile is gone, replaced by grim determination. "Okay. Um, want to go out to dinner? I'm starving."

"Yeah." I nod. "That sounds good." And safe. I need safe.

Going back to his house means spending time in his room, most likely rolling around on his bed and getting naked. And while I might kick myself for not going back to his house with him, I also know I'd be moving too fast if I did. I'm not ready to take that next step. I need more time. I don't want him to think he has me that easily.

There's nothing wrong with playing hard to get.

We go to a busy chain restaurant that's loud and crowded, the bar full of people watching Monday Night Football. Jordan doesn't seem interested in the game whatsoever, and after we're seated at a booth far away from the bar and the TVs, I lean over the table to say, "Don't you want to watch the game?"

He shrugs, his gaze locked on the giant menu open before him on the table. "Not really. I hate both teams."

"Not a Steelers fan?"

"Not even close." He sends me a quick, disgusted look. Of course, he manages to look both hot and disgusted. This boy is talented. "I've actually become a Raiders fan lately."

"Really?" He doesn't look like the type. Raider Nation is pretty crazy and they have a rough reputation. "Why?"

"Their QB is good. The entire team is good." He starts looking over his menu once more. "What are you going to have to eat?"

"I kind of want a burger." Huh. I wonder if he finds that not ladylike enough. Or am I overthinking things?

"Me too." He shuts the menu and rests his forearms on top of it. "I like that you're not afraid to eat in front of me."

"You just made me feel like a total pig," I tell him, and he laughs. "Seriously, did you date a lot of girls who didn't like to eat in front of you?" That's weird, but whatever.

"I don't really date."

"What do you mean by that exactly?" My dinner choice made, I close my menu as well.

"I just…I mean what I said. I haven't dated much. Lauren Mancini and I were a thing during our freshman year, but that didn't last long, and once we broke up, I never really went out with anyone else."

He is such a liar. He's had lots of girls. Plenty of girls. An endless stream of girls. "I hate Lauren Mancini."

Whoops. I probably shouldn't have said that out loud.

"She's kind of a bitch," he agrees.

Confirmation is so validating.

"Kind of?" I raise a brow.

"Fine, she's a total bitch. But back when we were fourteen, she wasn't so bad. She could be fun sometimes. Though she was also self-conscious and worried too much about what other people thought of her."

"I guess she hasn't really changed," I mumble. I hate hearing him say she was fun. That he had a good time with her. That they share a past. We share a past too, I guess, but it doesn't feel the same. That was so long ago, what he had with Lauren. Jordan was probably a different person then.

"Nah, she's changed. She acts like she owns the school and isn't afraid of anyone, but deep down inside, I bet she's still just as insecure as she was when we were freshmen."

Hmm, he used the word "we".

"Are you insecure?" Maybe I don't need to dig into his past with Em. Maybe I can figure everything out on my own. It might not be so hard to get him to open up to me after all.

"I have my moments. Don't we all?" His gaze locks with mine. "You make me feel insecure."

"Shut up. I do not." I absolutely don't believe him.

The waiter appears at that precise moment and takes our order, leaving us with promises to bring our drinks and the mozzarella cheese sticks appetizer Jordan spontaneously requested.

"You do," Jordan tells me once our waiter is gone. "I never know how to act around you. I always feel unsure."

"Why?" I'm shocked. I'm not a big deal, not like he is.

"It's like I see you and I lose all my brain cells. I can't think. Well, I can think, but it's only about you. All I want is to—" He covers his face with one hand, and I can hear the muffled chuckle behind his palm. "I probably shouldn't admit this to you."

"Admit what?" Now I'm curious.

He drops his hand from his face, his expression serious. "All I do is wonder when can I get you alone next. I want you all to myself." His voice goes deeper and his eyes get darker. "Always."

"Oh." I blink at him, slightly dumbfounded.

How do I respond to that?

The waiter reappears with our drinks, letting us know that the appetizer will be out very soon. Once he's gone, I unwrap my straw and dunk it into my cup before I take a sip of my Sprite. I'm agitated at the thought of Jordan constantly trying to get me alone so he can…what?

Come on. You know what.

"Is that all I am to you? Some sort of conquest?" That comes out snottier than I meant it to, but I must know. If this is only about having sex with me or whatever, then it's time to move on. I'm not going to give it up to him just so I can say I did it with Jordan Tuttle. That's not what this is all about.

I care about him. Actually, it's more than that. I'm in love with him.

If all he wants is sex, though…

"Of course not." He sounds offended that I would even suggest it. "This is a big deal to me." He reaches across the table and grabs my hand. "*You* are a big deal to me. I tried to tell myself that I didn't need you."

Ouch. I hate when he says stuff like that.

"But I was wrong. I pushed you away like an idiot, and once you were gone, I was even more miserable. So I've come to a realization."

"You have? What is it?" I'm whispering. My throat is raw. This moment feels…serious.

"I don't want to live my life without you in it."

Aw. I love it when he says stuff like that.

We stare at each other, a silly smile on Jordan's face, and I know I'm wearing one too. I told myself I didn't want to move too fast and then he has to go and say such sweet things. Act sweet. Look sweet. And just like that, I'm ready to forgive him for his past sins and take him back. Does that make me weak?

I hope not.

The spell is broken by the waiter returning and setting the plate of mozzarella sticks on our table. Jordan lets go of my hand and grabs one, dipping it in the marinara sauce before he shoves the entire thing in his mouth. His eyes go wide and he chews fast before he's taking a big drink from his soda.

"Too hot?" I ask amusedly.

"Yeah, but I'm hungry, so I sort of don't care." He grabs another one and downs it too. He's like a little boy who's been deprived of delicious food for far too long and now he wants to eat all the things. All I can do is watch him, occasionally sipping on my Sprite. Until I remember this one particular question I want to ask him.

"You're not going to eat a mozzarella stick?" he asks before I can get a word out.

I shake my head. "No thanks. So hey…can I ask you something?"

"Sure." He takes a drink from his soda and waits.

"Why weren't you at school today?"

"I was there," he says carefully, his gaze narrowing. "You saw me at practice, right?"

"Well, yeah, but I'm talking earlier. You weren't in class. I didn't see you in English, or at lunch. I didn't even pass you in the hallway." I watch him closely, searching for a reaction but he doesn't so much as flinch. "Where were you?"

"I had stuff to do." He shrugs those broad shoulders of his. "Took up most of the day."

"What sort of stuff?" I hate prying, but he's not giving me anything here.

"Just stuff, Amanda. You know, school stuff. Family stuff." He grabs another cheese stick and shoves it into his mouth, his gaze shifting away from mine. That's it. That's all he's going to give me.

His reaction tells me that maybe he does have something to hide.

chapter fourteen

"Hey." I settle in a chair across from Em. It's Friday, and the entire week has been incredibly busy with school and practice and homework and work and Jordan. I never got a chance to talk to Em about her Google research. When she saw me in the senior hall earlier this morning, she asked me to meet her in the library at the same table we were at Monday during lunch, so here I am. "What's going on?"

"I wanted to tell you about my Tuttle research." Em smiles, looking pleased with herself. "Would you like to know what I found out?"

Duh. "Yeah, but keep your voice down, okay? I don't want anyone else to hear us." I glance around the room before I move to the other side of the table so I'm sitting in the chair next to hers. That way we can whisper in each other's ears if we have to. I trust no one. Anyone could be lurking behind the stacks.

"Ooh, I like this. I feel like a spy." Em snatches the kettle chips bag out of my hand and munches on a couple before she starts talking. "I've been sneaking in searches when I can, and I was finally able to dedicate a few hours last night to the cause." The disappointment on her face is obvious. "I have to admit he doesn't leave much of a trail."

"You were searching for hours?" I'm shocked. Why would she waste that much time if she couldn't find much? Em only started in on this so-called investigation a week ago, and I haven't done any digging beyond that night he took me to dinner, and got absolutely nowhere.

It felt wrong, trying to dig into his life, searching for his secrets. So that was the last time I questioned him. And he's been readily available ever since. Always at school, at practice, driving me home or dropping me off at Yo Town when I had to work. My hours have shrunk so I'm only working one night a week and both Saturday and Sunday, and Jordan seemed pleased by that.

"I get to spend more time with you," he'd said just before he pulled me in for a kiss. That turned into another kiss. And another and another...

"I was bored," Em says, knocking me from my thoughts. "Didn't want to do my homework, was sick of looking at everyone's stupid Snapchat stories. So I went into full on investigative mode and dug up a few things. Not much though, so don't be too disappointed."

"I won't be disappointed. I feel bad that we're even doing this," I mumble, my appetite evaporating the more I think about it. I hand over my bag of chips to Em and she takes them gleefully, tearing into them like she's starving.

"Don't feel bad," she says between mouthfuls. "All of this information is on the World Wide Web. If he didn't want it known, he would've had the information wiped."

"Can a person actually do that?"

She sends me a look. "Come on. Of course, someone can do that. Especially if that someone has a ton of money, like Tuttle."

"Well, don't keep me in suspense! Show me what you've got."

"I don't have anything to show you. More like stuff I can *tell* you." She leans back in her chair and I lean forward, not wanting too much distance between us. Again, I don't want anyone to overhear. "His dad is cheating on his mom."

My mouth drops open then snaps back shut. "I already know that."

Em lifts a brow. "Really? What do you know?"

"I only know—that." I'm not going to spill to Em what Jordan told me. It doesn't feel right.

"Well, I saw photos of dear old dad with his arm around a woman who isn't Jordan's mom. So I did a little digging on the old man and discovered something very interesting. It seems that Mr. Tuttle likes to mess with girls who are barely legal. I'm talking women who are only a few years older than us. There are photos of him with all sorts of pretty blonde women all over the 'net. But there was one in particular who appeared in photos with him again and again. Every time I saw her, it bugged me because her face was familiar. More digging gave me her last name." She smiles triumphantly. "You will never guess who it is."

"Who?"

The smile fades, and her expression turns serious. "Lauren Mancini's older sister."

"What?" I shake my head, like I can shake some sense into it. "You're telling me that Jordan's dad is having an affair with Lauren's *sister?*"

"Yes, can you freaking believe it? I always knew Candace Mancini had a few tricks up her sleeve, but I didn't realize she actually turned real tricks." Em starts laughing, obviously pleased with her crude joke.

"Ha ha, very funny." I go over the information in my mind, remembering the woman we saw his dad with at the restaurant when we went out with Ryan and Livvy. That woman couldn't have been Candace Mancini. I thought she was older. And Jordan hadn't recognized her, not in that way. Surely he would've known and maybe said something about it to me?

But then again, maybe he knew and chose not to say anything at all.

"You have to admit, it's pretty scandalous," Em says just before she tips the mostly empty chip bag into her mouth and shakes out the rest of the crumbs.

"It is," I agree. "But what does it have to do with Jordan? Did you find out anything about him?" I feel guilty even asking the question. I don't care what his dad is doing—unless it affects Jordan. But this bit of information shouldn't matter.

"Oh, come on. It definitely has something to do with Jordan. His dad is boffing the older sister of his ex-girlfriend. That's so freaking scandalous, I feel like we're living in an episode of *Pretty Little Liars* here. Or *The Vampire Diaries*, without the vampires," Em says with a giggle. "This is juicy stuff."

And she's reveling in it. "So you didn't find out anything about Jordan?"

Em shrugs. "His relationship with his parents is awful. Word on the street is his mom is addicted to painkillers. He's the only one left in that house, so he bears the brunt of all the bullshit delivered by his parents, and that's gotta be a lot of pressure on his mostly capable shoulders."

I'm so relieved she didn't discover something awful about Jordan. At least this is just involving his dad. It would've been another thing entirely if she found out Jordan was the one having an affair with

Candace Mancini. "He doesn't like his parents much."

"Who would? They sound like awful people." Em leans in closer, her voice lowering. "Another rumor I've heard is that his dad is willing to pay the University of Oregon a lot of money to accept his son, especially since that's dear old dad's alma mater. But the normally dutiful son doesn't want to go there."

I already know this too. So there really aren't any deep dark secrets concerning Jordan.

"He's donated a lot of money to the football organization. Guess he was a Duck once upon a time and had dreams of becoming a professional football player, but then he blew out his knee and the dream died."

I lean away from Em so I can meet her gaze. "You did find out a lot of information, didn't you?"

"It wasn't that hard with the dad. He's a public figure. Mom keeps to herself. She's always at the spa, on vacation, or locked away in that giant mansion taking too many pills and drinking too much alcohol." Em frowns. "You think Tuttle will end up a total mess because of the way his parents are?"

"I don't know." I start chewing on my thumbnail. "I hope not."

"But he's kind of a mess already, right? Secretive when he doesn't need to be. Very standoffish. Doesn't have many close friends, yet he's always drinking and having parties."

I'm in immediate defense mode. "He's really smart. He does well in school, he always has. And he cares about his team."

"Does he care about you?"

"He says he does." The doubt creeps into my voice without my meaning it to, and Em latches on to it.

"But you don't believe him?"

"After everything that happened between us before..." I shrug. "I don't know what to believe sometimes. It's hard."

"I get it." She nods. "I trust no one, and that includes Cannon. He's just—*too* sweet. I'm waiting for him to do something awful. I know it's going to happen, and I just wish it would go down soon so we can get this over with."

The bitterness in her tone is telling. "You two are officially dating then?"

"I date no one." She sounds just like Jordan. "Relationships are a set up for disappointment. Remember?"

I do remember. But her down-on-relationships talk makes me feel stupid so I change the subject. "Hey, have you ever heard any rumors about a girl getting—raped by a senior when she was a freshman?"

"Are you talking recent rumors?"

"No, a few years ago. Like...I think it happened to someone from our class, but when we were freshmen." I bite my lip, hoping I haven't given away too much. If Kyla knew I was talking about what she told me, she'd hate me forever. And I'd deserve her hatred too.

"Amanda, I know you live in your sweet little protected bubble most of the time, but rape stories do circulate around this campus. More often than you'd think." Em shakes her head, her eyes sad. "But I don't remember hearing anything about a girl from our class getting raped by a senior when we were freshmen. And if it's true, that's just awful. Besides, don't you think we would've heard about it by now?"

Not if the victim kept it a secret. "Yeah, you're right. We probably would've." I frown and dip my head, hating that I doubted Kyla's story for even a second. I shouldn't doubt her. She was so upset, so traumatized just from our short conversation. Then she cleared right up and acted like nothing was wrong, which is totally not normal.

"Why do you ask anyway?"

"Oh." I lift my head and offer up a faint smile. "No reason. I Just thought I heard a story about a girl, but maybe it happened at another school."

"Maybe…" Em's voice drifts and she tilts her head, scrutinizing me. "Wait a minute. *You're* not hiding any deep, dark secrets, are you? About yourself?"

"What? No! I'm not talking about myself, I swear." I shake my head vehemently. "The most traumatic thing that's ever happened to me is Jordan Tuttle."

"Ha, and don't forget when you walked in on your ex-boyfriend and your best friend going at it at Tuttle's house," Em reminds me. Though how she knows about that, I have no clue. Maybe Livvy told her? Maybe the story spread so wide that everyone knows?

Probably.

"Great, thanks. I didn't need the reminder," I say sarcastically as I push back in my chair and stand. "I'm gonna go. Check out the cafeteria and maybe grab something to eat before the bell rings. Wanna come with?"

"Nah," Em says as I grab my backpack and sling it over my shoulder. "I'm going to stay here and catch up on some homework."

"Okay." I hesitate, then go ahead and say what's on my mind. "Maybe we should quit the investigation, you know what I mean?"

Em's surprised gaze meets mine and she lifts her brows. "Are you sure?"

"Yeah." I nod. "It—it doesn't feel right, sneaking around behind his back and digging into his life. I'd hate to find out he did something like that to me, so I don't want to do it to him."

"Hey. I get it." She nods and offers up a closed-lipped smile. "Your secret is safe with me."

I exit the library, trying to ignore the nagging feeling that Em might be lying to me.

*   *   *

It's always when you're minding your own business that the worst encounters happen, you know what I mean? It's so cliché, and I totally get it if you're rolling your eyes right now.

But guess what? I'm minding my own business, sitting in yearbook class and going over a new layout for the volleyball page spread when someone sits in the chair beside me.

I turn to find it's...Thad.

As in Thad the douche, my ex-boyfriend.

"Amanda." He gives me a chin nod, looking nervous. "What's good?"

Did he really just ask me *what's good*? He's ridiculous.

"What are you doing in here?" My tone is super snotty, but I really don't give a crap. "Aren't you supposed to be in band?"

He frowns, his forehead creasing. "Well, yeah, but I skipped out. Said I had to use the can." Lovely. He's so classy. What did I ever see in him again?

I check him out because I can. And then I remember what I saw in him. He may be a year younger than me, but he's cute. He always has a ready smile, and he made me laugh. He wasn't the best kisser and he had a habit of groping me when he got too intense with the kissing, but overall, our relationship hadn't been awful. It had been tentative and new and fun and exhilarating for a too-brief time.

The ending is what was awful. Finding him naked with my best friend Tara, actually having sex in one of Tuttle's guest bedrooms. That night, I thought I was the one who was going to end up doing it with Thad. Instead it was Tara.

I haven't spoken to either of them since. Until now.

A big sigh escapes me and I turn to face him fully. "What do you want, Thad?"

He ducks his head, his gaze focused on the table in front of us. "I feel bad about what happened."

"You should."

"Yeah." He lifts his head, his face sad. "Tara broke up with me. This morning. That's why I don't wanna be in band today."

I don't even feel a pang of sympathy for him. "Really."

Thad nods, his brown hair flopping into his eyes. He shoves it back irritably. "Said she couldn't be with me anymore. Something about me being too immature when she wants a man."

Well, maybe that's true. "And why are you telling me this again?"

"Because I've been feeling really guilty lately about…everything that happened between us. It's like you saw us that night, and that was it. You never talked to me or Tara again. You dropped out of band, you started hanging out with different people, you started going out with Tuttle, the most popular guy in school." Thad shakes his head. "It was weird. It *is* weird. Why'd you change so much and so fast, Amanda?"

This guy doesn't deserve an answer from me. Yet I still feel compelled to give him one. "I guess I was tired of the old me."

"Are you happy with the new version of yourself?" He watches me closely, waiting for my answer, and I take a deep breath, staring off into the distance.

Am I happy? I like the direction I'm going. Classes are good and I'm not scared of the future, otherwise known as college. I like my new friends, though that uneasy feeling about Em still lingers. I have a job that I like, but more hours would be nice. I don't miss band as much as I thought I would because I have new things to occupy my time. And then there's Jordan.

He makes me happy, even if that happiness is mixed with a healthy dose of panic and uneasiness.

"Yes, I'm happy." My voice is firm and when my gaze meets Thad's once more, I can see the sadness lingering in his eyes. Over what he lost?

I hope so.

"Then I'm happy for you too, Amanda." His voice is hollow, so I know his words are too. A smile plays upon my lips and I turn away from him, not wanting him to see it.

He's getting everything he deserves.

chapter fifteen

Jordan

It's been a little over a week since Cannon's party. The rumors died quick. Cannon and I took care of that, though I'm still pissed at him for interfering with Amanda and me in the first place. He needs to focus on his own problems. Like the fact that he likes Em, and she's just stringing him along. She's a hot mess. Yeah, I can admit she's definitely hot—but she's also crazy. Messed up in the head. Unpredictable. Who needs that?

Not me. I'm messed up enough.

Amanda's black eye has faded to almost nothing, and I'm fucking glad. Seeing her with that ugly bruise on her face every single day was tearing me up inside. The constant reminder that I did that to her sucked. Gave me all of those I-don't-deserve-her type feelings.

But I do deserve her. I deserve happiness too. I don't need to remain alone and focused only on school and football. I can have a life too. I can prove that to my parents and then they won't be able to say jack shit to me. Then they'll have to eat their words.

I've been keeping it slow with Amanda, just like I told her I would. There's no need to rush this, no matter how much just looking at her makes me burn. It's hard though. So damn hard. When she smiles at me, it's like my heart is in free-fall. And when I actually get to kiss her, touch her, pull her into my arms and hold her close? It's never enough.

Now it's Saturday morning and I got to sleep in since I was out so late the night before, thanks to the playoff game—which we won, by only a field goal. Meaning our defensive line couldn't hold them as well and the opposing defensive line sacked my ass more times than I want to admit. I'm sore and bruised and I'd sleep all day if I could, especially since my parents are gone and there won't be anybody around.

But I promised Amanda I would take her to work at eleven, so that means I need to get my butt out of bed and take a quick shower before I head over to her house.

I check my phone, scrolling through my notifications and smiling faintly when I spot the Snapchat from Amanda. I ignore all the other messages and open the one from Amanda. It's a stern-faced selfie and she's pointing her finger at me with the message, *Don't forget to pick me up at 10:45.*

I take a quick and serious selfie and include a message before I hit send.

How could I forget you?

She sends me back a pic of her standing in the bathroom with just a towel wrapped around her, her dark, wet hair spilling past her shoulders. Her face and neck are a rosy shade of pink and I think I can make out a few water droplets clinging to her skin, but then the photo's gone.

Stupid fucking Snapchat.

I take another quick selfie and include another message.

Drop the towel.

The selfie that comes back is of her smiling, one brow arched, and a message.

Send me a pic of your abs and I'll consider it.

My abs?

I sit up in bed and shove the covers off me, kicking them off the bed. I aim my camera at my stomach and take a photo, then send it.

Within seconds there's a new photo, and it's of her with the towel still on and she's pouting.

I need a better pic. Sexier. She also includes a blushing emoji.

Huh. All right. I'll deliver.

It takes a few minutes, but I finally have the pose down. It's a full body shot from my chest down, with one hand slipped just beneath the waistband of the black mesh shorts I only pulled on a few seconds ago. I thought about sending her a naked pic, but I don't want to freak her out completely.

Baby steps.

I caption the photo *Does this work for you?* And hit send.

A few minutes tick by and I'm starting to worry I pushed it, though I got the notification that she screenshot the image. Great. Will she use it against me later? She's not like that, so I doubt it.

Maybe she hates the photo. I run a hand through my hair, tug on the ends so hard that it hurts. Why hasn't she responded? What is she doing? I check the time. I need to get in the damn shower so I can be there to pick her up by ten forty-five.

Finally I get a reply and I open it to find a photo of her from the waist up, her hair still hanging in front of her now bare chest and one arm slung over her breasts. She's smiling and I screenshot it quick before it disappears. Then I call her.

"Tell me you're in the shower," she answers.

"Want me to send you a photo to prove it?"

"No! You need to go get ready so we won't be late."

"Your photo was a rip off."

"What do you mean?" I can hear the frown in her voice.

"I asked you to drop the towel."

"And I did."

"But I couldn't see anything."

"I did what you asked. I guess you needed to be more specific." I can hear the laughter in her voice, and I like it. Even though I'm irritated that I didn't get to see her actually topless.

"Okay, how specific is this for you?" I take a deep breath. "Send me a naked photo next time."

"Jordan."

"I'm serious."

"I know you are, but I don't have time for this right now. I have to get ready for work."

"So responsible." I hesitate before I ask, "What did you think of the photo I sent you?"

"It was nice," she admits softly.

"Just nice? Not sexy or groundbreaking or hot?"

"Oh, it was definitely hot. You have the best abs I've ever seen." She ends that sentence with a giggle.

And that giggle is like a shot powering straight through me, settling in my gut—and lower. "Remember that one time you licked them?" I ask her, my voice low, my thoughts dirty.

"Jordan! We are not having this discussion right now. Go get in the shower." She ends the call before I can say anything else, and I start to laugh. She's a bossy little thing when she wants to be.

I freaking love it.

After I get out of the shower and I'm towel-drying my hair, I see I have a missed call from my mom.

Shit. I do not want to call her back.

I finish getting ready and am halfway out the door when my cell rings. Mom again. Reluctantly I answer the call.

"I'm at the airport and I'll be home later this afternoon," she says to me in greeting. "We're having dinner tonight. You, me and your father."

"I have plans," I tell her gruffly, even though I don't. I'll make sure I do. I'll take Amanda out to dinner or to the movies or whatever. And if she can't I'll figure out something else. No way am I having dinner with my parents on a Saturday night. That sounds like a nightmare.

"Cancel them. We need to talk to you."

"What about?"

"Stop questioning me and just do as I say!" she practically screeches.

I pull the phone away from my ear. Jesus. "I'll bring a guest then." Hopefully Amanda will agree to go. I went to her family dinner, so it only seems fair.

"No. Absolutely not. This is a family matter we need to discuss. I don't want any interlopers trying to nose into our business."

"What time is dinner?"

"Eight o'clock."

"Fine," I bite out, hating that she's won. They always win. Despite the fact they're shitty parents, they have the upper hand because I'm a minor. And I hate it. When I turn eighteen, I swear to God I'm out of their house forever. I don't care if I still have school. I'll figure something else out. I gain control of my trust fund too, so it's not like

I won't have money.

"I'll see you then." I end the call before she can say anything else, and I hope like hell that pisses her off.

But that's not satisfying enough. I wrap both hands around my phone and hold the top edge of it to my forehead, closing my eyes. Trying my best to keep my anger under control. I want to throw something. Break something.

Instead I take deep, even breaths. Tell myself to get my shit together. Try to focus on the fact that I need to be calm and normal when I pick up Amanda. The last thing I wanna do is freak her out.

I drop my arms down to my sides and open my eyes. Catch my reflection in the mirror hanging on the opposite wall. I nod and grin, thinking the smile looks pretty damn real.

Even though it's totally fake.

chapter sixteen

Amanda

Since I've started working here, business at Yo Town has slowly died, mostly because of the cold weather. I guess no one wants to eat frozen yogurt in November—I can't blame them. Thanks to this, my hours have been drastically cut, and I rarely work with Blake, the Yo Town owners' son. I still see him around school, but we don't talk much. We have Honors English together along with Jordan, though I think Jordan intimidates him, so he pretty much ignores me.

But this afternoon, we're working together for the first time in a long time. From the moment I get there, it's pretty busy, customers constantly coming in, especially big groups of kids who always make a horrible mess. As the afternoon progresses, traffic quietly dies off. It's almost closing time and we're both cleaning up around the place when he asks me a question.

"So, uh, do you ever talk to Kyla?"

I look over at him, pretending to be nonchalant when I spot the nervousness written all over his face. It's kind of cute, how unsure he appears. If Kyla has a hard time trusting guys because of what happened to her, Blake would be a good choice as a date, even as a potential boyfriend. He's sweet, kind and smart. He's not drop-dead gorgeous, but he's cute.

Blake's the type of guy I would've gone for if Jordan Tuttle hadn't walked into my life.

"I talk to Kyla all the time," I answer as I wipe off all the sticky round tables. People are such slobs, especially kids. They let the frozen yogurt melt and drip everywhere. "Like almost every day."

"Really?" Blake sounds surprised.

"Well, yeah. We run the hydration station for the football team together, remember?"

"Oh yeah, that's right." His expression turns sheepish. "I forgot."

Really? I don't know if I believe him, but whatever. "You like her, huh."

"Well, um, kind of." He shakes his head, his cheeks turning pink. "But I don't think she likes me."

"How do you know?"

Blake shrugs, looking sad. "I don't know. She just—she doesn't seem that in to me. She's in a couple of my classes so we talk a lot, and everything seems like it's going great. We have a lot of stuff in common, she laughs at my lame jokes, but then just when I work up the nerve to ask her out, she seems to, like, mentally retreat. It's the weirdest thing."

I think I know why she acts like that, but it's not up to me to tell him. "Maybe she's just really shy."

"Yeah, maybe. I don't see her with guys much. She has a few close friends, and she seems to keep to herself a lot." He leans the broom against the front counter and goes to sit at one of the small tables, looking defeated. "I don't know if she's really interested in me, you know? What if she thinks I'm just a friend?"

"You'll never know if you never take a chance and ask her out," I suggest gently.

"I don't want her to reject me."

"You'd rather live with regret then? Always asking yourself 'what if'?" I'm trying to live my life without regret, but it's hard when certain things make you nervous. Like rejection. Like accepting someone back into your life even though you know they're most likely going to hurt you again.

I totally understand where Blake is coming from.

Blake drops his head, gazing at the table. "When you put it like that..." His voice drifts and he watches me helplessly. Like I have all the answers.

So I give him one.

"Just ask her out. I'm sure she won't reject you. Ask her to the movies or take her to dinner or whatever. Keep it simple."

"You really think she'll say yes?" He lifts his head so our gazes meet.

"Yeah, I really do." God, I hope she does. I will feel awful if she turns him down.

We continue cleaning and talking about school when the door swings open and in walks...Eli Bennett and Lauren Mancini. Holding hands. Laughing together. Looking very much like a couple.

What. The. Hell.

I turn to look at Blake and mouth, *I'm outta here*. I don't want Lauren or Eli to see me, though Lauren knows I work at Yo Town. She probably came here and brought Eli on purpose.

But to, what? Humiliate me? Last time I talked to him, he was still willing to chase after me, despite my obvious disinterest. The guy is persistent, I'll give him that, but his persistence can get annoying quick.

I'm almost to the door that leads to the back of the building when Lauren calls out my name. I freeze and slowly turn around, pasting a smile on my face. "Hey," I say weakly, offering a lame wave as a greeting. I glance down at my shirt, see the smear of chocolate right in the middle from the melted M&Ms I cleaned up earlier.

"Having another fun afternoon selling frozen yogurt?" Lauren asks brightly, her eyes wide, her smile as friendly as a shark's.

"Amanda, I didn't know you worked here." Eli grins and lets go of Lauren's hand, moving toward me like he's going in for a hug. His arms are wide open, but I dodge around him at the last minute.

"I'm surprised Lauren didn't tell you," I say, leaning against the wall and crossing my arms. I don't care how defensive I look. I don't want to go back out there and help them or ring them up. The second they turn around I'm going into the back and staying there until they leave.

"Nah, she didn't." Eli glances over at Lauren and she smiles sweetly in return. Gag. "It's good to see you, though you're…kind of a mess."

Ah, leave it to good ol' Eli Bennett and his annoying honesty. "This is what happens when you have to actually work for a living," I tell them both, annoyed. "Sometimes life is a little messy."

"How does Jordan feel about that?" Lauren asks snidely.

"Feel about what?" I am so done with this snobby, rude, inconsiderate *bitch*. "And do you really have the right to use his name like that?"

She rests a hand on her chest like I shocked her. "It is his name, isn't it?"

I hate how superior she acts all the time. "No one ever calls him Jordan. Even the teachers call him Tuttle."

"She's right," Eli adds, earning a dirty look from Lauren. "What? It's true. Everyone calls him Tuttle."

"*I* don't call him Tuttle," Lauren says, turning her venomous gaze on me. "Considering we used to be together, I think I'm allowed to call him whatever I want, whenever I want."

"But that was a long time ago, wasn't it? Like when we were fourteen?" Extra heavy emphasis on the word "fourteen", because come on. How serious could their relationship have been?

"Such a long time ago, I barely remember it," another very familiar voice confirms from behind Lauren and Eli.

My gaze lands on Jordan's scowling face and I can't help but smile at him. My own personal hero, always to my rescue.

He has impeccable timing.

"Jordan!" Lauren practically squeals when she turns and sees him. If she starts hopping up and down and clapping, I might cut a bitch. "What are you doing here?"

"Picking my girlfriend up from work," he says easily, dropping the word *girlfriend* like it's no big deal. The disappointment on her face, in her body language, is painfully obvious. "What are *you* doing here?" He sends Eli a quick look. "Isn't he a little young for you, Lauren?"

"Um, we just had a sudden craving for frozen yogurt," Lauren says, ignoring Jordan's rude comment. "Come on, Eli." She grabs hold of Eli's hand and starts to drag him over to the yogurt machines. "Let's go pick out what flavors we want."

"Hey, Tuttle," Eli says as he walks past, but Jordan doesn't say a word. He doesn't even look at them.

He only has eyes for me.

They're long gone and I still can't move. I feel pinned in place by Jordan's smoldering gaze. "You're early," I finally manage to say.

"I was hoping we could leave now and your *co-worker—*" He says this word snidely. I don't know why he doesn't like Blake. It's weird. "—can close up without you. What do you think?"

Excitement bubbles deep within me. Wanting to get out of here now sounds promising. "Why do you want to leave now?"

"I have plans."

He says the words with such finality, I realize quick those plans don't include me. What else could he be doing? I should ask him.

But instead of asking him, I say, "I'll go check with Blake," and walk away as fast as I can.

Because really? I'm annoyed. There he goes again, being completely closed off and not telling me anything. I can't read his mind. And I can't figure out his mood either. This morning when he came by my house to pick me up, he'd seemed so happy, and fun too. Sexy and flirtatious and full of delicious kisses. At one point I'd been tempted to call in sick to work so I could spend the entire day with him.

Now he's acting standoffish. Like he doesn't want to tell me anything, and I hate that. As his official/unofficial girlfriend, I think I have a right to know what's going on.

Don't I?

I go behind the counter where Blake is waiting at the register for Eli and Lauren to finish so he can ring them up. "Do you mind if I leave a little early? My ride has somewhere he needs to be."

Oh, I sound so bitchy, but I don't care. I'm mad.

Blake frowns, tilting his head to the side. "You okay, Amanda?"

I nod. Shrug. "Sure. Why do you ask?"

"No reason." He glances around the room, making a face when he hears Eli and Lauren giggling over at the toppings section. I would bet big money they're destroying it. He lowers his voice. "Do you not want to leave with Tuttle? Is that the problem?"

"Why would you ask that?" I frown.

"I don't know. You seem upset. And you weren't upset until Tuttle walked into the place," Blake points out. He stands a little straighter, squares his shoulders. Like he's going to rush to my defense and fight Jordan. He'd get smashed in an instant. "If he's not treating you right, let me know. You don't deserve to be with an asshole."

What is it with guys always rushing to my defense? A few seconds ago, I loved it. Now I hate feeling so weak. "He's not an asshole, Blake." *Well, maybe he is.* "He's never hurt me." *He broke my heart, but I guess that doesn't count.* "And I was sort of upset at Eli and Lauren when they came in, remember?"

But Jordan did make it worse. Not that I want to admit it.

"As long as you're sure..."

"I'm sure," I say firmly. "But I'll stay if you need me to. I'm scheduled to close and I don't want to ditch you."

"No, it's okay. If you want to go with him, go." Blake chuckles, trying to lighten the mood I guess. "You'll just have to return the favor sometime." He smiles easily and I lunge toward him, giving him a quick hug and a kiss on the cheek. Why I'm so happy he gave in, I don't know. I'm still angry at Jordan.

It's cute, though, how Blake's face turns bright red, and when I release him, I glance over my shoulder to find Jordan watching us.

Glaring.

Frowning.

Looking ready to tear Blake's head off.

Our gazes meet and I tell myself to look away, but it's like I can't.

"Ready?" Jordan asks, his voice tight, his eyebrows up. He crosses his arms, his biceps bulging, and I remind myself to focus on my anger.

On his anger.

Not his sexy muscles straining against his sleeves.

Ugh.

"Let me get my purse," I tell him, turning toward the doorway that leads to the back office. I spot Lauren and Eli still standing by the toppings bar, though they've forgotten all about the candy and are blatantly watching us. The look on Lauren's face is nothing short of pure malice mixed with amusement. If she wasn't holding that giant cup of frozen yogurt, she'd probably be rubbing her hands together in anticipation of spreading this particular story around school come Monday. Or even better, on social media. Instagram. Snapchat.

We're putting on a show for everyone to see.

chapter seventeen

Jordan

I'm trying my best to keep my shit together, but it's difficult. I don't say a word as we walk toward my car and neither does Amanda. All I can focus on is that moment between her and Blake from just a few seconds ago. When she hugged him, and gave him a kiss on the cheek, beaming up at him like he just made her day. Her night. Her entire year.

Christ. I wanted to rip his hands off when they touched her. Wanted to demolish his face with my fist when she kissed his cheek. I know it was an innocent gesture. I know she wasn't trying to provoke me.

But it almost feels like she did all of that to drive me crazy and it fucking *worked*.

I open the passenger-side door for her and she climbs into the SUV, biting out a quick, "Thank you," right before I slam the door shut. Her lips part as we stare at each other through the window, and I'm overcome with the need to kiss her.

Pushing the urge out of my mind, I jog around the front of the Range Rover and get in on the driver's side. I start the car and glance over my shoulder, hooking my hand around the passenger-side headrest as I quickly back out of the parking spot. I could use the backup camera, but this gives me an excuse to possibly touch her.

And I do. Touch her. I wrap a silky strand of dark hair around my finger, tugging on it gently just before I let it go and remove my hand from the seat. I put the SUV into drive and tear out of the parking lot, hitting the gas so hard, my tires squeal across the pavement. Amanda gasps as she reaches for the grab handle above the door.

"Sorry," I mutter once I turn onto the road. I barely glance in her direction, almost afraid of what I might find. Like her overwhelming disapproval. "Didn't mean to scare you."

"You didn't scare me." She lets go of the handle and primly sets her hands in her lap. I think she's trying for dignified, but her hair's in a messy braid with wild strands around her face, there's mascara smudged under her eyes and her shirt is a disaster.

But she's still beautiful. And her ass looked damn good in those jeans when I was walking behind her just a few minutes ago.

We remain quiet as I continue to drive, and when I stop at a red light, I can't stand it anymore. "You're mad."

She shrugs, but otherwise remains silent.

"Why?" What did I do wrong? If anyone is in the wrong here, it's her. She's the one who grabbed Blake. She's the one who kissed him. I may have called her my girlfriend to Lauren and Eli, but we haven't made anything official. Hell, I feel like I walk on pins and needles around her almost all the time, scared I might do something wrong that'll send her away from me forever.

What right do I have to be angry over her hugging and kissing Blake? Are we even officially a couple yet?

"Because you said you wouldn't keep things from me, but you still do. You're exactly the same. You've got all of these deep, dark secrets you keep hidden away, and you're so standoffish sometimes. If we're supposed to start working on our relationship, Jordan, you actually have to talk to me, you know?" She exhales loudly and turns away so she's facing the passenger-side window.

I say nothing. Just stew over her words as I continue to drive. She doesn't live too far from Yo Town, so we arrive at her house quick. Pulling up to the front, I notice there are no lights shining through the windows.

"No one's home?"

She keeps her back to me. "My parents are out of town, picking up my brother at college," she tells the window. "It was a last minute thing. I guess his car broke down."

"Your old car?" The one I said could barely run that first time I picked her up after a late shift at Yo Town.

Guess I called that one.

"Yeah." Her shoulders slump a little. "They took Trent with them and they'll be back tomorrow. Sometime in the early afternoon."

"So you're staying home alone tonight." And she never mentioned this to me before. Not even this morning when I drove her to work and everything was so good between us.

Well, more like when I was trying to convince myself I was okay with my mother bossing me around and demanding that I come to our messed up family dinner. Instead of thinking about that bullshit, I focused on Amanda and how happy I was to see her. How good she tasted when I kissed her. How right she felt when I pulled her into my

"I've done it before. Stayed by myself overnight. It's no big deal." She finally turns to look at me, and I see a flicker of pain in her eyes, but then it's gone. My heart feels like it's cracking. I'm the one who put that pain there. I'm the one who hurt her.

"Why didn't you tell me?"

"I only just found out while I was at work. And I was going to tell you, but I wanted to make it a surprise." She sighs, her shoulders slumping. "But now you have other plans. Plans you won't tell me about."

"It's not that I don't want to tell you, it's just that what I'm doing isn't going to be fun. Trust me," I say firmly.

"What exactly are you doing?

"My mother demanded I come home for a family dinner." The sarcasm is heavy on those last two words. "More like it'll be two hours of them giving me endless shit. I don't want to go." I hesitate for a moment before admitting, "But I have to."

"Maybe..." Her voice drifts, and she clamps her lips shut. They curve into this mesmerizing little smile as I stare at them, and I'm tempted to lean over and kiss her.

"Maybe what?" I ask when she remains quiet.

"You should come over tonight. After your dinner." She sinks her teeth into her lower lip, like she can't believe she just said that and she's trying to stop the words from leaving her. "If you want to."

"I want to," I say immediately, giving in to my impulses and leaning over the center console, pressing my mouth to hers in a gentle kiss. "I definitely want to," I murmur against her lips.

She smiles and pulls away, her gaze locked with mine. "Are you sure?"

"Yes." I reach out and cup her cheek, stroke her soft skin. "Want me to text you when I'm done?"

Amanda nods.

"Will you be okay all alone?" I don't want her scared.

I want to protect her in every way I can.

"Yeah." She nods again.

"I'll see you later tonight then." I lean in and kiss her once more. This one is longer, my lips lingering, our mouths clinging. When I finally break away she has this dazed expression on her face and her lips are swollen.

Every time I look at her, I swear she gets more beautiful.

chapter eighteen

Amanda

I decided to leisurely prep for my night with Jordan. First I took a shower, shaved everything I could and washed my hair with my favorite shampoo and conditioner. Once I dried off, I slathered on enough body lotion that I ended up smelling like the inside of a Bath & Body Works store. I'm figuring by the time Jordan comes over, it'll mellow out to the perfect, subtle scent.

I take my time drying my hair and then curl it with the curling iron Livvy left at my house. It has a big barrel and makes the most perfect waves. I pluck my brows. I brush my teeth. I debate wearing makeup and decide why not, then only put on a light coat of mascara and that's it.

Nerves make my stomach twist since I didn't really eat dinner, though I probably should. Mom calls to check up on me, and she makes me swear I have no one over at the house. Considering I don't have anyone over when she calls, I'm not lying when I swear I don't.

Yeah. Whatever makes me feel better, right?

Once I end the call with Mom, I go into my tiny walk-in closet and stare at my clothes. Boring, boring, boring. I want to wear something cute but casual. Something that doesn't look like I'm trying too hard because honestly? I am trying so hard right now.

If all goes as planned, I'm going to seduce Jordan Tuttle tonight.

Funny, right? He's the player. He's the one who's been with an endless list of girls. I'm the virgin who's made out with maybe a handful of guys. What do I know about seduction? Nothing, that's what.

But I'm bound and determined to get over my nervousness about having actual sex. I'm going to do it. With Jordan. In my bed. All night long.

Oh God. I think I'm going to be sick.

Determined to get over the nausea, I decide to focus on other things. Like what I'm going to wear. I go to my dresser and dig through the top drawer until I find the new lacy black bra I splurged on a few weeks ago, thoughts of Jordan in my mind as I purchased it. It's sat unworn in my underwear drawer ever since, along with the matching lacy panties I bought. I drop the towel I have wrapped around me on the ground and put them on, then check out my reflection in the mirror.

Ugh. There's no way I can greet him looking like this. What am I going to do? Just casually open the front door wearing only my underwear? Yeah, Jordan might appreciate it, but I'll feel dumb.

This seduction thing is hard.

Kneeling down, I pull open the bottom drawer and pull out a pair of black cropped leggings. Then I grab my favorite PINK gray, black and white sweatshirt and tug it over my head before putting on the leggings. I step into my old black slippers and then check my phone.

It's only nine-thirty. I've still got a long wait ahead of me.

I flop on the bed and text Livvy, asking what she's doing. Thankfully, she responds immediately.

> **You don't want to know.**

Huh. What does she mean by that?

I definitely want to know now.

> **You'll be mad at me.**

When am I ever mad at you?

> **This will make you mad.**

She's being so evasive. Meaning she's hiding something. She's doing something wrong. But what?

It's like a light bulb goes on over my head. I send her another text.

Please tell me this has nothing to do with Dustin.

No answer for a few minutes and then…

> **This has nothing to do with Dustin.**

Are you lying?

> **Maybe.**

OLIVIA!!!

I rarely bust out the full name, but this is deserved. What the hell is she doing with Dustin right now?

Are you with him?

I'm at his house. He's feeling really down because he broke up with

Brianne earlier. He asked me to come over, so I did.

They broke up?

Yeah. First thing this morning. Via text. So cheesy.

Now you're over at his house consoling him?

Yes! We're friends. That's what friends do.

She is going to get into a heap of trouble. I can just feel it.

What about Ryan?

What about him?

Where is he?

He had his friends over at his house and they're playing one of his dad's new video games.

Oh, that's right. His dad is a video game designer. But I thought Ryan hated video games?

Doesn't he hate playing video games?

Sometimes his dad asks all his friends over so they can test them out. I think that's what they're doing.

Suddenly, my phone rings and Livvy's name flashes on the screen.

"Why are you calling me?" I answer.

"It's a lot easier than typing. I'm feeling lazy. Plus, I just snuck outside." I hear a door close behind her and it gets a lot quieter. "Please don't be mad at me for going over to Dustin's. He sounded so sad and like he needed a friend. I couldn't say no to him."

"You should say no. It's going to get you into a lot of trouble when

Ryan finds out," I warn.

"Oh, screw him. What does he care? I'm sort of over his bullshit."

How many times have I heard this? And they haven't been together very long. It's kind of crazy. "If you're over his bullshit, then maybe you should break up with him."

"I'm not ready for that yet."

"But you'll go over to Dustin's house like no big deal."

"Stop. You're making me feel bad." Livvy pauses for a moment. "What are you doing right now?"

"I'm alone. My parents are gone." I explain to her how they left to go help my older brother George with his car. I'm starting to wonder if that was a made up story. It sounds bogus.

"Wait a minute. So you're in your house completely alone?" Livvy sounds shocked.

"Yeah. What's the big deal?"

"Are you having Tuttle over tonight?" Her voice lowers and I can tell she's teasing me.

I decide to use her answer from earlier. "Maybe."

Livvy sucks in a sharp breath. "He *is* coming over there, isn't he? Or is he already there? Ah, you're going to do it tonight, aren't you?" She is screaming so loud I pull the phone away from my ear.

"Oh my God, Liv! Go ahead and let the entire neighborhood hear you."

"Sorry! I'm just so excited! I can't believe you two are finally going to do it!" Livvy squeals, making me wince.

"I don't know if anything is going to happen," I tell her. "So don't get your hopes up."

"Come on, you're alone in your house and he's coming over, right? You never did tell me where he is."

"He's having dinner with his parents right now. Then he's coming over."

"Oh." She says nothing else and I'm immediately defensive.

"What do you mean by that?"

"Remember that time we went out to dinner and we saw his dad?"

How could I forget? It was an awful night.

"Aren't you worried that if his dinner with the parents is anything like that night, Tuttle will come over to your house all pissed off and ragey?"

"Ragey?"

"Well, yeah. It's like he's full of pent up rage. And that makes him ragey. Get it?"

"I get it." My stomach growls and I realize I'm hungry after all. "Listen, Livvy, I gotta go. Don't do anything too crazy, okay?"

"I won't, I promise. We're just talking. That's it." Livvy giggles. "But I want you to do as many crazy things as possible tonight, okay? And I want a full report tomorrow!" She ends the call before I can say anything else. I check the time.

Well, that killed fifteen minutes.

I'm munching on chips and a grilled cheese sandwich I just made when I finally get a text from Jordan.

I'll be at your house in less than five.

I swallow hard, nearly choking on cheese and bread. He'll be here in less than five minutes?

"Shit!" I yell out loud as I grab my paper plate and dump everything in the trash, including my half eaten sandwich. I turn off the kitchen light and run to my bathroom, where I hurriedly brush my teeth to get rid of grilled cheese and Dorito breath. Of course, that's when the doorbell rings, me with a mouthful of toothpaste, foam around my lips and dripping down my chin.

I spit in the sink, rinse out as fast as I can before I wipe my face with a towel. I'm literally running to the door and when I finally get there and throw it open, I'm relieved to see Jordan standing on the doorstep. Looking windblown and vaguely irritated.

Oh, and super hot. Like, wearing a plaid flannel shirt and jeans and boots hot. Like I want to rip his clothes off hot.

"Hi," I say—or more like I squeak. I sound like a mouse.

"Hey." He nods toward me. "Can I come in?"

"Of course." I back up out of his way and he walks inside, stopping just in front of me. His gaze drops to my chin, lingering there, but he doesn't say anything. "Is something wrong?"

"You have something." He reaches out and swipes at my chin, his fingertip covered in white. "On your face."

Oh my God. How embarrassing. "Yeah, it's toothpaste."

"You were brushing your teeth?" His brows shoot up.

"Well, yeah. You texted me when I was eating Doritos and a grilled cheese sandwich." Ack, why'd I tell him that? "I didn't want to have Dorito breath."

"You're cute." I lift my head to watch as he slips his finger in between his lips and sucks the toothpaste off. That's sort of gross. But it's also rather…intimate, in a weird way. "Minty fresh."

"Jordan!" I go to shove his chest and he grabs hold of my wrist, keeping my hand pressed against him. "You're so weird."

"Come here." He pulls me into his arms, crushing me against him and I go willingly, slipping my arms around his waist and holding him tight. "I missed you," he murmurs. "Your hair smells good."

"Thanks," I whisper. My plan worked—he likes the shampoo. "I missed you too." We only just saw each other a few hours ago and it had been tension-filled. Crap, we'd almost gotten into a fight. But now I just want to melt into him. Hold on to him and never let him go.

"Let's get inside." He walks me farther into the house and kicks the door shut. He seems just as reluctant to let me go as he turns the both of us toward the door so he can lock it. "Wanna sit on the couch?"

"Okay," I say weakly, thankful he's not taking me back to my bedroom first thing. I'm nervous enough. We need to lead up to this slowly.

He takes my hand and we settle onto the couch, our legs pressed next to each other's as he slips his arm around my shoulders. I lean my head against him and breathe in his woodsy scent. "How was your dinner?"

"Total bullshit."

I lift my head so I can look at his face. His jaw is tight, his eyes narrowed as he stares straight ahead. I refuse to let his closed off expression deter me. "You don't want to talk about it?"

Jordan exhales loudly and gives a slight shake of his head. "Not really, but I don't want to shut you out either."

So that's what it feels like when your own words are thrown back at you. "If you'd rather talk about something else, I understand. I know your parents are a—sensitive subject."

He glances down at me, his expression sincere. "I honestly don't know what to say. It's the same thing with them, every single time. They try and tell me what to do. They try and control every aspect of my life, especially my father. They spent the entire dinner talking *at* me and not listening to a word I said, so eventually I shut up and tuned them out."

That sounds so awful. No wonder he acts the way he does. It sounds like no one has ever treated him nicely. Or shown him any love. Not even any kindness. "Why do they want to control you so much?"

"I don't know." He shrugs and I rest my head on his shoulder once more. "Because they can? Because they think they own me? It's not like they care about me or about what I do. Only if it messes with their idea of what's proper or not."

His parents sound like monsters. I met them both only once, and that one time we saw his dad doesn't really count. Though the time I met his mom had been incredibly awkward too.

I rest my hand on his thigh and give it a squeeze. "I'm sorry."

"For what?"

"That you have such awful parents."

"It's not your fault my parents are awful." He goes quiet for a moment. "Sometimes I wonder why they even bothered having me. I feel like I'm more of a nuisance to them than anything else. They've always done whatever they want—who cares about the kid? They've never given me any of their time, even when I was younger and really needed it, you know?"

We always need time from our parents, but I don't say it.

"Yet they have these endless expectations on me. All of these demands that supposedly mean something to them and our family name. My father likes to say that a lot. Keeping up the family name. It's a bunch of bullshit." He sounds absolutely disgusted. "And if I don't meet their expectations, if I don't do exactly what they want, then I'm a complete disappointment."

"Are you serious?" I'm outraged. Like seriously outraged on his behalf. "How can you not meet their expectations? You're smart, you're a star football player, you don't get into trouble—"

He interrupts me. "Oh, I've gotten in trouble. You just don't hear about it because my dad pays off whoever he has to so he can keep it under wraps."

My curiosity shoots way up but I can't focus on that right now. "Whatever. Don't we all get in trouble sometimes?" Well, not me. Not until last summer when I started hanging out with Jordan. Not that he makes me a bad person, but...

He makes me want to do bad things. With him.

"You know what the real problem is? They want to have complete control over me. I'm turning eighteen soon, and they can't stand it. I'll come into my trust fund and I won't need them anymore."

A trust fund? I'm stunned. "You have a trust fund?"

"My grandfather died when I was a baby. He left me a trust fund and my father has invested well on my behalf over the years. It's about the only good thing he's done for me," Jordan says bitterly.

I knew he was rich, but I didn't realize he'd have his own money. He'll be completely independent and could probably move out of his parents' house if he wanted to.

"What are you going to do when you turn eighteen?" I ask.

"What do you mean?"

"Are you going to stay home and finish out the school year? Or are you going to—leave?" Oh, God. What if he leaves? Once he finishes out the football season—which is in a matter of days—he has nothing keeping him here. He's probably completed enough classes that he could graduate now if he wanted to. When's his birthday anyway? I feel bad that I can't remember. And what are his plans? He hates his parents so much I wouldn't blame him for wanting to leave this place and never come back.

"I'm not going anywhere. I'll finish out the school year and graduate, just like everyone else." His voice is soft and I can hear it rumble in his chest. "I'll have money in January when I turn eighteen, but I don't know where'd I go, Amanda. My parents are rarely home anyway, and I don't think I want to live on my own. Thinking about that kind of shit is…"

Scary. He doesn't need to say the word out loud. I know what he's thinking, and I can't blame him. It *is* scary sometimes, to think of the future. I told myself at the beginning of the school year I need to live my life day by day and not worry about tomorrow. So far, that's been working out fine.

But I don't have rotten parents like Jordan does. I know he has financial security, but money can't buy you happiness. And it definitely can't buy you love. I think he realizes that.

I don't know what else to say. An apology isn't good enough and like he said, it's not my fault his parents are such assholes. So I remain quiet and close my eyes, enjoying this moment of just sitting with Jordan and not talking about anything at all. I listen to his even breaths. The sound of his heartbeat, steady and true. His fingers skim over my shoulder, his thumb slowly tracing the seam of my sweatshirt, and I swear if he keeps this up, I could fall asleep like this…

"Amanda."

Jordan's deep voice snaps me awake and I lift away from him in a hurry, sitting up straight and looking around, pushing my hair out of my face. My head feels heavy and my vision is hazy, and when I look over at Jordan, I notice he looks just as tired as I feel.

"Did we fall asleep?' I ask groggily.

"Yeah." He grabs his phone out of his pocket and checks the time. "For at least an hour."

"Really? Wow." I run a hand through my tangled hair, then slip my finger beneath each eye to check for smudged mascara. Of course, my finger comes away black. I can't ever get it right with this guy, I swear.

"Do you want me to leave?"

"What?" I turn to look at him. "No. Why would I want that?"

"You want me to stay?" He rubs his eyes and my heart melts. He looks like a sweet, sleepy little boy, and the urge to pull him into my arms and keep him forever is strong. "I don't want to do anything, I promise. Just sleep."

"Oh." I'm disappointed. But I'm also…relieved. Maybe tonight isn't the night for my sexual liberation. Maybe tonight is the night I get to indulge and cuddle with Tuttle.

Oh, crap. I'm going to need to hashtag that and post it on Snapchat somehow. He might get offended, but screw it.

It's a chance I have to take.

chapter nineteen

"So you really didn't have sex with Jordan Tuttle, huh?" Livvy's tone is clearly disbelieving. But why would I lie about that?

"No, I really didn't have sex with him," I say firmly.

We're sitting on the floor in Livvy's bedroom on Sunday afternoon. I didn't work at Yo Town today, but I still need to be home by five for our weekly family dinner. My parents brought my older brother George home, so he'll be there too. I guess he's staying here for the next few days, maybe even weeks. I heard Mom say something about academic probation and Dad freaking out over George dropping out of college, but I stayed out of it.

At least their focus is on my brother and not me. They have no clue Jordan spent the night at our house last night. Though nothing happened. Not a thing. Only a few quick kisses and the two of us twisted around each other all night long, sleeping peacefully. We woke up around ten, I made him breakfast—cereal and toast and coffee—and then kicked him out in fear of my parents showing up unannounced.

He didn't seem to mind, though. He gave me a thorough kiss goodbye, whispering against my lips, "Remember our Snapchat conversation from yesterday morning?"

I nodded, wondering where he was taking this.

"We could still do that, you know. Send each other—photos. No one will have to know. They'll just disappear." He smiled and kissed me one last time, most likely knowing he's shocked me. "You can trust me."

That particular conversation has been on my mind ever since.

"What are your thoughts on, um, sending nude photos?"

Livvy pauses in painting her toenails and lifts her head, the surprise on her face obvious. "Say *what?* Don't tell me Jordan's asking you for nudes."

Of course, Jordan's asking me for nudes. He's almost eighteen years old. I'm sure he *lives* for nudes. He might even have a...collection?

Ew, a tiny detail I really don't want to know about.

"Kind of," I tell her.

"What do you mean?" Livvy frowns.

"He asked for one this morning after we kinda flirted around the topic."

"How? Tell me exactly how it went down."

"Well, I sent him a photo of me wrapped in a towel after getting out of the shower yesterday morning." I bite my lip and duck my head, not wanting her to see my embarrassment.

"Ooooh, I didn't know you had it in you! Dirty girl." I look up just in time to see Livvy wink at me. Which of course sends us both into hysterical giggles.

Once I compose myself, I continue. "So he sent a photo of himself in return and told me to drop the towel."

Livvy's eyes light up. "He asked you to or told you to?"

"He told me to."

"So demanding. That's kind of hot." The dreamy sigh that escapes her makes me smile despite my worry. "Did you drop it then?"

"Kind of." I explain how I took the photo and how I posed. She shakes her head when I'm done.

"That isn't how you take a nude photo, Amanda." She says this like I should know, her voice full of disappointment.

"Well, I have no clue what I'm doing, so I thought it was okay." When she sends me a knowing look, I blow out an exasperated sigh. "I'm not going to just send him a bunch of nudes with my legs spread or whatever. That's gross."

"It's hella gross," Livvy agrees as she screws the cap back on top of the nail polish and sets it on her bedside table. "You don't want to look like a photo shoot out of *Hustler*. That magazine is absolutely disgusting, by the way."

I've never even heard of *Hustler*. And I'm not about to ask Livvy how she knows about it.

"But yeah, you definitely want to tease him," Livvy says with firm authority. "Show a little bit without showing the whole package, you know what I mean? Guys love that. A glimpse of a side boob. The bottom half of your ass cheek. The illusion of nudity without you actually being naked."

I'm frowning so hard I'm probably going to give myself wrinkles. How does she even know all this stuff? "You really think I should send him nude photos? Just bare it all and hope for the best?"

"You won't need to *bare it all*, but yeah. Why not?" Livvy shrugs. "Everyone's doing it."

"Just because everyone's doing it, doesn't mean we should too." I watch her closely. "Have you sent nudes to Ryan? Be honest."

She quickly shakes her head. "No way. I don't trust him."

"What?" Now it's my turn to be totally shocked. "But you guys are, like, *together*. You're boyfriend and girlfriend, in a serious relationship. You've had—" My voice drops to a whisper. "—*sex*."

"Yeah, so?"

Livvy is acting so nonchalant about her lack of trust in her boyfriend. It's kind of blowing my mind. "You gave up your virginity to Ryan, yet you don't trust him. Don't you think that's kind of weird?"

"I don't know. Maybe? I'm too scared he might do something awful when we split up. Like show the naked photo I sent him to all his friends or whatever. That would be beyond humiliating."

"You seriously believe he'd stoop that low if you broke up?"

"It's a risk I don't want to take. Even with Snapchat and setting the photo to, like, one second before it disappears, I still wouldn't send him a naked photo. We're probably going to break up and he'd figure out some way to use that photo against me." Livvy shakes her head. "Honestly? I don't know how much longer this relationship is going to work."

Just like that, the subject changes. I feel like I've been waiting in nervous anticipation for her to drop this bomb. I choose my next words carefully. "Are you thinking about breaking up with him?"

"Sort of. It's been on my mind a lot lately. I'm not as happy as I was when we first got together, I know that." She shrugs and touches the corner of her big toe nail to test if it's dry or not. "It was nice talking to Dustin last night. It made me realize how much I miss him." Her voice is quiet and she keeps her focus on her dark burgundy painted toes.

"What, so now you want to try out a relationship with Dustin?"

Okay, I'm not going to judge. But—and this is according to Livvy—their friendship hasn't always been the best. In fact, from what Livvy told me, before she started dating Ryan, she and Dustin were pretty toxic for each other. Lots of back and forth, *we're friends, we're not friends, we're gonna make out and do things to each other, oops we don't like each other anymore* type stuff.

Why would she want to go back to that? And why would he want to take her back?

"No. I don't know. Dustin and I have a long past. He's been such a huge part of my life and we just—stopped talking. It's been hard." She shrugs. "I mean, Ryan's sweet and he's a great kisser. Plus, he's really good in bed. But is that enough to keep going out with him? I'm not sure."

He's really good in bed? Maybe I didn't want to know that? Then again, maybe I do want to know. I'm sort of fascinated with the many possible reasons why he's so great. "Do you have other guys you can compare notes with?"

"What are you talking about?" Livvy frowns.

I probably phrased that all wrong. "Well, you said Ryan's good in bed. Which means you think he's good at—sex." I pause and meet her gaze. "So. Is he? Good in bed?"

"Yes. Most definitely." The look that crosses her face is nothing short of dreamy.

"And you've been with how many other guys?"

Her frown returns. "Dustin and I messed around a lot, but we never had actual sex."

"So you've been with Dustin and Ryan and that's it?" Livvy nods. "Then how do you know Ryan's any good? If you haven't really been able to compare him to anyone else."

"Whatever." She waves a hand, dismissing my words. "That part doesn't matter, Amanda. When it's good, you know it's good. Trust me."

Yeah, I don't know if I can. But I just smile and nod and try to steer the conversation back to where I want it to be.

"I'm just saying don't throw away your relationship with Ryan just because you heard Dustin has a big dick or whatever," I mumble, feeling dumb.

Livvy bursts out laughing. "Remember, I've *seen* his dick, my prudish friend. And while I wouldn't call it huge, I can definitely say it's pretty decent, for a dick."

I will never, ever look at Dustin in the right way again. "Has he ever sent you nudes?"

"Dustin? No way. Though he asked me for some once when we were fifteen and being stupid." She smiles serenely. "I told him I wasn't going to provide his beat off material and he never asked again."

"You did not," I breathe. I can't even imagine saying something like that to Jordan. I'd be too embarrassed.

"I did so! That's all he was looking for, you know?" She studies me carefully. "You and Tuttle never really did it, huh."

I slowly shake my head. "No, we never really did." Just thinking about it makes me nervous. I don't understand why being a virgin is such a big deal. Why do we have to *give* it away? Or *lose* it? Why is so much tied up in it? I do everything else but actual intercourse with Jordan yet that somehow keeps me pure? Saves me from…what?

When I think about it too hard, it's kind of ridiculous.

"But you two did—other things. Right?" Livvy asks.

"Yeah. Just not the actual deed." I start picking off the nail polish I just painted on my fingernails. This conversation makes me feel jittery. Nervous. How can I measure up sexually with any of the other girls

Jordan's been with? How can I measure up to Jordan himself?

"Well, he's going to want to," she says with all the authority of someone who knows. "Probably soon too. Are you ready?"

"I don't know. I want to say yes, but…." I clamp my lips shut. What's holding me back?

"But what? I mean, I get it if you're nervous. Having actual sex is *such* a big deal."

"Why?" When Livvy looks at me strangely, I continue. "Why is having sex a big deal? We've already done so much. Why do we put such heavy expectations on actual intercourse?

"Oh God, you just said intercourse." Livvy collapses into a fit of giggles, which irritates me. I'm trying to have a serious conversation. I let her giggle for a few minutes, and when she finally gains some control, she answers me. "It's, like, society who puts the expectations on intercourse and virginity and girls saving themselves. Boys get laid and it's considered a rite of passage. Girls have sex and we're considered sluts. It's totally unfair. You know what I mean?"

"I know exactly what you mean."

Livvy mock pouts and crosses her arms. "We shouldn't be judged so harshly just because we want to explore our sexuality."

"I totally agree," I say with an enthusiastic nod. This is what I want. A serious conversation about sex. "Who cares if we're having sex, right? We're practically adults. We should be able to do whatever we want."

"Yeah!" Livvy throws her arms into the air like she's cheering at a football game. "So you're ready to just do it with Tuttle then? Get it over with? Liberate yourself?"

My heart trips over itself just hearing Livvy say that, and all my righteous enthusiasm disappears. I swallow hard, fighting the nerves battling it out in my stomach. "Maybe?"

"Maybe's not a real answer," Livvy teases, wagging her finger at me. "What happened to your sexual liberation of two seconds ago? You go from wanting to send nudes and having sex with your hot boy to... maybe?"

Yeah, where did it go? One mention of doing it with Jordan and I quietly panic. "I guess it's one thing to talk about it, and another to actually do it?" When she sends me a stern look, all I can do is shrug.

But come on. What's the real problem here? Do I not trust Tuttle like Livvy doesn't trust Ryan?

Well, Livvy doesn't seem to trust Ryan whatsoever. I do trust Jordan with some things, but not...everything. Like my heart. He's broken it once already, yet I keep going back for more. After a while he's got to think he has me no matter what.

Will he take advantage of my weaknesses? Will he keep hurting me because he knows he can't lose me? How much more can I take?

Am I already setting us up to fail?

chapter twenty

"You should come with me to the quad for lunch," Livvy suggests as we walk down the hall after fourth period, headed for our lockers. It's lunchtime on Monday and the idea of sitting in the quad with all the popular people kind of makes me nauseous.

"Will Lauren Mancini be there?"

"Yes, only because she's hanging around Eli all the time and he can't leave campus." That's a senior privilege only, and considering she's dating a freshman…she's stuck. Unless she wants to sneak him off campus in her car. I wouldn't put it past her to try it.

"No thanks." I pick up speed as we draw closer to our lockers. "I'm going to the library. I need to catch up on reading anyway."

"I really don't want to be there alone," Livvy admits just before she goes to her locker and starts to open it, her back to me as she speaks. "Please come with me, Amanda. I need you."

I dump a few books into my locker and shut it before going to stand next to Livvy. She sends me a quick glance, her expression sad, and I swear she almost looks ready to cry.

"Hey." I touch her shoulder. "Are you okay?"

She offers up a little shrug before she shuts her locker door and turns to face me with glassy eyes. "Not really. It's weird right now. Everything feels so strange."

"What exactly do you mean?"

"I mean, I don't think I want to be with Ryan anymore." She drops her voice extra low and it trembles. "The two of us together, we're a total mistake. It won't work. Like, ever. All we do is fight. I'm irritated with him all the time, and I think he feels the same way about me. Our relationship is pointless. I want out."

"Oh, Livvy." My heart aches for her. I hate that she's hurting so much. I hate that she wants to break up with him. I know they've had their ups and downs, but I didn't think it was this bad.

"I want to be with Dustin." She clamps her lips shut and I swear her eyes well up with tears. "I can't do this anymore."

"Do what?"

"Fake that I'm happy with Ryan. I'm not." Now the mascara-tinged tears slide down her cheeks and I can't help myself. I pull her into my arms for a big hug, holding her close while she cries into my shoulder, getting my sweater wet.

"Forget the quad," I tell her as I smooth my hand up and down her back. "Come with me to the library."

"No way," she says, her voice muffled against my shoulder. "I know you see Em in there a lot. I do *not* want to deal with her right now."

They're still circling each other, and I doubt their friendship will ever be the same. "Fine, then let's go off campus together and we'll go out to eat. You brought your mom's car today, right?"

"No. She needed it because she has an early shift." Livvy pulls away, furiously wiping at the tears streaking her cheeks. "We're stuck here."

"No, we're not." I pull my phone out and impulsively send Jordan a quick text. I have no idea what his answer is going to be, but I'm hoping it's yes.

Can I borrow your car?

His response is quick.

Are you freaking serious?

Yes, I'm serious. I need to take Livvy to lunch somewhere off campus.

I can drive you both.

I'd rather take her alone. She really needs to talk about some stuff.

He doesn't respond, and my stomach twists with nerves.

"Who are you texting?" Livvy asks, and I hold up a finger to silence her.

"Hold on, I'll tell you in a minute. Let me work on this." I stare at my phone screen, willing him to text me back but so far, nothing.

"Maybe we can sit in one of the study rooms," Livvy suggests. "No one goes in those during lunch."

"Please, people use them at lunch all the time," I tell her, my gaze locked on my phone. Ugh, I'm going to be so frustrated if Jordan doesn't respond soon. I really want to do this for Livvy. It would mean a lot to her, and to me.

"What do you mean?"

I glance up and meet Livvy's gaze. "I mean that I've caught a few people in those rooms at lunch or after school hooking up."

Livvy's mouth drops open. "Are you serious? Really?"

"Yes. Really." I nod and check my phone yet again, relieved to see he's texting me. "It's the perfect place to hook up privately. The teachers never check those rooms as long as you're quiet."

I remember the first time I discovered a couple making out in one of those private study rooms. I'd been a freshman, and I think they were seniors. The girl sat on the guy's lap, straddling him, her legs spread and tiptoes poised on the floor, his hands on her breasts, their mouths fused until I opened the door. Their lips broke apart and she glared at me, reaching for the table. When she tossed a book at me, I ducked while the guy threw back his head and laughed.

My fourteen-year-old mind had been blown.

"Hmm." There's a glimmer in Livvy's eyes as she grabs her phone and starts doing some texting of her own. An uneasy feeling slithers down my spine as I watch her when my phone buzzes in my hand.

I never let anyone borrow my car. Ever.

But I'll let you take it.

Because I trust you.

Not to wreck it.

So don't.

Wreck.

It.

A little smile curls my lips. This feels like a big deal.

"Okay, I have plans," Livvy announces, making me look up at her with a frown. "I really appreciate your help, Amanda. Like, really. But

I'm good now. I've got it handled."

I raise a brow. This is suspicious. "Who are your plans with?"

"Um." She nibbles on her lower lip and takes a step closer to whisper in my ear, "You gave me a good idea with the private room thing in the library. So, uh, Dustin is meeting me in one in five minutes." She checks her phone. "Make that four. I gotta go."

"Livvy." I grab her arm before she can leave. "What are you doing? If Ryan catches you, he's going to be furious. What if someone sees you two together and tells him? Is that how you want him to find out about you and Dustin—sneaking around?"

"I don't want him to find out anything, so I *really* hope no one tells him." She sends me a pointed look and I'm offended. Does she truly believe I'd rat her out to Ryan? What the hell is wrong with her? "Guess it's the risk I have to take, though," she says, her tone flippant. "Dustin needs to talk to me. Privately." She extracts herself from my grip and without another word, she's gone.

My phone buzzes again and I check it.

I'm out in the parking lot. Meet me at my car and we can go over a few things before you take it.

Growling beneath my breath, I stalk down the hall and push through the double doors that lead outside. I can't believe Livvy's going to meet Dustin in the library and do…what? Make out? Or worse? She's freaking crazy. And she's still with Ryan, so she's basically cheating. I despise cheaters, especially after what Thad and Tara did to me. I don't want to think less of Livvy, but she's not giving me much choice.

This sucks.

I'm walking through the senior parking lot when I spot Jordan standing near his black Range Rover, leaning against its side. He's wearing a white Henley shirt, his arms crossed and his biceps bulging beneath the long sleeves. The breeze ruffles his dark hair across his forehead and he stares off into the distance, every inch the troubled, broody boy that he is.

He looks so freaking good, I'm momentarily distracted by him. I stop and stare, my lips parted, my breath becoming shallow. It's still hard for me to believe that this guy, this gorgeous, sweet, annoying, smart, strong, wonderful, awful boy likes me. That he might even care about me.

"Hey." His deep baritone knocks me from my daze, and I head over, stopping just in front of him. "Where's Livvy?"

"She made last minute plans. With someone else." I don't say anything else. Livvy's secret isn't mine to tell, and I'm afraid if I start talking about it, I'll get really pissed. So I leave it alone. "Guess I don't need to drive your car after all, but thank you for offering. I sense it was huge deal."

"It is," he agrees, tipping his head toward me. "But you're worth it."

Oh. He says things like that and I'm left speechless.

"You don't have any plans?"

"No." I shake my head, feeling tongue-tied.

Jordan grabs my hand, lacing our fingers and giving them a squeeze. "Then let's go to lunch together."

"Don't you want to stay here?" He usually does. He's always out at the quad, holding court over his loyal subjects. I used to sit out there with him, with all of them, just basking in his presence. But once we had the so-called breakup of our so-called relationship, I stopped going. One, because I couldn't stand to be near him knowing he wasn't mine anymore. Besides, most everyone who would hang out with Tuttle is annoying. Frustrating. Awful.

All of the above.

"No, not if I can sneak off campus somewhere with you." He tugs me closer, his expression serious, his voice low. "Let me treat you to lunch, Amanda."

When he talks to me like that, looks at me like that, I tend to give in easily.

"Okay," I say softly, a jolt pulsing through me when he runs his thumb over the top of my hand. Sometimes the simplest touch has the most devastating effect. "Where do you want to go?"

"Whatever you want."

"The Corner Bakery Café?" It's my new favorite restaurant, though I don't get to go very often.

He makes a face. "You like that place?"

"It's delicious." I take another step closer, so I'm practically invading his personal space. He doesn't seem to mind. "Have you eaten there since it opened?"

"Once. With my mother." That face he just made? Now it looks worse. "Not the most pleasant experience."

I'm starting to think every experience with his mother is the furthest thing from pleasant. "Well, take me there instead and we can make it a better experience." I grin at him, unable to stop myself.

He smiles and drops a kiss on my lips. Then another, this one longer, and with the slightest bit of tongue. I rest my hand on his chest, my fingers curling into the soft fabric of his shirt. His free arm circles around my waist, and I swear I hear someone yell his name, but I ignore them. I'm too in shock that he's kissing me in the parking lot while everyone walks by, so I'm not arguing.

I like it.

"*Jordan Tuttle!* Get your hands off that girl right now! I'm writing you up for PDA!"

Jordan leaps away from me and we both turn to find the vice principal, Mrs. Maddox, glaring at us, her arms crossed in front of her ample chest, her mouth set in a firm line. Every so often the PDA police—as we all like to call them—roam the campus and scream at couples for putting on overt public displays of affection. It's freaking ridiculous, how strict they are.

What makes it worse? We're getting yelled at for an innocent kiss while Livvy and Dustin are most likely hooking up in the freaking library.

"Sorry, Mrs. Maddox," I tell the vice principal, who's glaring at us with disgust, hating how shaky my voice sounds. I never get in trouble, like ever. This is a huge deal for me.

Mrs. Maddox's face falls, disappointment shining in her eyes. "Amanda Winters? Is that you?"

"Yes, ma'am," I say miserably.

She looks at me, then over at Jordan before her gaze returns to mine. "The both of you, in my office. Now."

"Are you serious? But we're going to lunch," Jordan starts, but she silences him with a look.

"You're going nowhere," she says firmly, her bright fuchsia lips forming a thin line. She's older, probably in her late fifties or early sixties, and she's super grumpy most of the time, even with the good kids.

"But Mrs. Maddox—" Jordan starts again, and she shakes her head, cutting him off with just a look.

"Trust me. You're only making it worse." Mrs. Maddox starts walking. "Follow me. And no talking to each other," she calls over her shoulder.

We both fall into line behind her, Jordan sending me a secret, slightly irritated look before he lets me walk ahead of him. Jordan's annoyed, but I'm terrified. What if Mrs. Maddox calls my parents? I'll never hear the end of it, especially if she tells them what I'm in trouble for.

All three of us walk back into school, Mrs. Maddox taking us to her office. She points at the two chairs across from her desk as she settles into her seat, the stern look on her face telling me that she means business.

"I am so incredibly disappointed that the two of you are in my office right now," she starts out, her shrewd gaze sliding to mine. "Especially you, Amanda."

I duck my head, my cheeks hot with shame. If she's trying to make me feel like absolute crap, it's working.

"You both sign the student code of conduct every single year while you attend this school, so you should know the rules, especially now that you're seniors. Public displays of affection are strictly against school code, especially—*kissing* on campus," she continues.

I am going to die of embarrassment.

"What's the punishment?" Jordan asks, sounding bored. I chance a glance at him, noting how he's slouched in his chair, his expression a combination of arrogance and annoyance. It's like he doesn't give a crap if he's disrespecting Mrs. Maddox.

"Excuse me?" By the look on Mrs. Maddox's face, she is not amused.

"I asked, what is the punishment." Jordan leans forward, his gaze intent as he stares at her. "You can skip the lecture. Just tell us what you want us to do."

"A week's detention," Mrs. Maddox snaps, anger flashing in her eyes. "For one hour, right after school, starting today."

"A week?" I gasp.

"I have practice," Jordan says easily, like she won't challenge him. "Can't make it."

"You can and you will," Mrs. Maddox says as she pulls a pink pad of paper out of the top drawer of her desk and starts filling out the detention slip. "I won't tolerate your rude attitude toward me, Tuttle. You must adhere to the rules just like everyone else in this school. You're not a special snowflake."

If it was any other time I would totally laugh over her special snowflake comment, but I keep my head bent so I don't have to look at either of them. It's easier this way.

"But we have the regional championship coming up." He sounds the slightest bit panicked and I lift my head, hating how worried he looks. That worried expression is gone in an instant, though, and replaced with anger. "I can't miss practice. Coach Halsey is gonna have a coronary."

"That's not my problem. And you should've thought of that before you accosted Amanda Winters in the senior parking lot." Mrs. Maddox scrawls her signature across the detention form before she tears the paper off and hands it to him. "You may go, Jordan."

Oh. Someone else who calls him Jordan. Surprising.

He rises to his feet, crumpling the detention slip in his hand. "What about Amanda?"

"I'm going to talk to her for a few more minutes." She sends him a pointed look when he doesn't budge. "Alone."

Jordan looks over at me. "I'll wait in the hall for you."

And then he's gone, the door shutting behind him with a loud slam, making Mrs. Maddox wince and me flinch.

We sit quietly for a moment, the only sound the scratch of her pen across the pink detention slip as she fills it out. She tears the slip off the pad and hands it over to me. I take it, hating how my hands shake.

"Amanda." Her voice is much more pleasant now, though that tinge of disappointment is still there. "What are you doing?"

I frown. "What do you mean? You know what I was doing. That's why you're writing me up for a PDA vio—"

"Not that," she interrupts with a brisk shake of her head. "What are you doing with Jordan Tuttle?"

"Oh." How is this any of her business? I don't have to answer her, do I? "We're, uh, friends."

"Really." Her voice is flat. She doesn't believe me, but I don't know how else to describe us. "Is that what you call what I witnessed just a few moments ago? A friendly kiss?"

"Um, yeah?" If she considers tongues friendly, then most definitely.

"Amanda." She sighs and tilts her head, examining me closely. "You're a good girl. You get terrific grades, you never get into trouble, yet here you sit in my office, and I'm going to send you to detention. Do you know what your problem is?"

I'm slightly taken aback by her question. "Um, no?"

"Jordan Tuttle, that's what." She leans over her desk and lowers her voice, like she's sharing a secret with me. "He's—troubled. Most likely too much trouble for a girl like you."

Now I'm just flat out offended. "What's that supposed to mean?"

"You can do much better, dear." This is said in a whisper, and then she smiles. "Don't you think?"

I rise to my feet, my entire body trembling, I'm so angry. I can't believe she's warning me off Jordan. If I wanted to report her to someone higher up, like in the superintendent's office, I bet she'd get in a lot of trouble. "Is that all you wanted to discuss?"

She gapes up at me, clearly surprised by my reaction. "Yes, but—"

"I'll report to detention this afternoon." I walk out of her office without another word, ignoring her when she calls my name. I'm totally stunned by her words, by my reaction, by my disregard for the rules. I'm all about the rules, I always have been. I would never go against an adult's wishes, especially one who's in charge of me.

But Mrs. Maddox was so rude, so incredibly awful just now. What does she know about Jordan's personal life? Absolutely nothing. And where does she get off calling him troubled? Warning me about him?

My blood feels like it's boiling, I'm so flipping mad.

I stride through the main office, ignoring everyone sitting behind the counter or in the chairs by the window, though I know I heard someone call my name. I'm too angry to talk, too angry to do anything but just operate on autopilot and I push the main office door open with all my might, making the door creak loudly with the force of my strength.

Stopping short, I'm surprised to find Jordan leaning against the opposite wall in the hallway, scrolling through his phone. His eyelids rise, his turbulent gaze meeting mine, and without a word I go to him, take his hand and lead him out of the building.

I have to get out of here before I lose my mind.

chapter twenty-one

"Where do you want to go?" Jordan asks once we're in his car and driving down the road, away from campus.

"I don't know. I don't care. Just get me out of here," I say irritably. I roll down the window and let the late fall air wash over my face. It's barely fifty degrees outside but it's sunny, so the air feels extra cold. It's like a slap of reality against my cheeks, and I shiver.

"You should close the window."

"Are you cold?" I turn to look at him.

He shrugs. "I'm always hot." *Indeed.* "But I don't want you getting cold."

"Such a gentleman," I murmur as I hit the button and roll up the window. "I think I'm too angry to be cold."

He smiles to himself and shakes his head. "You do seem fired up."

"Mrs. Maddox is a total bitch."

"Whoa, simmer down, Winters. Tell me how you really feel."

I ignore the fact that he's teasing me, that he can make light of the situation when he was just as pissed as I was only a few minutes ago. But I can't tell him why I'm so angry. No way am I repeating what Mrs. Maddox said about him. The both of us don't need to be mad at the same time. That'll just make everything worse. "The PDA rules are stupid."

"Yeah, they are."

"We're practically adults. Why can't we kiss on our lunch break? What does it matter? We weren't even in the school."

"But we were on school grounds," he points out.

I send him an irritated scowl. "What? Are you defending her now?"

"No. I think the no-PDA rule is stupid. And I think Mrs. Maddox must have a bug up her ass that makes her run around campus and bust people on an almost daily basis. It's messed up." He's quiet for a moment and his silence starts to make me antsy. "But I think I can get us out of this mess."

"How?" I ask incredulously.

"Coach Halsey will bail us out."

"He'll bail *you* out." I slump in my seat and cross my arms, staring ahead morosely. The lunch period is almost over and we're going to be late getting back to school. For once in my life, I don't care.

"He'll take care of you too. You're our water girl, remember?" He reaches out and runs his big hand over my knee. "It's going to be okay. I'll take care of this."

"What if Mrs. Maddox calls my parents?" I slap my hands over my eyes and groan. "I *never* get in trouble. They'll probably want to kill me over this, especially since I got caught kissing you. They already don't like you. We don't need to give them any more reasons to not like you."

Jordan remains quiet for a moment, and I drop my hands to find him staring straight ahead, that tic in his jaw starting up again. "I wish I could change their minds."

I wish he could too, but that's going to take time. I decide to change the subject. Sort of. "Do you think Mrs. Maddox will call them?"

"Honestly? No. This is your first offense. Mrs. Maddox seems to like you. She can't stand me. If we get caught kissing again, then she'll probably call your parents. Or if we don't show up for detention, she'll call them."

"I thought you said Halsey will get you out of detention?"

"He'll definitely get us out of detention. But we have to go today. That's what will freak coach out. I won't be at practice and he'll get mad, figure out I'm in detention and demand I get out of there. Then I'll tell him he needs to get you out too, and boom. We're done." He smiles, looking pleased with himself.

But whoops, I'm still stuck on one particular thing he mentioned earlier in the conversation. "You said this is my first offense. Is this your first PDA offense, too?"

His expression turns to stone and he keeps his gaze fixed on the road. "No. It's actually my third," he bites out.

I sit up in my seat and gape at him, but he's still not looking at me. "Your *third?* Are you serious?" My mind is going haywire trying to figure out who he got busted with for the PDA thing. "Shouldn't Maddox suspend you or whatever?"

"I think our chances or whatever restart with every school year, or something like that. My first two offenses were during my freshman year, and I haven't got in trouble since."

Realization dawns. Meaning his first two offenses were...

"With Lauren?"

"Yeah." He doesn't look at me. Still. So I stare straight ahead, stewing over what he just said, my mind clicking through all the many scenarios that might've happened between them.

Stupid Lauren Mancini. She has so many...*moments* with him. They share a history that I can never have and it makes me jealous. There. I can admit it. I'm jealous of her and what she and Jordan shared. I don't care if it was four years ago. They still spend a lot of time together. He plays football. She's a cheerleader. And she's linked to him because supposedly her older sister is having an affair with his dad, which is so freaking bizarre I can barely wrap my head around it.

The entire scenario is twisted and dark and weird. Makes me wonder what I got myself into.

"Was she your first?" I blurt out, unable to contain the question.

"My first what? Girlfriend? Sort of. If you don't count the girl I messed around with at camp the summer after seventh grade."

"You messed around with a girl the summer after seventh grade?" God, the more he says, the less I want to know.

"It was pretty innocent." He shrugs. "Lots of hand holding and experimental kissing."

"What do you mean, experimental kissing?" I snap. Oh, I sound like a jealous girlfriend right now. But it's like I can't help myself.

"I don't know. I had zero skills. I was thirteen and clueless. She helped me out. We helped each other out."

I am jealous of a nameless, faceless thirteen-year old from summer camp that he probably hasn't seen since. I'm also clearly insane. I need to stop. "And then you practiced those skills on Lauren?"

Whoops, there goes my mouth again.

He sighs and makes a left turn into the parking lot of the Corner Bakery Café. He pulls into a spot right in front of the restaurant, puts the SUV in park, kills the engine and turns to look at me. "I'm going to say this one more time, Amanda. Lauren Mancini doesn't mean *shit* to me."

I blink, unable to respond.

"She flattered my fragile ego at a time when no one seemed to give a crap about me. She was cute, she was fun, and I went for it. Our relationship only lasted a few months, and it deteriorated fast. You know this. She was a pain in the ass. We argued a lot. I never met her needs, she said. I don't even know what her needs were, and it's not like she told me," he says, sounding irritated. "I think she expected me to be a mind reader."

"Oh." It's all I can manage to say. I'm feeling really stupid right now. If I don't want to drive him away, I need to get over these jealous feelings. They're going to ruin me.

Ruin us.

"And she wasn't my first, if you're talking about sex." He says nothing else. Doesn't give up any more information.

I don't ask for it either. It's none of my business. If he ever wants to tell me, fine. But I can't keep asking.

"Would you like to know how long I had a crush on you, Amanda?"

A self-depreciating laugh escapes me and I finally look over at him. "You really had a crush on me?"

He doesn't even hesitate. "For-fucking-*ever*. Since seventh grade. Maybe even sixth grade? I can't remember exactly. I was a real prick back then, and you were always nice to me. Remember when you sat in front of me in English our eighth grade year? Every time you passed something to me, you'd always smile. And it was a real smile, your eyes would sparkle and everything."

I sort of remember that. I just wanted him to be friendly, yet he always scowled at me. He scowled at everyone. "I was scared of you."

"Really?" He looks surprised. "Well, you scared me too. I'm still scared of you, Amanda. The way you make me feel when I look at you, when you say my name, when you smile at me…it's freaking terrifying."

God, he says the best stuff. And he doesn't even realize it. He's just raw and open and honest and I love it. "Why didn't you say anything back then? Or—try anything?"

"I didn't think you were interested. Not like that. Plus, I didn't think I was your type."

"I didn't know you were my type until you started talking to me," I admit.

Jordan frowns. "What do you mean by that?"

We've had this conversation before. I guess I can't get over it, though I need to before I drive him away for good. "You were so popular and I wasn't. We moved in different circles. I thought you were untouchable. Then you took care of me last summer at your party, after I discovered Thad and Tara together. I was a total drunken, emotional mess and you were so sweet, so thoughtful."

His eyes seem to catch fire as he studies me. "My thoughts about you that night were anything but sweet or thoughtful."

"Really?" He must be joking. He wasn't thinking of—jumping me, or whatever. "What were you thinking?"

"I couldn't believe I actually had you where I wanted you, and you were really upset, so I couldn't do anything about it. No way was I going to try anything when you were drunk and sad and crying. That would've been a total asshole move," he explains.

"But I thought you are an asshole." I keep a straight face, hoping he knows I'm teasing him.

"Oh, I am." The slow smile he sends me makes my skin tingle and my breath catch in my throat. "But I never want to be an asshole when I'm with you."

Swoon. All I want to do is squeeze him tight and never let him go. But I'm also hungry, so I have to make a suggestion before I die of starvation. "Let's get our lunch to go and eat it somewhere else."

"We're going to miss fifth period," he points out with a wicked smile.

"Who cares? Let's skip the rest of the day and get back just in time for detention," I suggest."

He raises a brow. "Feeling rebellious today, Amanda?"

"I think you bring out the bad girl in me," I tease him.

Jordan chuckles. "I wish."

*   *   *

WE END UP at a park my parents used to take me and my brothers to when we were little, but I haven't been here in years. I remember the reason why we stopped coming too. When we were younger, it only cost a dollar a carload. Now it's up to five dollars a carload. My parents couldn't justify the expense. We started going to the much smaller, much more boring free park down the street from our house instead.

Jordan finds a parking spot directly in front of a giant pond and we sit in the car eating our sandwiches and watching the ducks as they glide by on the water's surface. People walk along the pond's edge, and there's an older couple sitting on a nearby park bench, the woman's gray head leaning on the man's shoulder.

It's cute.

"We used to bring bread crumbs to this pond and feed the ducks," I say after I finish the first half of my sandwich. I was going to wrap up the other half and save it for later, but screw it. I'm still hungry, so I might go for it.

"Yeah?" Jordan takes a sip from his drink. "Your parents would bring you with your brothers?"

"Uh huh. Trent was too little, so he just sat with my mom and dad. George and I used to get in fights over who got to feed the ducks first. One time a duck bit his hand and he howled and cried like that stupid duck bit his finger clean off." I giggle at the memory. "My brother was always really dramatic."

"Is he still?"

"Oh yeah." I go quiet for a moment, thinking about George. "He came home from college this past weekend. He's not doing good there. The school is putting him on academic probation next semester and he's finishing two online courses from home. I guess he withdrew from the rest of his classes—it was either that or he'd fail them. My parents are so mad."

"Is that why your parents were gone this weekend? They went and picked him up?" Jordan asks.

I nod. "He wrecked our old car almost two weeks ago, but he only just told them a few days ago. Once he started talking to my mom, she figured out quick he wasn't going to school hardly at all. He's too busy partying and hanging out with his friends, I don't know. My parents aren't talking to me about it, and I don't pry. George has holed himself up in his room and barely comes out, not even to eat. It's really tense at my house right now." Unbearably tense. I don't like going home. I miss working at Yo Town—this week I'm only scheduled Saturday afternoon, that's it, and I need the money. Once football is over for good, I probably need to find a new job.

Luckily enough, I'm busy at school and that keeps me away from the house, but only till around five, and then I have to go home. If Livvy's going to constantly chase after Dustin, then I don't want to hang out with her anymore. At least, not right now. I don't want to play a major part in the demise of her relationship with Ryan.

"I know how to help you with that." When I look up at him in confusion, Jordan's face is impassive. Downright innocent. "Your stress. I can help relieve the tension."

"How?" I ask warily. This is usually the point where Jordan says something dirty and I'll call him a pig and then we'll both laugh because we know I don't mean it.

But he doesn't say anything like that. Instead, he grabs the rest of his sandwich and starts tearing up the bread in little bits, tossing them into his empty chip bag. "Let's go feed the ducks."

Okay. That's not what I expected him to say at all. "Seriously? You'll sacrifice your sandwich for me?"

"I shouldn't eat the bread anyway. Too many carbs." He tears up the rest of the bread from his sandwich, tossing it all in the chip bag until it's gone. "Wanna help me feed them? I don't want them to bite me, and it sounds like you have more experience with that."

He smiles. I smile back. I'm helpless to this. His charm. His sweet ways. He's trying so hard. I see that. I want to give him a chance.

Really? I'd probably give him a thousand chances, though I'd never tell him that. I don't want to stop seeing him. Talking to him. Kissing him.

I like kissing him a lot.

"Let's go," I tell him right before I open the car door. We both climb out, Jordan clutching the chip bag full of torn up bread and me with my phone at the ready. I'm totally documenting this moment.

The ducks see humans approach the pond and they become frantic.

They all start quacking as they make their way to the pond's shore, each of them waddling out of the water and rushing for us.

Jordan sends me a slightly panicked look. "They're pushy."

I start to laugh. "Don't be scared. Start throwing them bread crumbs and they won't jump you."

He holds the bag out toward me. "You want some?"

"Sure." I reach inside the bag and grab a handful, then start scattering the crumbs onto the ground. The ducks go crazy, their quacking reaching high decibels as they all scramble for the bread at once. I take a step back, bumping right into Jordan, and he sneaks an arm around me, his hand resting flat against my stomach as he pulls me closer to him.

"They are a little pushy," I admit, my voice shaky. Not because of the ducks, more from Jordan's nearness. He's so tall behind me, so big and firm. I feel protected snuggled so close to him.

"I know," he murmurs against my hair. With his free hand, he dumps the rest of the breadcrumbs on the ground and the ducks go wild, incessantly quacking as they peck at the ground, fighting over the last of the crumbs. "Think they'll try to eat our shoes?"

"Only if they think our shoes look like bread," I joke.

The ducks swarm around us for a while in search of more snacks, but eventually they give up and head back out into the water. Jordan and I remain in the same position, both of his arms wrapped around me now, squeezing me tight. He leans down so he can rest his chin on my shoulder and I tilt my head to the side, my knees weakening when I feel his warm breath waft across my neck.

"Wanna make out in the back seat of my Rover? Like that one song by the Chainsmokers?" He says the last few words against my skin, his mouth tickling. I laugh, turning so that our gazes meet.

"You really want to make out in the back seat of your car?" I lift my brows.

"We have at least an hour before we have to get back for detention." He lowers his voice, his gaze locked on my mouth. "And I'd make out with you wherever you'd let me, Amanda."

I pull out of his arms and take his hand, leading him back to his car. I'm giddy, my stomach fluttering with a thousand butterflies in anticipation of what we're about to do. "Let's go make out then."

He's grinning. And it's so cute he takes my breath away. I like seeing him like this. Playful and light, as if he has no worries in the world. I don't think he gets enough of this in his life.

Maybe I can give that to him.

I let him take the lead as he goes to unlock the back door of his Range Rover, and he holds it open for me, the grin still plastered on his face. I get in and he climbs in after me, shutting the door behind him, cutting off the outside noise. All I can hear is my heart hammering in my ears and I take a deep breath, wondering which one of us is going to kick this off first.

"Come here," he murmurs, grabbing my hand and tugging me close.

I go willingly, until I'm sitting on top of him, my legs spread around his hips, knees braced on the seat. He tilts his head back and leans against the headrest, his gaze roaming over my face.

"How'd I get so lucky?" he asks, his voice soft.

"What do you mean?"

"Having you back in my life. You should've told me no. You should've told me to stay the hell away from you." He reaches for my face and cradles my cheek, his thumb stroking over my skin back and forth. Back and forth. Mesmerizing me. "But you didn't. I'm thankful for that. For you. You're the only good thing in my life right now."

His words break my heart. It makes me sad, all the love he hasn't experienced. He wears such a tough shell, never letting anyone close for fear of getting hurt. Not that he'd ever say that. He wouldn't call it getting hurt. He doesn't believe he *is* hurt.

But he so is. He's damaged. Though not broken. I can't fix him, I don't want to fix him, but I can be there for him and show him what it's like. That it's okay to let love into your life.

Oh, I sound corny in my own head, but it's true.

He slides his hand around the back of my neck and pulls me down toward his mouth. "Do you think this is too public a place?" I ask just before he kisses me.

He lifts his lids, his gaze meeting mine. "I don't really care who sees me kissing you, Amanda. And I don't think there are any PDA police patrolling the park, so we should be good."

I laugh, but he smothers the sound with his mouth, silencing me completely. It's a hesitant kiss at first, a little unsure, which is totally unlike Jordan Tuttle. We take it slow, our lips lightly connecting. Breaking apart. Reconnecting. Lingering longer with every pass. His fingers tighten around my nape and I run my hands up his chest, feeling every defined muscle beneath his tight shirt until I'm clutching his broad shoulders.

His other arm slides around my waist just as he parts my lips with his tongue. I open for him easily, a low moan leaving us both when our tongues connect. Our hands roam as our kiss deepens, and when his hand slips beneath the hem of my sweater, his hot fingers pressing into my bare skin, a full body shiver moves through me.

"You're always so responsive," he whispers against my neck after he breaks the kiss. His mouth is hot against my sensitive skin and I shiver yet again. "I wish we had time to go back to my house."

"Jordan," I whisper, a whimper escaping me when he gently bites my neck. That shouldn't feel so good, I swear. "Isn't it fun to just…kiss for a while? And nothing else?"

He lifts away from my neck and faces me, his gaze slumberous, his lips swollen from the kisses we just shared. Chill bumps race over my skin at the way he's looking at me. Like he wants to—devour me. It's hot. *He's* hot. "Yeah." His voice is rough and he clears his throat. "Though with you, I always want more."

His admission makes me brave. "I want more too." I lean in, pressing my forehead against his and closing my eyes. "But I'm—scared."

"Of what?" He strokes my hair away from my face, his fingers gently raking through the strands, and I want to purr like a kitten. "Of me?"

"Of everything. Of giving myself to you and never being able to get it—*me* back." I bite my lip, worried. Should I have just admitted that? I lift my forehead away from his and open my eyes to find him already watching me.

He frowns, his brow creasing. "What do you mean? I'll only take what you're willing to give me, Amanda. I would never push you for anything."

"I know, and you never have pushed me." I touch his cheek, run my fingers along his jawline, the stubble there sharp against my fingertips. "And we've done a lot, but…it's still scary, you know?"

"We'll take it slow." He kisses me. A warm, sweet kiss that makes my heart feel like it's going to fly right out of my chest. "I promise."

We kiss some more, and I'm in no hurry to stop this. A car pulls up beside Jordan's and a butt load of kids fall out of it, all of them screaming as they run toward the pond. I barely notice.

Jordan doesn't notice at all. He's too intent on making me want to lose my mind with his mouth.

"Should we go back to school?" I ask fifteen minutes later. I'm out of breath. My mouth is sore and my entire body feels charged with electricity.

"Yeah. Soon," he murmurs just before he kisses me again.

And I let him. I need the distraction.

At least for a little bit.

chapter twenty-two

Friday night. It's the regional championship game and it's at home. Jordan and I only served one day of detention before Coach Halsey lost his mind and went to Mrs. Maddox, demanding that she excuse the rest of the detention "sentence" for the both of us.

I don't know what Coach Halsey said to her, but she dismissed us from detention with no argument.

I've spent the entire week with Jordan. I'm too annoyed with Livvy to hang out with her and she knows it. I think it's her guilty conscience that's keeping her away from me too. She still hasn't broken up with Ryan. And I'm sure she's still seeing Dustin on the side.

So not cool.

The football team has had longer practices throughout the week to prepare for the biggest game of the season, so I've focused all my energy on my hydration station duties. Kyla and I have been working—and talking—nonstop. Spending so much time together has helped us get closer. I like her a lot. I consider her a good friend, and I hope she considers me one too.

But yeah. It's Friday night and the stadium is full of people on both sides. The crowd is roaring and waving signs, but the game hasn't even started yet. The band is playing in the stands, getting everyone pumped up and Kyla is pacing behind the hydration station, her constant back-and-forth and the intense expression on her face making me nervous.

"You're freaking me out," I tell her when I can't take it any longer.

"Why aren't you already freaked out? Your boyfriend is about to play the most important game of his life at this very moment, and you're acting like it's no big deal." Kyla shakes her head, clearly exasperated with me. "There are recruiters here tonight. I'm sure all of them will be watching him play."

"I'm sure," I say as I glance around the field. The boys are already out there, tossing the ball back and forth to each other with ease. Trying to intimidate the other team, I guess. I turn to look at Kyla. "Do I look stupid?"

Her eyes go wide. "What do you mean?"

"I mean this." I point at the number eight I drew on my cheek in sparkly blue paint. "What I'm wearing. Is it too much?" My hair is in a high ponytail, tied with blue and white ribbon. I'm wearing a long-sleeved white T-shirt beneath one of Jordan's old jerseys, which he brought to school for me a couple of days ago. So yes, his last name is emblazoned on the back of the shirt, along with his number.

"I think you look cute. You're supporting your boy." Kyla smiles and her eyes sparkle. I know she means what she says. "And the Tuttle jersey is a nice touch. I'm sure when Lauren sees that she'll lose it."

"Please." I make a dismissive noise. "She's too into Eli right now."

Kyla bursts out laughing. "That is just the weirdest matchup ever."

"Not really. I think they're perfect for each other," I say sarcastically.

"Kind of like you and Tuttle?" Kyla raises a delicate brow.

"Exactly!" I clap my hands and bounce up and down like...a cheerleader. What's wrong with me? Oh, I know. I'm finally nervous and excited about tonight. This is the ultimate make-or-break game for our team. "Hey, can you take a picture of me for my Snapchat story?"

"Yeah, sure," Kyla says. "How do you want to pose?"

I've had this pose in my head for weeks, because I'm weird and obsessive like that. I hand Kyla my phone and then turn so my back is to her, showing off Tuttle's name and number. I'm glancing over my shoulder with a knowing smirk, the eight on my cheek and my hands on my hips.

Kyla takes one photo and checks it. Deletes it, then takes another, repeating the process until she's satisfied. "What do you think?" she finally asks when she hands my phone back to me a few minutes later.

I stare at the photo, pleased that it looks exactly how I envisioned it. "It's good." I glance up at her with a frown. "It's not too much, is it?"

"No, it's perfect. Girls will die. Tuttle will love it. It'll be so obvious the two of you are together." Kyla nods her approval with a smile. "Now post it. Then go find him and wish him good luck, okay? I think he needs it. He looks antsy."

I turn toward the field and spot him out there, yelling at one of his teammates. Yeah, I bet he is antsy. And nothing I can do or say will calm him down, though I'll try my best.

Focusing on my phone, I tap out a caption for the photo before I post it to my story.

Good luck tonight, Jordan! You got this! #TuttleisBae #eightisgreat

I can't help giggling as I stash my phone in the back pocket of my jeans and make my way to the sidelines in search of Jordan. I stop next to Coach Halsey, who is screaming his head off so loud he's making me wince. I take a step away from him and he sends me a sheepish grin just before he launches into another tirade, cupping his hands around his mouth so everyone can hear him.

Like they can't already.

"Amanda." Jordan takes off his helmet and is jogging toward me, his mouth grim, his gaze steely. I know that look. He is in full on concentration mode, and a shiver moves through me. It's sexy when he's so intense. "You okay?"

Look at him, concerned about me when he should be focused on the upcoming game. "I'm fine." I smile and take a step toward him. "How are you?"

"Trying to keep my shit together," he says in all seriousness.

I want to laugh, but I don't. Instead I move even closer, grab hold of his hand and interlace our fingers. "You've got this. I know you do."

His eyes are warm as they scan my face, lingering on my cheek. "I like seeing my number on you."

"Do you?" I raise my brows. "I feel like I've been branded."

Just like that his eyes shine with a possessive gleam. "Yeah. I really like it." His voice lowers and then he's pressing a quick kiss to my lips. I can feel the coach glaring at us, probably dying to say something, but he doesn't. "Now everyone knows you belong to me."

"There you go again, acting all possessive." I act like I'm complaining, but his words send a shiver down my spine.

"You love it." He knows me too well, and when he kisses me again, it's like Coach Halsey can't take it anymore.

He explodes. "Tuttle! Get your skinny ass over here. Now!"

Jordan sends me an apologetic smile and I squeeze his hand. "Good luck," I whisper. "You've totally got this."

"Thanks, baby," he whispers, and oh my God, I want to faint when he calls me baby. I am such a girl, I swear.

I watch him go, startled by the subtle clearing of someone's throat coming from behind me. I whirl around to find of all people standing there but...

Em.

"Hey," I say weakly. "Long time no see."

"How's it going, Amanda?" Her chin-length hair is tucked behind her ears, there's a lot of black liner circling her eyes, and she's wearing a white choker along with a navy blue T-shirt and white and blue stripes painted on both of her cheeks. I don't think I've ever looked so school spirited.

"It's really...good," I admit, realizing that I mean every word. Things really are good. Like extra good.

"That's—good." Em smiles, and we both laugh.

"Why are you here on the sidelines?" I ask. I don't recall ever seeing her attend a football game before, but hey, maybe she's here for...

"I came down to wish Cannon good luck. He asked me to." Her cheeks turn the faintest shade of pink. "He said he needed a good luck charm, so I offered to be his for tonight."

My eyebrows go up, but I say nothing. I don't want to freak her out. Em's even more skittish about relationship-type stuff than Jordan ever was.

"Want to stay down here with us and work the hydration station during the game?" I ask. That way she can stay close and it'll probably be so crazy, we'll need the extra hands.

Em appears taken aback by my offer and she slowly shakes her head. "Oh, I couldn't do that. I don't think." She hesitates, shifting on her feet. "Really? You don't mind?"

"As long as you don't mind us putting you to work, yeah, we could use the help." I look over my shoulder to find Kyla standing nearby. "You don't mind if Em helps us tonight, do you?"

"No way, that's a great idea. I'm sure we can put her right to work." Kyla smiles and waves at Em. "Hey, Emily."

I had no idea they knew each other. Being isolated in band for all those years, it was all I focused on, so I didn't pay attention to other friendships.

"Hi, Kyla." Em takes a deep breath, her gaze meeting mine, a fixed smile on her face. "Fine. I'll help you guys, but don't get mad if I screw up." She sounds put out, but I know she's faking it.

I know she wants to be close to the field so she can watch her boy.

"There's no way you can screw up. Trust me." I take her arm, link it through mine and lead her over to the hydration station. "Besides, this way you can keep watch on your boy all night. It's a win-win situation."

"He's not my boy," she mutters, but I send her a knowing look, calling her on her bullshit without saying a word. She briefly sags against me and ducks her head with a laugh. "Fine. It'll be nice to watch my—boy—while being so close to the game. You got me."

"It's okay to admit you like him," I tell her quietly as we go behind the hydration station. I let go of her arm but she stays close, her gaze meeting mine. "It's not a crime to care about someone."

Her gaze drops and she gives a little shrug of her slender shoulders. She looks so tiny, so vulnerable, and I swear even her chin wobbles. Like she might cry. When she lifts her gaze to mine once more, though, her eyes are dry and all that raw vulnerability disappears like it was never even there. "It's just hard to believe something can be this—*good*," she admits. "That someone can be so nice and fit with you so perfectly, like you were meant to be. It's almost too easy. And that's scary. Do you know what I mean?"

I think of Jordan. I wouldn't call our relationship easy, but this past week, it's been exactly that. Easy. Fun. Perfect. "I know exactly what you mean," I murmur.

And I do.

chapter twenty-three

Jordan

We're winning.

Barely.

I don't want to jinx myself or the rest of the team, but I'm feeling confident for the first time since the game started. It's almost done too. With a little less than two minutes left in the fourth quarter and us ahead by ten, the rest of my team is strutting around like they've already got this. High-fiving each other on the sidelines, sitting on the bench, and out on the field between plays. With plenty of smack talk going back and forth with the other team, the air is full of frustration, adrenaline and testosterone.

But we shouldn't get too confident. The other team is getting ready to score a touchdown, and I'm pretty sure those bastards are going to do it too, which means *we* need to score another touchdown, or at least a field goal, to cinch this game. A field goal would be nice, but I don't think it's good enough.

I need to throw that last touchdown. I want the glory moment. I want whoever catches it to have that glory moment too. Ryan and I have been talking it over the last few minutes while watching our defense work their damnedest to hold the opposing team back, and we have a plan in action.

A plan we don't tell Coach Halsey, though hopefully he's confident enough to realize we won't let him down, especially when what we're planning is in our playbook. We're still going by the rules.

We're just doing it on our own terms.

"Go get hydrated, stat, before you head back out onto that field. You two have played extra hard tonight," Halsey says from behind us, making Ryan and me turn to look at him. Coach's mouth is set in a grim line, his eyes narrowed. He's sweating profusely and his face is red. He looks like he's going to have a heart attack at any moment and drop to the ground.

"You okay, Coach?" Ryan asks, squinting at him as he shakes his hair out of his eyes. He nudges me in the side, sending me a what's-up-with-him look, and I try to keep a straight face.

"Don't stress," I tell Halsey, clapping him on the shoulder as I start to walk past him. "We've got this."

"Christ, I don't think I can take much more of this," Halsey mumbles just as Ryan starts singing "We Are the Champions" as loud as possible, making the other guys on the sidelines laugh. "Don't get too confident, Bennett!" Halsey yells after us. "I mean it!"

Ryan shakes his head and mutters a string of curse words under his breath. "That old man has no faith in us, I swear to God," he says, chock full of arrogance, as usual. The kid is a good football player and he freaking knows it. "We're gonna blow his mind in approximately forty-five seconds, don't you think? Wish I could see his face when I catch the winning touchdown. I've been practicing that back flip for the last two weeks. Tonight I'm going to bust it out right after I score. Spiking the ball in the end zone won't be near satisfying enough."

"Keep your voice down," I tell Ryan irritably. He's too much sometimes. Too showy, full of too many words, too many hand gestures. I appreciate his confidence, and I can admit I have my own fair share of it. It's what makes us better players. But I never clown it up.

Ryan, though? He'll get in people's faces and brag about how great he is. He'll sing loud songs and brag and shit talk until you want to tell him to shut the hell up. It's annoying. No wonder his little brother Eli is such a cocky shit. He gets it all from his lame-ass older brother.

"What's the problem? Bro, you are way too uptight. We have *got this*. I'm just ready to mow them down and make them eat their shitty words when it's over. Did you hear that one guy right before the first half ended? Said I had chicken legs. Started making clucking noises." Ryan shakes his head, disgust written all over his face. "Motherfucker."

I did hear that guy and he knew just what to say to irritate the crap out of Ryan. And it worked. He's most sensitive about his skinny legs. Yeah, you need physical abilities when you're playing this game, but it's one hundred percent a mental game too. If you're thrown off by a few taunting words or a couple of rough hits, forget it. You could lose the entire game just because some asshole decides to call you chicken legs.

"Forget that guy," I tell Ryan as we approach the hydration station. "He's just jealous because you can actually run while he can barely move." That defensive guy slinging insults Ryan's way was huge, built like a tank and slow as hell.

Ryan keeps chattering and I nod like I'm listening, but I'm not. I'm looking for Amanda, searching until I find her standing just behind the hydration station, talking to Em. My chest goes tight when she lifts her gaze to mine like she can feel me watching her, a little smile curling her lips when she spots me. I smile back, unable to stop myself.

I love having her on the sidelines during the games, especially tonight. It's like I need her here to get through the game. Just seeing her wearing my old jersey and my number painted on her cheek makes my chest want to puff up with pride. Or yell out to anyone who'll listen to me, "Hey, see that beautiful girl over there? She's mine."

But I don't need to say any of that. Everyone already knows she's mine.

"Man, you have got it so freaking bad for Amanda. You look like a total sap right now," Ryan says irritably.

I'm immediately annoyed. "What's wrong with that? You have it bad for Livvy," I say as we stop in front of the hydration station. Kyla hands us each a water bottle and we take them from her.

"Nah, not really. It's been rocky with her lately. She's become distant. And I can't remember the last time we had sex." He swishes the water in his mouth before he spits it on the ground.

Whatever. I take a drink, though not too much, because the nerves are starting to kick in. I know for a fact he and Livvy freaking did it not even a week ago, since he bragged to everyone about it. But I guess he forgot.

"I'm moving on," Ryan continues. Another fault of Ryan's? He talks too much right before we have to go out on the field. "Got some other fine ass girls lined up for when we split, because it's coming soon. I can feel it." Ryan grins. "Gotta keep my options open, you know."

The crowd suddenly roars and we both turn to watch the other team run the ball in. Wonder if they'll try for a two-point conversion. Then we'll only be winning by two points and chaos could break loose if we don't watch it. As in, they could sneak up and win this game.

Hell.

Halsey's yelling for us. The other team is setting up, and since their kicker didn't come out onto the field, I know they're going to try and run it in. Ryan hands off his water bottle to Kyla and he's already jogging back toward the bench where his helmet is.

I need to go do the same.

In a second.

"Hey."

Turning, I see Amanda standing right in front of me. She places her hand on the center of my chest and lifts up on her tiptoes, brushing her lips against the side of my jaw. "Good luck," she whispers close to my ear.

Damn. That kiss wasn't good enough.

I grab her hand and tug her close, pressing my mouth to hers in a quick, searing kiss. She backs away, blinking up at me, and even though that moment lasted maybe ten seconds, tops, I know I just rocked her world like she's always rocking mine.

"See ya," I tell her with a grin before I toss the water bottle to her. She catches it with ease and I turn to head back to the bench, grab my helmet and run out onto the field. The opposing team made their two-point conversion. We're only leading by two and there's a minute twenty left in the game.

It's go time.

chapter twenty-four

Amanda

I f I had nails, I would've bitten them all off already. But since I don't have them, it's like I'm just nibbling on my fingers, I'm so nervous. It's totally disgusting, I know it is, but I can't stop.

This game is killing me. It's killing all of us. Kyla has resumed pacing and she's wearing a path into the ground from her constant back and forth. Em has completely thrown herself into her new hydration station duties, staying focused on cleaning up and keeping fresh water bottles for the team versus actually watching the game.

She told me during halftime she couldn't stand watching. It made her too nervous. And right now, Cannon isn't even on the field. But it doesn't matter. She's purposely avoiding looking at the field.

But I'm watching. I can't *not* watch. I'm sending up silent prayers that Jordan can do this. That if he can't score a touchdown, at least they can wind down the clock and end the game with the win. They're leading by only two points and they currently have the ball, but it's still so incredibly nerve-racking.

Jordan remains unruffled and I don't know how he does it. They huddle, they get into position, I hear him call out the plays, and slowly but surely, he moves them down the field. The crowd is going wild, both sides of the stadium yelling and cheering. The cheerleaders are chanting, "Move it on down the line," and for once, Lauren Mancini's extra loud voice doesn't grate on my nerves.

I'm too focused on watching Jordan.

"I can't take it." Em appears beside me and I glance over at her, our gazes locking. Her eyes are wide and the eyeliner is smudged, giving her dark circles that make her look like a raccoon. She appears totally frazzled, I'm guessing by both the tense game and how busy we were tonight working the hydration station. I don't know how we could've done it without her. "I have to watch," she tells me. "It's almost over, right?"

"Yeah, it is. But one minute could last five, so be prepared," I warn her.

"Ah, come on. What's the big deal? Cannon's not even out there." Kyla is standing on the other side of me. She leans over to look at Em, and I can tell by the light in her eyes that Kyla's teasing. "That's why you're here, right? To watch your boy? Because you and Cannon are a—thing?"

"No," Em immediately says. I jab her in the ribs and she grunts, glaring at me. She huffs out a breath and rolls her eyes. "Fine. Yes, we're a thing. I'm not his girlfriend or anything like that, but we are…seeing each other."

"Aw, that is so cute." I smile at her and she rolls her eyes again, but she's smiling too.

We go quiet and turn our attention to the field, but both teams are on the sidelines.

"Why isn't anything happening?" Em asks, looking confused. When it comes to football, she really is clueless. Working tonight hasn't helped; she's barely able to concentrate on the game.

"The other team called a time out. Trying to mess with their heads," Kyla mutters. "They can do this, though. Mentally, our boys are tough."

I say nothing. Our boys are mentally and physically tough, but tonight they've been extra cocky too. Sometimes that's a good thing and sometimes...

It's a really bad thing.

Our offensive line jogs back out on the field and I breathlessly watch as they get back into formation. Jordan talks to his team, his voice ringing above even the roaring crowd, and my heart is in my throat when he gets the ball and passes it to the running back.

But that was a fake pass. Jordan still has the ball and I glance toward the end zone—Ryan is hauling ass toward it. I start hopping up and down, grabbing the girls' arms. "Watch Ryan, watch Ryan, he's going to catch it. He's going to catch it!"

The ball sails through the air and Ryan...

Catches.

It.

He lunges toward the end zone, sliding between two massive defensive linemen to land on the ground, the ball still clutched in his arms, the touchdown made.

The crowd jumps to their feet screaming their joy. The band launches into the most raucous fight song I've ever heard and the cheerleaders practically leap out of their shoes as they yell themselves hoarse and shake their pompoms.

It's over. They won.

Jordan did it.

We three all make a break for it and run toward the field along with the cheerleaders and the rest of the team, the coaches, the fans and the local media. The offensive line swarm Jordan and Ryan as they hug each other and rap their knuckles on each other's helmets. I can see their smiles—they're big and proud and I'm swept by the overwhelming sense that I will never forget this moment. That I will carry it with me until my last days, never able to forget the night Jordan Tuttle threw the final touchdown and won the regional championship game.

"Amanda!"

He's calling me and I go to him without thought, moving through the crowd of towering football players who surround Jordan. He's standing in the middle of the crowd, his helmet gone, his dark head sweaty, the black lines beneath his eyes smeared down his face. He's grinning from ear to ear. I don't think I've ever seen him smile so big, and when I get closer, when he actually spots me, it's like nothing else matters.

His gaze never leaving mine, he makes his way toward me, swoops me up into his arms and spins me around, his mouth meeting mine in the briefest, sweetest kiss.

"You did it," I whisper against his lips.

"We did," he agrees, slowly lowering me to my feet. Cameras are going off, the many flashes of light making me wince, and Jordan laughs, shaking his head. "Looks like everyone caught that kiss. Think Mrs. Maddox will bust my ass for PDA?"

I burst out laughing. "She might let you slide tonight."

"Tuttle!" Coach Halsey appears, grinning yet looking furious, all at the same time. "Come with me."

"I gotta go." Jordan leans in and kisses my cheek. It feels like we're getting carried down the field by the crowd surrounding us. I haven't taken a step, yet I've somehow moved. "Give me some time. Wait for me, okay?"

I nod. "Just text me."

He squeezes my hand and then the coach leads him and Ryan away. The rest of the team exits the field and I follow after them, heading straight for the hydration station so I can help Kyla and Em clean up and put everything away. But when I get there, I find Kyla is the only one cleaning up.

"Where's Em?" I ask her.

"With Cannon, I think." When I open my mouth to protest Kyla shakes her head, cutting me off. "Don't get upset. It's no big deal. She didn't have to help us tonight. I'm just thankful she did."

I snap my lips shut. Kyla's right. Why am I complaining—about anything? "What a game, right?"

"Totally amazing," Kyla agrees with an enthusiastic nod and a big smile. "I'm sure you're really proud of Tuttle."

"I think we're all really proud of the entire team," I say, but Kyla's right. I'm so incredibly proud and impressed by the game Jordan played tonight. I knew he had it in him. I've watched him play for years while in band and now this season, working so closely with the entire team. He's a talented football player. I bet he'll have a list of colleges who wish he'd come play for them.

The realization sobers me up and I go about my clean up duties on autopilot, my mind awhirl as the stadium slowly empties. Jordan is going to have so many opportunities. And it's not like he needs them either. He's already set with the trust fund so he never has to worry about money. A tinge of envy washes over me and I try to push it away but it's so hard.

He has it all, and everything for me, my entire future, feels like a huge struggle.

I'm almost finished cleaning up when I hear a familiar voice calling my name. I turn to see Livvy running toward me, her hair flying behind her, her expression animated. "We won! We won!"

I laugh and nearly fall over when she tackle-hugs me. "Yeah, we won," I tell her, my voice muffled against her shoulder as she squeezes me close and hops up and down. "It was such a good game."

"The best. Did you see the way our men worked so well together?" Livvy asks when she pulls away from me.

Huh. Now Ryan's her man again because he's the star of the game? "They work really well together," I say, though I know most of the time Ryan drives Jordan nuts.

"It was such a great game." Livvy laughs and shakes her head. "I've missed you, friend! You've been so busy this week."

"So have you." My voice is cool, my judgment on high alert, and I can't help it. Livvy and her Dustin antics have been bugging the crap out of me all week. I knew I'd get angry when I'd next talk to her and look at me.

I'm getting angry.

Livvy frowns. "Are you mad at me?"

I glance around, making sure no one else is nearby, before I step closer to her, my voice lowering so no one can overhear us. "What's going on with you and Ryan?"

"There's nothing going on."

"Right. So tell me what's going on with you and Dustin?"

Her brows go high. "We're friends. That's it."

"That's why you've been sneaking off meeting him all week? Comforting him after his breakup with Brianne Brown?" Oh, I sound snide as hell, but Livvy's behavior is totally triggering me. Making me think of Thad and Tara and what they did to me, how devastated I'd been. How their betrayal totally changed me.

I hate to see it done to someone else.

"Not that it's any of your business, but *nothing* has happened between Dustin and me. I've been a good friend to him while he mourns his breakup with Brianne. That's it. He needed someone to talk to and I've been there for him," Livvy explains, her voice flat, the sparkle in her gaze gone.

Great. Now I've made her mad. I feel awful, but I can't help my reaction, especially to suspected cheating.

"I'm sorry, Liv," I tell her with a sigh. "I don't mean to attack you or whatever. It's just that, when everything happened between my ex-boyfriend and best friend, it was so devastating. I have a hard time with the cheating thing."

"I'm not *cheating* on anyone. Trust me." Her tone is clipped and her expression is closed off. Almost like she has…

Something to hide?

Stop being so suspicious!

"I wanted to find you and see if needed a ride to Tuttle's house." When I frown at Livvy, she continues. "He's having a party. A huge bash to celebrate the win. It's being catered and everything so it's already set up, I guess. People are over at his house right now."

I'm blinking at her in confusion, unable to find the words to speak. He never mentioned a party at his house after the game. Why wouldn't he?

God, he's such a guy sometimes.

"He and Ryan are meeting with some recruiters, so they're going to be tied up for a while." The strained smile Livvy sends my way makes me feel bad for ever opening my fat mouth. Why'd I have to stir up trouble tonight? "He asked Ryan to ask me to bring you over to his house."

"Oh." I press my lips together and glance over my shoulder to find Kyla nearby, gathering her things. "Hey, Kyla. Are you going to the party over at Tuttle's right now?"

She sends me an odd look, one that says, *you know I don't go to those parties.* "I'm not going to be there, but tell everyone congrats for me." Kyla's out of there before I can say anything else.

"What were you going to do, invite her to the party?" Livvy asks incredulously.

"Of course I would ask Kyla to the party. She's become a good friend. And she's an integral part of the team."

"She's also kind of boring and no fun." Livvy grabs my hand and gives it a squeeze. "I'm sorry about the whole Dustin thing too, okay? I'm being totally honest with you right now. Dustin and I have talked a lot, but nothing has actually happened between us. I wouldn't cheat on Ryan, I swear."

She's mind cheating on him, and that's almost as bad. Maybe even worse? Though with guys, the emotional stuff doesn't bother them as much as the physical. So maybe Ryan wouldn't care?

Yeah, he probably would. But whatever.

"It's okay. You don't have to apologize," I tell her, though I'm glad she did. "Who am I to judge you?"

"Oh, you've been judging, but I get why. I can't imagine what that was like..." Livvy's voice drifts and she shakes her head. "I totally know what it feels like. How could I forget? When Em and Dustin hooked up over the summer and broke my heart."

"Em helped us out a lot tonight," I say, changing the subject. I don't want to discuss the whole Em/Livvy/Dustin/Ryan love rectangle scenario again tonight. We've already gone over that situation enough times that we've completely exhausted it—there's nothing more to say. "With the hydration station."

"Oh, that's nice." Livvy makes a face.

Uh oh. "I thought you two were finally working it out and trying to become friends again? Sort of?"

"Not really. I mean, we talk on occasion, but not for long, and usually only over social media. I know she's got her own man now and I shouldn't have to worry about her trying to steal Ryan away from me, but..."

"You think she'll try and steal Ryan away from you," I finish for her.

Livvy nods. "Or maybe even Dustin if that...ever happens. I don't know. What's worse, she'd be justified in doing it, you know? That's the really messed up part of it all. I stole from her and so she should steal from me."

"It doesn't have to be that way. You two can forgive and forget and move on. She's not interested in Ryan. She likes Cannon. A lot," I tell her.

Livvy waves a hand, dismissing our entire conversation. "I don't want to talk about that anymore. It's too confusing. Let's head over to Tuttle's house and get some of the catered food before it disappears. What do you think?" She smiles.

I nod and smile wearily in return. I'm exhausted. And even though I got my parents' permission to go, the last thing I want to do is hang out at a party with a ton of people, the majority of whom I don't even consider my friends. But I *am* hungry, so...

"Sounds good. Let's go."

We start walking, but then Livvy stops me. "You think we should go back to my place, change and then head over to Tuttle's?"

"No." I shake my head. "Let's just go as is. Show some team spirit."

"You're right." Livvy offers me her arm and I hook mine through it. "Let's do this."

chapter twenty-five

When we arrive at Jordan's house, the place is already crawling with people. There are cars parked everywhere, all along the road, leading up the driveway and in the field that surrounds his home. I instruct Livvy to park in front of the garage because Jordan would want us to.

At least, that's what I tell myself because, hello, I'm practically his girlfriend. That has to come with some perks.

The music is pumping loud as we make our way through the house and I see lots of familiar faces. Most of the football team is already here, and I spot most of the cheerleaders as well. Including my absolute favorite one.

Yes, Lauren Mancini is still in her cheer uniform and Eli Bennett is standing next to her, one arm slung around her waist and his hand spread wide over her butt.

Classy as usual.

The gigantic dining room—a room I've never been in—is filled with tables of food. There's no liquor in the house that I can see, but everyone was clutching beer cans or red Solo cups outside when we first came to the house, so I'm guessing this particular party is an alcohol-is-prohibited-inside type of event.

I'm guessing his mother had a hand in that decision.

"They're still not here," Livvy says, the disappointment clear in her voice as she scans the room. "What's taking them so long?"

"They should get here soon," I reassure her, then discreetly check my phone for about the hundredth time. But there's still no word from Jordan. I know he's busy tonight. There are recruiters and reporters and a team meeting, and I'd bet a million bucks he's totally exhausted and overwhelmed.

All I want to do is take care of him.

I make myself a plate of food because I'm starving and Livvy follows along behind me, swearing she's not that hungry after all and only grabbing a few things because I force her to. We eat in the kitchen, standing at the counter while surrounded by a ton of people who are doing the same thing. I swear there are more people at tonight's party than usual, and I'm guessing the offer of free food is drawing everyone out.

It kind of sucks. I know this is supposed to be a celebration for the team, but it's turned into a public spectacle. And these people aren't here to support Jordan and the rest of the team. They just want free booze and food and the chance to hang out at Jordan Tuttle's house.

"Think the cops will come?" I ask Livvy once I'm done eating my food. I swear the music has gotten even louder.

"They better not." Livvy makes a face. "That would ruin everything."

"I know." It wouldn't necessarily be a bad thing if you ask me, but I keep my mouth shut before I get myself into trouble by sounding like a jerk. "I just hope it doesn't get out of control."

"You're acting like a total mom right now, Amanda," Livvy says, her tone scathing. "Stop acting like a grandma and have some fun."

I'm so offended by her words I don't know what to say at first. And when I finally do come up with the right response, Lauren Mancini has to swoop in and make everything that much more difficult.

What else is freaking new?

"Ladies, I'm guessing you two are incredibly proud of your boys tonight, am I right?" Lauren beams at us and I'm immediately suspicious. Let's be real. Saying nice things isn't Lauren's style.

"Yeah, we're pretty proud," Livvy says for both of us. I just stand behind her, keeping my expression neutral.

"They both played such an amazing game," Lauren gushes. I wonder where Eli is. I wish he'd come over and drag her away with him. I'm thinking I won't get that lucky. "I know they were meeting with recruiters after the game. I'm sure all of their groupies were waiting for them too."

Groupies? Is she for real? And if anyone is a football groupie, it's her. "If you're trying to freak us out because Jordan and Ryan aren't here yet, Lauren, it's not going to work," I tell her wearily.

"What?" Her eyes go wide. If she's trying for the innocent look, she's failing miserably. "I would never want to do that," she says with a sly smile.

"Oh my God, you are such a bitch, Lauren," Livvy says, stepping in between us so her back is to me. "Go pick on someone else. Even better, go find your little boyfriend, you sick child predator."

Freaking ouch. That was a low blow. But Livvy isn't scared to deliver rude insults, not like I am.

"At least I'm not cheating on my boyfriend with my ex-best friend/ hookup partner," Lauren throws back at her, her tone snotty.

Livvy glares, mutters some ugly words, and then…

All hell breaks loose. People immediately scatter when Livvy lunges for Lauren, her fist connecting with Lauren's nose in a sickening, bone-crunching sound. I didn't even know Livvy had it in her, and I don't think Livvy knew it either, because she's swinging her hand like it's hurting her and Lauren is bent over howling, both hands covering her face, specifically her nose.

I grab hold of Livvy from behind, my arms hooking through hers as I steer her away from Lauren. People are yelling and phones are out, documenting the entire thing. What is it about violence breaking out in kitchens at parties? I lead Livvy out of the kitchen, Lauren calling after us that she's going to call the police. *Yeah right.*

She's going to call the cops and have Livvy arrested for assault. *Uh huh.*

She's going to tell Eli's parents and Livvy will get in trouble. *Hmm.*

That one's valid, considering Lauren and Livvy are dating brothers.

"I hate that smug bitch," Livvy says once I have her locked away in a small bathroom. I set the toilet lid down and instruct her to sit there so I can tend to her hands.

And tend to them I do, hoping I'm not ruining the pristine white guest bathroom towels when I mop up the blood dripping from Livvy's knuckles. She winces and groans when I gingerly dab at her roughened knuckles. I wish I could put a bandage on her hand, but it won't stick so there's no point.

"I'll be fine," she says with a nod after I rinse out the white washcloth for what feels like the millionth time. "It's just a scratch, don't you think?"

Definitely more than a scratch, but she's in good shape compared to Lauren, so I'm not going to correct her. "It'll heal just fine," I tell her. "But I'm guessing it'll be pretty painful the next few days."

"Hitting her in the nose is worth the pain," Livvy says with a little laugh. "Did you see her face when I did it? She was so shocked. I bet no one has ever hit her shitty little face before."

"I'm sure," I murmur as I finish taking care of Livvy. My phone buzzes and I pull it out of the back pocket of my jeans to find a Snapchat from Jordan.

I toss the bloody washcloth into the sink and turn on the water, then open the app.

It's a selfie of him with the trophy, his eyes half closed, his lips pressed to the trophy itself, like he's having a romantic moment, the weirdo. I read the caption that accompanies it.

I'd rather be kissing you. Where are you?

Awww, at least he'd rather kiss me versus the trophy. I take a photo of Livvy slumped on the toilet, glaring at the camera. I send it to him, letting him know exactly where I am. He responds quickly.

Give me a few and I'll come rescue you.

Smiling, I close out the app and shove my phone back into my pocket.

"Are you talking to Tuttle?"

I smile dreamily, excitement coursing through my veins knowing that I get to see him soon. "Yeah."

"You two are really disgustingly cute together," Livvy says with a slight shake of her head.

"Um, thanks?"

She rises to her feet, tilting her head to the side, examining me. "Hey. Did you ever send any nudes to Tuttle?"

I slowly shake my head, wondering where that came from. "It's just never been the right time."

"Huh. Well, make sure it's *never* the right time. Ignore my earlier advice. You shouldn't do it, unless you're one hundred percent comfortable. And even then if it doesn't feel right, that means it isn't. Go with your gut," Livvy says with a final nod, just as there's a knock on the door.

"It's Jordan," I tell a wide-eyed Livvy before I turn to the door and open it.

Jordan's standing there, filling the doorway with his presence, his sheer size, an amused look on his handsome face. His dark hair is damp and slicked back, like he just got out of the shower, and that fills my head with all sorts of distracting images. His gaze scans the tiny bathroom, landing on Livvy, and he smiles.

"I hear you kicked someone's ass," he teases her.

Livvy's face turns pink. "Not one of my finer moments. But Lauren deserved it."

"I kick out dudes who fight at my parties. I have a strict no-violence policy when I host parties at my house. It's the only way I've been able to keep my mom's valuable possessions intact," Jordan explains, his expression solemn, though I see amusement sparkling in his gaze.

Livvy laughs and I do too, though weakly. I wish she would leave. I want to be with Jordan by myself, and give him another congratulatory kiss.

"Your boy is here," Jordan tells Livvy, making her stand at attention. "In the kitchen. You should go greet him."

"I will." She stops beside Tuttle and gives him the quickest hug. "Thank you, Tuttle, for being so understanding about the stupid fight. I'm so embarrassed."

"Shit happens and she probably asked for it, so no worries. Go find Ryan." He smiles as Livvy edges out of the bathroom, and the moment she's gone he's shutting the door, locking it and grabbing hold of me by my waist, making me squeal. He lifts me up and places me on the edge of the bathroom counter, bracing his hands on the tiled edge and caging me in. "Hi."

I smile, feeling ridiculous. "Hi."

"You look pretty, though your eight is fading." He traces the painted eight on my cheek thoughtfully, his gaze locked on his finger as it moves across my skin. "I've missed you," he says, his voice low.

A shiver moves down my spine at his intimate tone. "I've missed you too."

"I have to warn you, I'm on a total adrenaline high."

"Isn't that a good thing?"

He cracks a smile. "Probably, but it also makes me a little bit too—much sometimes."

"As long as you don't get too crazy, I don't mind."

He shifts closer and I spread my legs wider, so he can step in between them. "I can definitely get a little crazy when I feel like this."

"In a good way or—" I suck in a sharp breath when he slips his arms around my waist and pulls me in so our lower bodies are flush together. As in, I will be able to feel *everything*. I sort of can already feel *everything*. "—or a bad way?"

"Depends on your definition of good." He leans in just as I close my eyes and tilt my head to the side, nuzzling his face against the side of my neck. "And bad."

Hmm, so winning an important game makes Jordan Tuttle horny. I get it. I'm feeling that way too.

He lifts away from my neck and then his lips are on mine, hungry and coaxing, his tongue sliding into my mouth, tangling with mine. He tastes delicious, cool and minty fresh, and I sink my hands into his damp hair, holding him still as we devour each other.

Someone knocks on the door, startling us apart. "Occupied—find another bathroom!" Jordan yells and when his gaze meets mine, we both start to laugh. "Maybe we should go up to my room."

I frown. "Don't you want something to eat first? Maybe talk with your friends and hang out for a bit?"

He grimaces. "I'm not hungry. And none of those people out there are my friends. Not really."

Hmm, I don't believe that, but whatever.

"I just want to be with you, Amanda." He drops a kiss on the tip of my nose and my heart flips over at the sweet gesture, the sweeter words. "My parents put together this stupid party. They just want to show off my big win. I want no part in it."

"Your parents are here right now?" I pull my arms away from his neck and lean back so I can meet his gaze. I thought they were gone. They're always gone when he has a party.

"Yeah." He shrugs. "Somewhere. Who knows? I don't care."

Realization dawns and I'm a little in shock. "Wait a minute. Would they still have had this party for you if the team lost?"

His expression goes dark, his lips thinning almost into a sneer. "Losing was never an option."

Say what? Of course it's an option. I hate to think it, but the team could've lost. And yes, it would've been awful and depressing, but life does go on. "Are you saying the Tuttle family can't lose? Ever?"

"Not when so much is riding on it."

How can he live up to these high expectations all the time? No one can. It's impossible—and unhealthy. It almost feels like his parents purposely set him up to fail. But he keeps on winning, keeps on accomplishing the impossible, just to prove them wrong.

"And what exactly is riding on this win?" I ask.

"My future, my reputation, the entire family's reputation." He shakes his head, that tic in his jaw back. The one that lets me know he's irritated, frustrated, a combination of both. "You wouldn't understand."

My mouth pops open. "I wouldn't understand? Why? Because I'm not rich like you? Because my parents don't put ridiculous expectations on us all the time? I want to understand, Jordan. I want to be there for you. I just—I'm having a hard time wrapping my head around everything you're telling me right now."

He grabs my cheeks and forces me to look up at him, his touch gentle despite the fury blazing in his eyes. "I don't want to fight with you tonight, Amanda. It's been a rough day, but a good one too. I just want to be alone with you." He presses his forehead to mine and inhales deeply. "I want to lose myself in you. But if we're going to keep talking about this, it might get ugly."

He's giving me an out, and I'm taking it. "I don't want to fight with you either," I admit, my eyes sliding closed when he slips his fingers into my hair and starts to massage my scalp. "I'm sorry."

"I'm sorry too." He rains kisses on my face and I want to melt. Both at his apology and how sweetly he's treating me. "Do you want to hang out downstairs for a while? I don't mind if you want to."

I open my eyes and stare up at him. His expression is earnest, all traces of his earlier anger gone. He wants to please me. Even though he doesn't give a crap about this party and would rather avoid it, he'll walk around and socialize for me.

For me.

"I don't want to make you do something you don't want," I murmur, and he smiles, diving in for a quick, hot kiss. "I mean it, Jordan. We can forget the party and go up to your room."

"Let's compromise. We'll go talk to people and act like we're having a good time. And then in like thirty minutes, we'll meet upstairs in my room and have a *really* good time." His smile is downright wicked. "What do you think?"

I swallow past my nerves and smile in return. "That sounds like the perfect plan."

chapter twenty-six

Jordan

This party is boring as shit, but I'm trying to deal. I check my phone for the time. Only seventeen minutes left until I can go upstairs.

Thank God.

Amanda and I went our separate ways on purpose, and that was her doing. Sometimes I don't get what my girl is thinking. Or what her motives are. They're never bad, but I always think she has some sort of angle.

This comes from years of never really trusting anyone and always being wary of their intentions. Amanda is slowly teaching me that putting my trust in someone is actually a good thing.

"Mingle with your people, Jordan," she told me at the foot of the staircase. She pressed her hot body against mine, teasing me with a smile, a touch, a kiss that I would've taken deeper, but she wouldn't let me. Instead she gently shoved me away from her and waved. "I'll see you in thirty minutes."

And then she left me standing there, dumbfounded as I watched her walk away, staring at her perfect ass in those tight jeans. It took me a few seconds to get out of my Amanda-induced stupor before I started to wander.

I immediately become irritated. There are so many people here, I can barely move from room to room. I find my mother holding court in what she calls the sitting room, surrounded by cheerleaders and members of the drill team, most of them sitting on the floor and listening to her college cheerleading stories with rapt fascination.

The woman is a total narcissist. She loves an audience—when she's composed and not strung out on prescription pills.

I'm sure the majority of those girls sitting there listening to her drone on about frat parties, hot football players and shaking her pompoms think that if they get in good with my mother, somehow they'll get in good with me. I'm not being arrogant when I think this— it's pretty much fact. The problem? I despise my mother. I don't believe she thinks too highly of me either.

The way to my heart isn't through her.

I bolt before anyone sees me lingering by the sitting room, because it feels like a trap. I go in search of and finally find a familiar face— Cannon sitting in an overstuffed chair in the living room with tiny Em perched on his lap. She's balancing a plate on her hand that's full of food and she's feeding Cannon like he's some sort of invalid. I'm about to give him shit for it, but the expression on his face is the happiest I've ever seen him, so I let it go. We make small talk for a few but Em keeps batting her eyelashes at him and murmuring stuff I can't hear. They're so into each other, I feel like an intruder. So I leave them too.

My teammates are in clusters throughout the house and I congratulate them all as I see them. Ryan and Livvy are standing in a corner in the hall near the front door, her arms crossed, his expression thunderous. Looks like another storm is brewing there.

Pass.

I find Eli Bennett and Lauren making out on the front porch, and she pulls away from Eli when she realizes I'm standing there, a drunken smile fixed on her swollen lips. "Jordan, hi!"

I feel like I can do no wrong when it comes to this chick, and it sucks. She needs to get over me for once and for all. "What's up?" I say to the both of them.

"Great game tonight," Eli says with genuine enthusiasm as he slings his arm over Lauren's shoulders and pulls her in close. She doesn't fight him either. She's fully embracing this weird relationship. "That last play was fucking amazing, Tuttle! Is Halsey forever indebted to you and my brother now or what?"

I ignore his question. "Thanks. Your brother did an outstanding job tonight." I clap on Eli's shoulder and give him a shove. "You'll have some major shoes to step into when it's your turn."

His eyes light up and then he goes into complete Bennett bragging mode. "Aw, I've got this. By the time I'm the quarterback they'll be saying, 'Tuttle who?'"

Lauren laughs nervously, sending me an apologetic look. I smile, but I know deep down inside they'll never say that.

They'll always remember who I am.

"You two have fun tonight," I tell them as I start to walk away, but I hear Lauren tell Eli something and then she's chasing after me, calling my name and trying to get me to stop.

Shit. I take a deep breath to prepare myself for the Lauren onslaught and turn to find her standing in front of me, expectation written all over her questioning face. "What do you want from me, Lauren?"

She seems faintly taken aback by my gruff tone and irritated question, but she flips past it quick. "I wanted to talk to you. About…" Her voice drops and I lean in a little closer so I can hear her. "My sister."

I frown. "What about Candace?" If people think Lauren's a nightmare, they haven't met her older sister. Candace is a holy terror. One of the biggest bitches you will ever meet, guaranteed. Almost as cold and calculating as my mother.

And that's saying a lot.

Lauren frowns. "You know what's going on with her, right?"

I hate it when she plays games. When anyone plays games. Why can't people be straightforward with me for once? "I have no clue what's going on with your bitchy sister and I don't really care either." I'm about to walk away, but Lauren stops me with a hand on my forearm. I turn to look at her, see the concern on her face. The confusion.

Dread sinks like a stone in my stomach. Whatever she's about to tell me, it's not going to be good.

"What is it?" I ask, my voice sharp. "Just spit it out, Lauren. Tell me."

She sighs and lets go of my arm. "My sister. She's having an affair with…your father."

I go completely still, my blood running cold. Okay. That was the last damn thing I expected her to say.

"I thought you knew, Jordan. It's been going on for a while now. A few months at least. She first told me about it a couple of weeks ago, said she threatened your dad that she was going to tell your mom and he practically dared her to do it," Lauren explains, looking miserable. "She wants a real relationship with him and he told her she's never going to get it."

"He's right," I say, trying to push past the heavy weight that feels like it's settled firmly on my chest. "He will never give Candace a real relationship, because he doesn't know how."

Lauren's voice drops to a low whisper. "I don't know what to do. She's dropped out of college. She won't listen to my parents and they're this close to kicking her out. But she has nowhere to go. Mom and Dad don't know what she's doing, but if they found out, they'd probably cut her off forever. She's on this downward spiral and your father is making it happen."

I take a step back, trying to get away from her accusatory tone, her angry eyes. "What do you expect me to do about it? I can't fix him, Lauren. He's completely unfixable. And he definitely won't listen to me, he never has. He doesn't give a shit about me, just like he doesn't give a shit about your sister. The biggest mistake she could've ever made was to get involved with him."

"So you won't help?" she asks incredulously.

"I *can't* help. There's nothing I can do for you. Or for Candace." Like they've ever done anything for me anyway. Why should I help them?

Lauren is slowly shaking her head, the disappointment on her face clear. "I thought you were becoming kinder, Jordan. I thought maybe somehow you being with Amanda would make you a more caring person, because she's so nice and she does something for you that no other girl ever has. But I guess I was wrong," she admits, her eyes filling with tears. She blinks them away, and I can feel the frustration radiating from her.

I can't believe she called Amanda nice. I can't believe she thought I could change. I start to laugh, unable to help myself. "I haven't changed,

Lauren. I will *never* change. It doesn't matter who I'm with or what I'm doing, I am who I am. And if that makes me a rude asshole just like my father, then so be it."

Lauren's lips part, her gaze going just beyond my shoulder, and I whirl around to find Amanda standing there, her mouth dropped open in shock, her pretty cheeks blazing pink with…what? Embarrassment? Disgust? Worry? Anger?

"So you're not going to help her?" she chokes out, her voice raspy.

I frown and take a step toward her, but she backs away, like she doesn't want to be near me. "You actually *want* me to help her?"

Amanda's lips snap shut, her eyes narrowed. She looks seriously pissed. On Lauren's behalf? I find that hard to believe. "Why wouldn't you? She needs you, Jordan."

I can't freaking win with either of these girls, I swear. "She just wants to cause trouble between us, can't you see that? You're always complaining about her. Always insecure when it comes to my past with Lauren."

Amanda flinches, like my words physically hurt her. "This has nothing to do with Lauren and everything to do with her sister and your—*father* having an affair. You actually *want* him to cheat on your mother?" She mirrors my earlier question.

"I never said that—"

"You don't really care though, do you," she interrupts.

Lauren takes this moment as her cue to leave. The chicken. Not that I can blame her.

"What my parents do is none of my business. Or yours," I say once Lauren is gone. I take a step closer to Amanda, grabbing hold of her arm so she can't escape. "Their marriage has been in trouble for a long time, Amanda. I can't stop them from doing anything to hurt each other."

"You could tell your dad to leave Candace alone, but you won't, will you? Because you don't care. You'd rather focus on yourself and screw everyone else." She jerks out of my hold, her eyes blazing with anger. "Lauren's right. You haven't changed at all."

"You're right. Is that what you want to hear? That I haven't changed? That I'll never change, despite us being together?" I glare at her, frustration bubbling up and bursting out of me like an erupting volcano. "You can't turn me into a different person, no matter how hard you try. Lauren's right. I'm not nice, just because you are. And that's something you're going to have to deal with if you want to be with me."

Her lower lip trembles like she's going to cry and I immediately wish I could take back everything I said.

"I don't want to change you," she whispers, wrapping her arms around her middle. "I just hoped..." Her voice drifts and she shakes her head before she slowly turns away.

"Amanda. Wait—" I start, but my words are meaningless.

She's gone before I can say another word.

And like the asshole I said I am, I don't chase after her either.

chapter twenty-seven

Amanda

It's been three weeks. Yes, you heard that right, it's been three long, painful, miserable weeks since I talked to Jordan Tuttle, and I feel like I'm slowly dying with every single day that passes.

Dramatic, right? Yes, I am in full blown dramatic mode right now and it freaking sucks. No one wants to be around me, and I can't blame them. Thank goodness the football season is over so I won't have to be around the team and see Jordan on a daily basis.

Stupid Jordan Tuttle and his big mouth and sullen attitude. He's not been in school much. Too busy being courted by the various universities who want him to go to their school in the fall. His options are endless. He's a freaking local star, and someday he'll probably become a national star too.

Me? I'm doing my best. Going through the motions. At night, after I finish my homework, I work on my college applications. I can only apply to five because that's the limit Mom and Dad will pay for application fees. My SAT scores are strong. My extracurricular activities are a plus and my grades are excellent. I can probably get into plenty of good colleges, but can I get a scholarship too? There's not enough money to take care of my education without me having to contribute heavily.

I don't know how I'm going to do that.

The hours at Yo Town are pitiful, so the weekend after the big game, I go on a job search and find one at a small gift shop in the mall. It's not the best job—the hours are going to suck since I'm working mostly the closing shift and the mall doesn't close until nine most nights. But I can't complain. It's money. My parents were able to get George's car fixed and they gave it back to me, so I'm able to drive to and from my job.

They see me trying, which is a hell of a lot more than what they're getting from George, who's barely passing his online courses, so right now, I'm winning in the Winters household.

Plus, Mom knows I'm hurting. She doesn't ever say anything mean or awful. Doesn't tell me Jordan Tuttle doesn't deserve me or that I'm better off without him. For those first couple of nights right after we argued over those crappy things he said to me and to stupid Lauren Mancini at his party, Mom came into my room, sat on the bed with me and held me without a word while I cried into her shoulder. It was just the comfort I needed.

In gossipy news, Cannon and Em are going strong. They're an official couple. They walk all over campus with their arms looped around each other, and they look kind of funny. Big ol' Cannon and tiny Em. But they're so happy when they're together. You can see the happiness radiate from them both. It's downright magical.

Yes, I'm still a romantic. Jordan didn't totally kill my vibe.

Ryan and Livvy broke up. Yes, they broke up. Can you believe it? It was for the best, though. Those two were fighting almost every day, and during one of their infamous quad arguments, when she threw out the words, "Maybe we should just break up then and get it over with," Ryan finally agreed.

I think his answer shocked her, but they ended it then and there with little protest.

And trust me, they didn't mourn the relationship for long. Ryan found someone new—a pretty girl on the drill team who's a former gymnast and has really long legs. Supposedly Ryan has found a new appreciation for girls who can do the splits and backbends.

Gross, right?

Livvy and Dustin aren't together, but they're not with anyone else either. They've fallen back into that "just friends" mode they were in before, the one that got them into so much trouble in the first place. But I think one of them is going to make a move soon, and make their relationship official.

On a side note, Livvy's mom ended it with her creepy boyfriend Fitch, and Livvy was so happy, she wanted to have a party. But then she realized her mom was really broken up over it, so they've been hanging out more, doing mom and daughter stuff, which is nice.

Kyla and Blake have started dating. They are moving so slow you'd think they were turtles in another life, but that's okay. Kyla's delicate, and Blake is shy. They have a lot in common, and Kyla's confided that he makes her laugh. I don't think Kyla's had much laughter in her life these last four years, so I'm thinking that's a good thing.

On the friendship front, we've forged a new group. Me, Livvy, Kyla and...Em. Surprising, right? It's early days and I'm not sure how long this might last, but I feel good so far. It's a step forward for Em and Livvy, and though they're not extremely close like they used to be, they're friendly. They can laugh together. And that's major. I also convinced Livvy that Kyla isn't boring. She's actually a lot of fun, she's just quiet, and they're the ones who've gotten close fast. It's nice. I have a clique, a group, and we're all good friends.

So yeah. Everything's coming together. We had a week off for Thanksgiving break and it was nice to get away from the drama that is school. Between both jobs, I worked a lot, spent the night at Livvy's along with Kyla one night, helped my mom prepare for Thanksgiving since we host it every year, and I worked my first Black Friday, which sucked.

Now it's Monday morning and I'm back on campus, dumping a few things in my locker before I go to first period. Livvy's waiting for me so we can walk together, and I don't notice the note caught up in the vents of my locker door until I'm just about to close it.

"What's that?" Livvy asks from over my shoulder, pointing at my door.

Oh. My heart leaps and I tell it to settle down. Even if it is from Jordan, I should tell him forget it. Seriously. Why hasn't he talked to me? Apologized to me? Told me that he misses me and wants me back and he screwed up so damn bad that he hates himself?

Yeah, that's never going to happen.

"Looks like a note," I mumble, grabbing the paper from the vent and unfolding it carefully. I recognize the writing from that last note I received in my locker. The one Jordan never claimed to have written, though I always sensed he had.

There are paragraphs scribbled across the paper, and I squint, trying to read the messy, slashing handwriting.

"What's it say?" Livvy asks curiously, but I shush her so I can read it.

I'm sorry. So sorry.

For everything.

I was an idiot for letting you go and not chasing after you. I should've. You're worth chasing after. What Lauren had just told me blew my mind, and though it has nothing to do with you, I guess it does because everything I do affects you as long as you're in my life. I didn't realize that until you left me.

But I wasn't lying when I told Lauren I would never change. This is who I am, Amanda. Flaws and all. I have a lot of them. I'm a lot to deal with, I know this. But I want you to know I never, ever meant to hurt you. It kills me to know you're in pain over something I did. I wasn't lying when I said I was an asshole. I bet you're nodding your head and agreeing, aren't you? I can't blame you.

But I want to be better. Better for you.

I miss you.

I miss your laugh.

Your smile.

Your lips.

Your eyes.

Your hair.

Your body.

Your brain, because you're the smartest person I know.

Maybe you're not ready to have this conversation face to face yet, and that's okay, so for now I'm going to leave a note in your locker every single day until you're ready.

Love,

Jordan

My heart is cracking in two. I clutch the paper to my chest and breathe deep, closing my eyes, fighting the tears that are always right there, ready to fall. They're gone fast and I open my eyes to find Livvy staring at me, her head tilted and her lips pursed.

"You okay?"

I nod, too afraid to speak. I might babble like an incoherent idiot.

"Is the note from Jordan?"

I nod again and she smiles, though she's shaking her head.

"How many chances are you going to give him?"

I clear my throat. "As many I can handle."

Her shoulders slump. "Amanda."

I mimic her. "Olivia."

"I'm being serious. He's hurt you so many times already..."

"Yes, he's hurt me, but I don't think he can help it." I hope I'm not making excuses for his crappy behavior.

"You make too many excuses for him."

Oops, Livvy is a mind reader.

She sends me a stern look as I carefully fold the note and stash it in my backpack before shutting my locker. "I'm exercising tough love on you right now," she says. "And I hate to say this, but he probably doesn't deserve another chance. You're too good for him."

"I was waiting for him to do something like this." We start walking toward our first period classes, ignoring the early morning chaos that surrounds us in the hall. "I know how he operates. He's like an animal who needs to retreat in the woods and lick his wounds until he's fully healed."

Livvy makes a face. "That sounds disgusting."

"Go with me here," I say with an irritated sigh. "Anyway. He's back. He's ready. And I think—I think I'm ready to hear what he has to say."

"That must've been some note," Livvy says, her eyes sparkling, though she's still frowning. "Maybe you should let me read it."

"No freaking way," I say vehemently, making her laugh.

Some things are better kept private.

*　　*　　*

I'M IN AMERICAN Government during sixth period when someone delivers a dreaded yellow slip from the office to my teacher Mr. Woodward. He reads the note, his eyes widening beneath his thick glasses before he lifts his head, his gaze locking on me. "Mrs. Maddox would like to see you in her office, Amanda."

Oh. Shit. My stomach bubbles with nerves as I gather my things, shove them all into my backpack and go to his desk, taking the slip from him before I leave the class.

The hallway is quiet as I make my way toward the office. So quiet I can hear my Converse sneakers squeak across the floor's shiny surface. I'm about to round the corner and turn right toward the main office when someone grabs my arm and pulls me deep into an alcove that's tucked just beneath the stairs that leads to the teacher's lounge.

I recognize his touch, his scent, the heat of his body immediately.

It's Jordan.

Of course.

"You scared me." I slap lightly his chest and he takes a step back, away from my still-waving hands. "Let me go."

"Did you get my note?"

"Yes." I stare up at him, hating how good he looks. "I thought you were going to send me one every single day because you knew I wasn't ready to talk to you face to face yet."

Jordan shrugs. "I got impatient and I wanted to see you."

Argh. He makes it sound so simple. He drives me bananas. "I can't stay here, Jordan. I need to go see Mrs. Maddox."

He smirks, and it's the sexiest thing ever. Gah. "More PDA trouble, Winters?"

"Stop." I shove him this time but he barely moves. "Seriously, Jordan. I have to go. She called me to her office."

"*I* called you to her office." He points his thumb at his chest.

I lean against the wall, confused by his admission. "What do you mean?"

"I, um, convinced someone who works in the office to fill out one of those slips to get you out of class. Looks like it worked." His expression is smug. He's very pleased with himself.

I, on the other hand, am not pleased with him at all.

"You only did that because you knew I wouldn't willingly go with you anywhere," I tell him, completely irritated by his bold move.

"True." He tips his head toward me, his expression solemn. "I messed up. But I also took this time away from you to really think about what I want, and what I want to give to you."

"Oh really." My voice is flat and I drop my backpack at my feet so I can cross my arms. "What have you been doing the past three weeks while you've ignored me, huh, Jordan?"

"A lot. I checked out a few colleges. I flew up to Oregon again with my father and we met with the coaches, but he finally realizes I don't want to go there. So he's on board with my decision."

"What's your decision?"

"USC. That's where I'm dying to go. I went and toured their facilities, met with the coaches, and it looks like I'm in." He grins, and I'm so tempted to throw my arms around him, I almost do.

I stop myself just in time.

"That's wonderful," I say, my voice weak. I really am happy for him. "You're getting everything you wanted."

"Not quite." His smile turns bashful and he shoves his hands in the front pockets of his jeans. "I fucked up with you, Amanda. I should've followed after you that night at the party."

My heart cracks at hearing his words. "I didn't like hearing you tear yourself down."

"I can't help it."

"Well, you should stop. It's annoying. And worse, it's untrue. You're *not* an asshole. You're *not* like your father. You're a good guy." I stare into his eyes, desperate to make him believe me. "I wish you could see it."

"You're the only one who ever does see it," he admits softly.

He's breaking my heart I swear.

"Did you and Lauren ever resolve your—mutual problem?" It's probably none of my business, but I have to know what's going on.

Jordan sighs and runs his hand through his hair, messing it up thoroughly. He's wearing a black Nike hoodie and jeans, and I want to jump him. Like usual. "Sort of."

Vague as usual. "What do you mean?"

His gaze locks with mine. "I talked to Candace. And then I talked to my dad. I told them both I knew what was going on and that they needed to stop, or I'd tell my mother."

My mouth drops open and I squeak. Then immediately slap my hand over my mouth to keep anymore unwanted sounds from escaping. "Are you serious?" I ask, my voice muffled.

"Yeah. I don't know if it helped anything, but I realized you and Lauren were right. I can't just stand by and let my father get away with his selfishness."

I drop my hand from my face. "Do you think the conversation helped?"

He shrugs. "I don't know. Maybe. Maybe not. My father kicked me out of his office. Candace told me I can't stop her from seeing my father because they're in love. I did what I could."

I sigh. "At least you tried. That's all that matters. You're a good person, Jordan. Despite what you think, you can change. You *have* changed. You're nothing like your fath—"

Now it's his turn to rest his hand over my mouth, silencing me. "Trust me. I'm *exactly* like my father. I also told him if he didn't let me go to the college I wanted, I would tell my mother he cheated on her with the sister of my ex-girlfriend."

My eyes go wide. He still hasn't removed his hand from my mouth and we watch each other. I'm sure he's prepared for me to spit on him or whatever, but I don't think less of him for doing what he did.

More like he just stooped to his father's level and dealt with him in a way the man understands. How else can Jordan make his point?

"It was a low move, but I don't give a shit. It got me what I want." His gaze is imploring as he continues to watch me. "Does that bother you, Amanda?"

I slowly shake my head.

"Do you think less of me?"

Another shake of the head.

"I've missed you," he whispers, his hand loosening around the front of my face.

He notices my barely-there nod.

"I've fallen in love with you." He says those words and then drops his hand, taking a step back. Like he needs the distance. "Being away from you was hard, but I needed to do it. I had to work on myself before I could be worthy of you, Amanda. I know you don't think that's true, but I do. And I need you to respect that."

I'm still stuck on those first words he just said to me.

I've fallen in love with you.

My heart feels like it's ready to soar straight out of my chest, I'm so giddy.

"I respect it," I whisper. "I respect you, Jordy."

He makes a face. Whoops, I think I just blew his mind. "Did you just call me Jordy?"

I giggle. "Do you mind me calling you that?"

"Uh, maybe? Maybe not?" I'm thinking he doesn't know how to answer. "If I let you call me that, will you forgive me?"

"Always." Oh, I probably shouldn't have said that, but...

Who cares.

"Or have I run out of chances?" His expression turns somber. "I understand if I have. I get it. I don't deserve another one."

It's my turn to rest my hand over his mouth to shut him up. "Stop," I murmur, giving his face a gentle squeeze. "You have to stop running away from me every time things get difficult, Jordan. I can't keep doing this." He nods. "If something bad happens, come to me. I won't turn you away. We can work on your problems—and my problems—together." I drop my hand from his face before I whisper, "I've fallen in love with you, too."

He smiles, and his entire face lights up. I remember thinking how I've never seen him so happy than at the end of his last game, but that's not true.

Right now, stuck in this dark alcove with me at school during sixth period, just after he admitted he loved me and I just admitted that I love him. This is the happiest I've ever seen Jordan Tuttle in my life.

This.

Right now.

I don't want to ever forget this moment.

chapter twenty-eight

Jordan

We're in the back of a limo, just Amanda and me. She somehow convinced me to take her to winter formal and considering it's our last one before we graduate and I get to bring the girl I'm in love with as my date, I figured I could tolerate one stupid formal school dance.

Turns out I don't regret going to this dance at all. When I went to pick Amanda up at her house and she greeted me at the door wearing a short, form-fitting dark blue velvet dress, I wondered how I was going to be able to make it through the night without grabbing her and doing something vulgar. She smelled so good, and her hair and makeup and that dress...*Jesus*.

I was done for and we hadn't even left her house yet.

The dance was fun, loud and crowded and full of bad music. I sat out the fast dancing and watched Amanda bounce around on the dance floor with her friends. More often than not, I was checking the hem of her dress, waiting for it to fly too high and give me a covert shot of her panties.

Then I got nervous and decided to go out there so I could protect her from other perverts' prying eyes. I couldn't be the only one checking her out.

Every slow dance belonged to me. I held her as close as I could without getting busted by Mrs. Maddox. She seems pretty lax at school dances, which is mind blowing. I saw plenty of grinding going on during the fast songs and the slow songs, but it's like everyone turns a blind eye.

There was only an hour left when I convinced Amanda that we should leave early. How did I convince her? I whispered all of the many dirty things I wanted to do to her when we get back to my place and she blushed prettily, squeezed my hand and said she was ready to go.

And that's how I ended up in the back of this limo—she said she didn't want a limo, but I wanted to pull off this winter formal thing right—with Amanda. She's practically sitting in my lap and my hand is on her thigh, fingers gliding forward so they can rest between her legs. Her skin is warm and smooth and the heels of her shoes are pressing into my knee, but I don't give a shit.

All I can think about is touching Amanda like this. I swear I can feel the heat from between her thighs and my fingers crawl higher, beneath the hem of her dress, farther and farther until I'm brushing against damp lace and she's breathing so hard I'm worried she might pass out.

"Jordan," she moans just before her mouth crashes into mine. I shove the dress higher, not caring about keeping this discreet, my fingers delving beneath her thin panties to stroke her delicate flesh.

She's coming so fast I hardly have time to react, and then she's laughing against my mouth, a sigh of relief escaping her once she's come down off her high.

"I've been waiting for that all night," she murmurs against my lips.

"I barely touched you."

"But you know how to touch me just right." She gives me a smacking kiss and then I'm removing my hand from her panties and she's tugging her dress down over her thighs. She's curled up next to me and I hold her close as we ride back to my house, which is thankfully very empty. No parental units in sight.

Tonight is special. Tonight is the first time Amanda and I are going to have sex. She wanted it to happen the day we admitted we were in love with each other, but I held her off. I didn't want to rush it. I wanted the moment to be memorable. Romantic.

She told me I was a total cornball and I didn't deny it.

"You smell amazing," she whispers against my neck just before she starts kissing it. The suit and tie I'm not used to, and it feels like I'm choking, especially when she slings her thigh over mine and starts climbing on top of me. I try to hold her back and she mock pouts at me, her dark hair falling into her eyes. "Why did you push me away?"

"We're almost to my house. You want me to walk out of the limo with a huge tent in my pants?"

Amanda bursts out laughing. "I don't care if you don't."

"Well, I care." I sound like a frumpy old man, but I can't help it. I'm not having sex with her for the first time in the backseat of a limo. That's every teenager cliché come true.

"Aw, Jordy. You're no fun."

I scowl at her and she bursts out laughing. Yes. She's seriously taken to calling me Jordy. And it freaking sucks. She knows I hate it too. That's why she keeps doing it.

I make like I'm going to tickle her and she dives out of the way, trying to avoid my groping hands. But she's not fast enough and there's not enough room in the back of the limo. I grab a hold of her and start tickling her ribs, making her squirm and giggle and try to fight me. Us messing around like this makes me hard as a rock and when I tackle her, pinning her so she's lying flat across the seat, I slowly press against her, letting her feel just how she's affecting me.

Her eyes go wide and she arches against me, her skirt riding up. She spreads her legs, accommodating me, and my eyes want to roll back in my head, that feels so damn good.

"I can feel you," she whispers.

"That's what you do to me," I whisper back.

She starts giggling and I wonder if she drank from the flask Livvy brought to the dance. "Are you drunk?"

"No way." She shakes her head. "I took a tiny sip from Livvy's flask, but that stuff was nasty."

"Mmmhmm." I thrust against her again, my entire body going tight and making me regret the move, but then she slings her arm around my neck and pulls me down for one of the hottest kisses of my life.

So hot, we don't even notice that the car has come to a complete stop until a few, kiss-filled minutes later.

"Think he tried to open the door for us and got a show?" Amanda asks with a lift of her brows.

"I hope to hell not," I growl, hating the idea of anyone seeing Amanda like that. No one else can look at her that way.

She's mine.

I lift myself off her and she sits up, pulling on her dress so she's covered, then smoothing her hair. Her lips are swollen and her cheeks are flushed. She's gorgeous. And soon I'll have her naked in my bed and I'll really make her mine.

Once and for all.

chapter twenty-nine

Amanda

I've been so nervous thinking about my first time actually having sex that when the moment is finally here, it's shocking how at ease I am about the entire thing.

The dance was so much fun. I'd never come to the winter formal before, and having Jordan Tuttle as my date was just...perfect. He looks dreamy in a dark suit and tie, and he brought me a beautiful white rose wrist corsage. I pinned a white rose boutonniere on his lapel and then we posed while my parents and Trent took photos on their phones. Well, Dad busted out his fancy camera first and took a bunch of photos, and then he let Mom and Trent have at it with their phones. Trent just wanted to get bad pictures of us so he can post them on his Instagram later, the little jerk.

I gave my phone to my mom and she took a bunch more for me. Then I opened the Snapchat app and took a selfie of the two of us together. I didn't have to do any retakes either. The photo was perfect. I added a caption before I posted it to my story.

My date for winter formal. #cuddlewithTuttle

I posted it to Instagram too.

Yeah, I have possessiveness issues, just like Jordan does.

But now we're at Jordan's house and we're in his bedroom. He's undone his tie and shed his jacket, rolling up the sleeves on his shirt, and wow, wow, *wow* is he hot.

If I think about what happened earlier in the limo, I'll get embarrassed. I can't believe how fast he made me…you know. All night at the dance had felt like foreplay. All the slow dance and teasing and flirting. The laughing and kissing and spending time with friends and hand-holding and heated looks across the table. Yeah, one big night of foreplay, so of course when he slips his fingers in my panties, I go off like a rocket.

Like I said, embarrassing. But only a little bit. I feel comfortable enough with Jordan that I can get over the embarrassment pretty easily. Besides, the boy knows just how to touch me.

Somehow, while I was lost in my thoughts, Jordan put on music and lit a couple of candles. He also got rid of his shirt, kicked off his shoes and is now lying across his bed wearing only the black dress pants, patting the empty spot beside him.

"Come join me."

It's not a question, it's a demand, and I don't mind, because I *want* to join him. I start to step out of my shoes but he slowly shakes his head.

"Keep the shoes on."

I'm smiling as I crawl onto the bed and lie beside him. He scoops me into his arms and holds me close, our mouths meeting in a slow, sweet kiss. He touches my face, his fingers gentle, his lips and tongue teasing, and my body instantly reacts, wanting more.

So much more.

I keep talking about unforgettable moments, and this is one of them for sure. Maybe a top moment in our lives so far, because hello, we're about to have sex for the very first time.

The very *first* time.

I'm so excited I can hardly stand it.

"Amanda." His voice is ragged against my neck and he's grabbing handfuls of my dress. "Let's take this off."

I help him get rid of the dress and when he sees me in only my black lacy thong and matching demi bra, he groans and covers his eyes like he can't stand it.

"Damn, you are trying to kill me, I swear."

"You're trying to kill me too." I reach for the waistband of his pants and slide my fingers beneath it, touching soft, hot skin and making him shiver. I slowly undo the button and pull the zipper down. "These need to come off, too."

He shucks them off fast, and then we're both only in our underwear. His erection strains against the front of his boxer briefs and I can't stop staring. *That* is going to be inside of *me* in mere minutes.

Will it fit?

Will it hurt?

Will I like it?

I'm guessing the answer to all three questions will be yes, yes, yes.

"You know I've never done this before, right?" I ask him, my voice shaky, my entire body shaky. I'm so nervous and excited.

"I know." He touches my cheek, his thumb streaking across my swollen lips. His face is somber, not even a trace of a smile as he says,

"You know I haven't done this before either, right?"

Wait.

A.

Minute.

I smile. Try to blow his statement off with a little bit of humor. "You're joking, right?" I ask with a nervous laugh.

He is as solemn as I've ever seen him as he slowly shakes his head no.

"I'm serious."

I close my eyes and now I'm the one shaking my head, laughing a little. Laughing a lot. He must be joking. This is a trick. A weird one, but a trick nevertheless. "Okay, you're so funny. The joke is on me, ha ha."

"Amanda." He tugs on my hand, and the next thing I know we're kneeling on the bed facing each other. "I'm dead serious. I've never done this before."

"But you're the blowjob king," I blurt.

He frowns. "What?"

"Well, not that you *give* blow jobs." Oh God, I'm messing this up so freaking bad. I need to shut up. Yet I can't. "But you let girls give you blow jobs like, all the time."

"Well, yeah, but I told you before that number was grossly exaggerated."

I blink at him. "So there isn't an endless list of girls you've hooked up with?"

He shakes his head.

"And you've never had sex with any of them."

"No." His voice is firm.

"Not even Lauren Mancini."

His irritable sigh tells me he can hardly tolerate my question. "Not even with Lauren Mancini."

My mind is officially blown.

"What have you done?" I ask, then shake my head. "Wait a minute, maybe I don't want to know."

"I've done a few things. I'm not a saint, I've messed around." He studies me carefully. "I'd never gone down on a girl before until you."

"Wait, what?" But he did it so...*well*.

He looks faintly embarrassed. His cheeks are ruddy and everything. "Yeah. I just went on pure instinct with that."

Oh my God. So he'll get better at it? Lucky me.

"The rumors about me are so overblown. And I never bothered arguing them. Most of the stuff people say about me is pure bullshit." He takes my hand, brings it to his mouth and kisses my knuckles. "You're the only one who knows the real me."

Aww. That is the sweetest thing. This entire night has been amazing. So amazing I can't take it anymore. I tackle him, sending him backwards on the bed so I'm on top of him, our underwear the only barrier between us.

"I love you," I whisper just before I kiss him. I can't stop kissing him. The kisses become more and more intense, and then his hands start to wander, and my hands start to wander. My bra is discarded. So are my panties. He rolls over so he's on top of me, I help him get rid of his boxer briefs and then we're naked. Skin on skin, hot and hard against soft and smooth, and oh my God, I am about to lose my mind right now.

"Let me get a condom," he says, grabbing the box from his bedside table and pulling out a packet. He tears open the wrapper and pulls away from me so he's on his knees, rolling the condom on.

I watch because it's fascinating and I'm in awe of everything that is Jordan Tuttle. His body is beautiful. I want to kiss him all over.

But I'm also nervous.

"Are you scared?" he asks when our gazes meet.

"A little."

His smile is almost bashful. "I don't want to hurt you."

"We should take it slow," I suggest.

"You see, that's always a problem with you. Taking it slow." He pushes me so I'm lying flat on my back and he's hovering above me. "I can never do that when it comes to you."

"Take it slow?"

"Yeah. You make me greedy." He starts kissing my neck. "Hungry." My chest, my breasts, licking and sucking and nibbling and oh God. "So fucking hungry, Mandy. I can't take it."

His mouth is everywhere. His hands are everywhere. He's positioned just above me, ready to slip inside, and I spread my legs wider, ready for him. His mouth is on mine, the kiss sloppy and wet and full of tongue and ever so slowly, he pushes inside of me.

I wince. My entire body tenses and he pauses, his breathing harsh as he hovers above me. "You okay?"

"Yeah." I nod and he slips deeper, making me gasp. "It just…hurts a little."

"Damn, Amanda." He sounds in agony, and then we're kissing again, my arms slung around his neck as I try to bring him in closer.

This is the part when I could say I see fireworks and we come together in a symphony of magical lovemaking. But that would be a lie. It's definitely magical, yes, because it's the two of us together, having sex for the very first time. We're in love with each other, and that makes it even more special. So it isn't just some casual hookup, you know?

But it isn't perfect. No, more like it's a little awkward and painful and kind of weird, but once we figure out what we're doing and I get over the initial pain, it's really good.

So good.

When we finish, our bodies are slick with sweat and we're both out of breath. The music has long stopped playing and the only light in the room comes from the two flickering candles Jordan lit before we started. He gets rid of the condom and crawls back into bed, pulling me close so I'm snuggled up to his side, our legs tangled, my head on his shoulder.

"Where do your parents think you are tonight?"

"Livvy's house." Like I could tell them where I'm really at.

"Where's Livvy at?"

"I think she's having Kyla over to spend the night." Livvy went to winter formal with—you guessed it—Dustin, but they're still not official. Talk about taking it slow. And Kyla went with Blake and they were so cute together.

"Would you rather be with them?"

"Um, no." I nudge him in the ribs, making him grunt. "This was a lot more fun."

He starts to laugh. "Fun? That's one way to put it."

"I bet it gets even better the more we do it," I suggest shyly.

Jordan glances down at me, his eyes glowing in the near darkness, his smile wide. "You want to keep doing it?"

"Don't you?" I ask innocently.

His hands skim my ribs and then he starts tickling me, making me laugh. Making him laugh. We roll around on the bed trying to tickle each other, but then we start kissing and it turns into something more and...

Yeah. It's even better the second time around.

And the third.

Maybe even the fourth.

You know what I mean.

chapter thirty

"You two make such an adorable couple." Mom is watching us sit together on the old, saggy couch that's been in our since I can remember. Jordan and I just smile at her, my hand clutched in his, his thumb absently stroking my skin. It's a far cry from that first time he came to the house for Sunday dinner and she asked him what he was doing with me.

Yeah, not one of my favorite moments.

It's the Sunday before Christmas, which just so happens to be Christmas Eve. Mom and Dad invited Jordan over for dinner and we've already eaten what felt like a ton of food. Now we're sitting in the living room, ready to open Christmas presents because my parents have completely come around and they embrace Jordan like he's a part of the family.

I think it's because they realize just how happy I am with him, and how good he makes me feel. When I'm around him, I can't stop smiling. Seriously, it's like I have some sort of smiling disease, and he acts the same way, I swear. We're good for each other, Jordan and I.

"Let's open presents!" Trent yells, making everyone laugh, with the exception of our mother.

She sends Trent a stern look. "Your daddy is almost done in the kitchen." He's making his famous spiked egg nog, though I'm sure he won't let us have any. "Once he's sitting with us, then we can open presents."

Mom is allowing all of us to open the few presents we have from relatives who live out of town. The majority of our present opening will happen tomorrow morning, and then again when my mom's family comes for Christmas dinner. It's going to be loud and crazy and our small house is going to be full of a lot of people.

It's going to be awesome.

"Are you sure you can't come over tomorrow?" I ask Jordan for about the thousandth time. He keeps turning down my invitation, telling me he doesn't want to interfere with our family's day. He doesn't understand that we think of him as family and we want him at our house.

I'm almost desperate to have him with us. I can't stand the thought of him spending Christmas alone. I'm pretty sure his parents are both out of town right now.

Meaning they are the absolute worst parents alive.

Jordan sighs and slings his arm around my shoulders, tugging me in close. Despite the shabbiness of our home, he never says a word, never reacts, never complains. I think he's comfortable here, and I love that.

I love him.

"Do you really want me here tomorrow?" he asks, his voice low, his gaze meeting mine. I see uncertainty there. Vulnerability. My heart cracks and I'm overwhelmed by the love I feel for him. "I don't want to intrude—"

I press my hand over his mouth, cutting him off. We do this to each other all the time now. "Stop. You're never intruding. We want you here."

"Yes, Jordan. We want you here," Mom says just as I drop my hand from his mouth.

He leans in to steal a quick kiss and then he's smiling at my mother. "All right then, I'll come over tomorrow."

"Great. Now let's open presents," Trent says irritably.

Dad and George walk into the living room and go straight to the tree twinkling in the corner. Mom cues up the Christmas music on the satellite radio and soon we're all opening presents. My mom knit Jordan a beautiful black scarf and he immediately wraps it around his neck. Trent tears into his presents so fast he sullenly watches the rest of us open ours, a cloud of wrapping paper surrounding him.

Jordan gives my parents a gift card to one of the fancier restaurants in town and Mom about hugs him to death when she sees it, saying, "You shouldn't have!" over and over again.

"Since you're coming over tomorrow, I'll wait and give your gift to you then," I tell Jordan once we're done unwrapping our presents.

"Well, I'm giving you yours now," he says, presenting me with a small box wrapped in gold foil paper and topped with a bright red bow.

Oh. It's small. Looks like jewelry, which makes me incredibly nervous. I take the box from him and unwrap it with trembling fingers, anxious to discover what's inside. The wrapping paper reveals a black velvet box, and when I slowly pop it open, I gasp at what I find tucked inside.

A ring. A delicate band of rose gold with a small sapphire in the center, flanked by tiny diamonds on either side.

It's beautiful.

"So pretty," I whisper as I take the ring out of the box and study it. He plucks the ring from my grasp and takes my hand, sliding the band on the ring finger of my left hand.

I actually hear my mom squeal when he does this.

"I love it," I tell him just before I lunge for him and wrap him in the tightest hug I can muster. "I love you," I whisper in his ear just before I kiss it.

He slides his fingers through my hair, skims them across my nape, making me shiver. "I love you too."

*   *   *

LATER, AFTER WE clean up the wrapping paper mess and eat Mom's homemade pumpkin pie while watching Trent play his new video game for a while, Jordan and I are about to go outside on the front porch before he leaves for the night when Mom stops us.

"Your father and I have discussed it, and Jordan, we'd like to invite you to stay the night if you want to," she offers. "Amanda mentioned to me earlier that there's no one home right now for you, and I hate to think of you alone on the night before Christmas." The tremulous smile on Mom's face tells me she's about to cry. The holidays always make her emotional. "Please say yes. All I can offer is the pullout couch, and it's not the most comfortable thing in the world, but we'd love to have you stay."

"I'd like that, Mrs. Winters." He smiles at my mom and she envelopes him in a quick hug before she pulls away. "Thank you."

"If you need clothes to sleep in or whatever, I'm sure George has some," Mom suggests, fluttering her hands around like she doesn't know what to do with herself. I have a strong feeling she thought Jordan would turn her offer down.

I'm so glad he didn't.

"I have my gym bag out in my car," Jordan tells her. "I have a change of clothes in there."

Mom beams, all traces of her near crying long gone. "Perfect. Go get it, but hurry! It's cold out there."

We go outside and I stay on the porch while Jordan runs to his Range Rover and grabs his gym bag. I watch him amble back up the porch stairs, my heart swelling at the sweet look on his handsome face, the excitement dancing in his eyes. He loves that my parents invited him to stay over.

I love that he's staying over too.

"Do you like the scarf my mom made you?" I ask him when he rejoins me on the front porch.

"Yeah. It's really nice. And warm." It's still twisted around his neck and he gives one of the ends a tug. "Did she make you one too?"

"Oh yeah. She does every year. I just haven't opened it yet." I grin. "I have a huge collection of Mom's homemade scarves, and so does the rest of my family."

"Guess I need to catch up then," he says sheepishly, and I can't take it anymore.

I tackle him right there on the porch, kissing him with all I have. I'm so forceful, he drops his gym bag on the porch and his arms go around me, holding me tight as he kisses me hungrily. We've been holding back all night, trying to be discreet in front of my family, and now it feels like a dam just burst.

"Okay, stop," he finally says minutes later, pushing me away from him. Though not too far. "Or we might get arrested for public indecency."

This makes me giggle. "Are you going to maul me on my front porch?"

The sexy look on his face tells me he's considering it. "Don't tempt me."

A shiver moves through me and he pulls me back into his arms. "Cold?"

"Yes." But happy. So happy. The porch is lit from the glow of the Christmas lights Dad puts up every year, and pretty much every house on our street is lit up as well. "Oh! I want to give you something."

He frowns. "What?"

I wiggle out of his hold and pull the small wrapped box out of the pocket of my cardigan. "This is for you."

His frown deepens as he stares at the box I'm holding before he lifts his gaze to mine. "I thought you were giving me my gift tomorrow."

"I have two presents for you. This is the special one. The other one can wait until Christmas." Tomorrow's gift is a bottle of cologne that will make me want to lick him every time I smell him.

A real win-win gift, if you ask me.

He takes the present from me and slowly unwraps it to reveal a simple black box. He pulls off the lid and finds the men's silver link bracelet I bought for him. Lifting his head, he smiles at me. "I love it."

"Really?" I stressed over his gift so much. I took the girls to the jewelry store and had them help me pick it out. They reassured me it was perfect, but I still worried he might not like it.

"Really," he says firmly, taking the bracelet out of the box. "Will you help me put it on?"

I take the bracelet from him and hook it around his wrist. It looks good on him and I smile, tracing my finger over the silver links. "You don't mind wearing a bracelet?"

"I will wear anything from you with no complaints." He drops a kiss on my cheek then runs his finger over my new ring. "Do you like your present?"

"I love it so much." I hold my hand out and spread my fingers, admiring my new ring. It's so tiny and dainty and perfect. "It's gorgeous."

"Not as gorgeous as you," he says, his voice low. I turn to meet his gaze and see the heat there. The hunger. Goosebumps sweep over me as he leans in and kisses me again, his tongue sweeping my mouth, his hand cradling my cheek.

The front door swings open, causing us to spring apart, and Trent is standing there with a disgusted look on his little face. "Mom says you two need to come in before you freeze to death, but I'm telling on you. Mom, Amanda and Tuttle are making out on the front porch!"

The door slams before I can hear what anyone else said.

"Should we go inside?" Jordan asks, his eyes sparkling with amusement. That he can tolerate my pain in the butt brother says a lot about his character.

"I guess so," I say with a little laugh.

"Hey," he says from behind me just before I open the door.

"What?" I turn to face him, startled by just how close he actually is.

He reaches out and tucks a wayward strand of hair behind my ear, his fingers lingering on my skin. "Did I tell you that I love you today?"

My cheeks go hot. Will I ever get used to Jordan so freely offering words of love to me? Probably not. "Yes, you did. But I'd like to hear it again."

Jordan tugs me into his arms and kisses me, his mouth warm

despite the freezing cold air. "I love you, Amanda," he whispers against my lips.

"I love you too, Jordan Tuttle." I touch his neck, his hair. I can't get enough of him. Ever.

"Forever?" he asks. It's our new favorite word and hearing it makes me smile.

"Forever."

Friends Series

One Night (Prequel)

Just Friends

More Than Friends

Forever

acknowledgements

This series would've never gotten off the ground without the enthusiastic encouragement from Nina Grinstead so Nina, this book is for you. Just so you're aware, she will fight each and every one of you to the death for Mr. Jordan Tuttle so watch out. #TuttleisBae

Thank you the bloggers and reviewers who read this series and helped me promote it. I can't do this job without your help so please I know I appreciate each and every one of you.

I always want to shout out to the readers because they are the reason I keep going. Thank you for reading.

And a huge thank you to my daughter and son and their friends for their constant source of inspiration. Even though it's middle school drama they're currently dealing with and not high school (though man, it is some major drama let me tell you), the stories they tell reside in my mind and many times end up on the page. Kk fam sorry bout it (my apologies, it's an inside joke).

about the author

Monica Murphy is the New York Times, USA Today and #1 international bestselling author of the One Week Girlfriend series, the Billionaire Bachelors and The Rules series. Her books have been translated in almost a dozen languages and has sold over one million copies worldwide. She is a traditionally published author with Bantam/Random House and Harper Collins/Avon, as well as an independently published author. She writes new adult, young adult and contemporary romance. She is also USA Today bestselling romance author Karen Erickson.

www.ingramcontent.com/pod-product-compliance
Lightning Source LLC
Chambersburg PA
CBHW010805250626
47156CB00010B/3000